THE
LONGEST
ECHO

ALSO BY EOIN DEMPSEY

Finding Rebecca

The Bogside Boys

White Rose, Black Forest

Toward the Midnight Sun

THE
LONGEST
ECHO

A Novel

EOIN DEMPSEY

LAKE UNION
PUBLISHING

Published by Lake Union Publishing, Seattle

www.apub.com

Amazon, the Amazon logo, and Lake Union Publishing are trademarks of Amazon.com, Inc., or its affiliates.

ISBN-13: 9781542014632
ISBN-10: 1542014638

Cover design by Faceout Studio, Lindy Martin

Printed in the United States of America

For my son Jack

AUTHOR'S NOTE

The Longest Echo is inspired by true events. However, characters, certain factual elements, and the timing of events have been altered for the sake of the narrative.

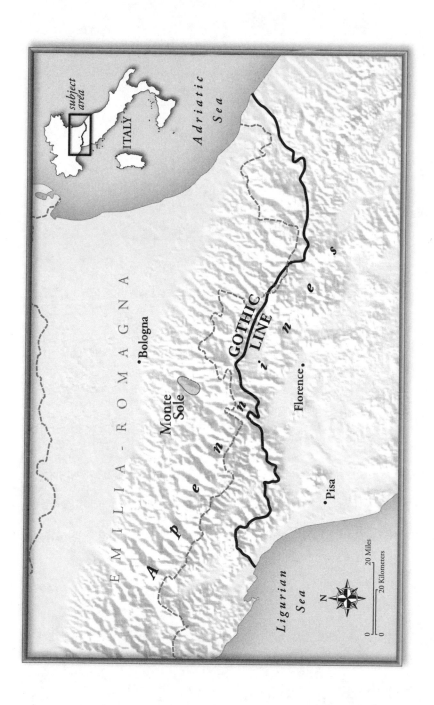

PROLOGUE

September 15, 1944—Monte Sole, forty kilometers south of Bologna, Italy

It has been more than a year since the Italian surrender compelled German forces to occupy the entire peninsula of Italy. Their goal: to protect the southern borders of the Reich. The mountainous Italian terrain has lent itself to a war of attrition, where every hill, road, and rocky crag is hard-won. Despite having liberated much of the country, the Allies have ground to a halt at the Gothic Line, sixty kilometers south of the city of Bologna.

Wedged between the Gothic Line and the prize of Bologna and northern Italy beyond, the traditional peasant people of Monte Sole await their fate. The wild, mountainous area they've lived in for hundreds of years has become a hotbed of partisan activity. The Stella Rossa, a ragtag fighting force consisting of locals, Italian Army deserters, and escaped prisoners of war, fighting back against Nazi and Fascist oppression, has become a thorn in the side of the occupying German forces. Rumors of retribution have begun.

PART I

CHAPTER 1

Liliana lit the ox-fat candle, now almost burned down to a nub. The sun was setting, shining orange on the tilted fields of wheat and grapes and corn on Monte Sole. She put both hands on the stone window-sill, almost pressing her nose against the glass as she peered up the mountain. A brook extended into the jungle of brush so thick that only threads of sunlight could penetrate it. She knew it all, every field, every farm, every mysterious path that appeared from nowhere and led nowhere. She knew every thorny bush, every acacia tree, every patch of grass choked by weeds. She knew the chestnut groves, their seeds covering the forest floor like a carpet, their woody musk wafting through the air. She knew the ginestra bushes, the spatter of their yellow flowers covering the mountainside. She knew the cypress trees, especially the ones in the field behind the house her family had lived in for two hundred years. Her father had planted one for each of his children, even baby Giovanni, who had never made it past his second year.

She sat back on her mattress in the bedroom she'd shared with her two sisters since they were babies. Martina's bed was made, the sheets pressed down, barely a wrinkle visible. Lena's sheets were strewn about, as they had been when she'd climbed out of bed that morning to help with her duties on the farm. The light outside was fading now, and Liliana picked up the book lying on her bed, leafing through to where she'd left off. The escape was instantaneous. Everything else faded with the sun outside, and she sat closer to the candle, the flickering light dancing across the pages. The book had been a gift from Mrs. Chilcott in Bologna, the woman whom her mother had sent her to work for. Mrs. Chilcott had recognized this thirst within her. The book was in English, in this place where most people couldn't read, where her sisters, like her parents and aunts and uncles before them, had left school at the age of twelve.

Liliana ignored the first call, waiting for the tramp of footsteps to come up the stone stairs that led to the bedroom. Her eyes raced against the sound of her sister's feet, and she didn't look up as Lena opened the door. She finished the chapter as Lena spoke for the second time. Dinner was being served soon, and their mother needed her help. Liliana nodded at her sister and placed the bookmark back into the novel, setting it down on her pillow for later. She thought of Mrs. Dalloway in London as she blew out the candle and followed her sister downstairs.

"One of the books the writer in Bologna gave you?" Lena said.

"The only one I still haven't read. She was adamant I read this one last."

"Maybe one day you can teach me to speak English, and what 'adamant' means too."

"Just let me know when."

"Maybe after dinner."

"That's what you said last night."

Their mother, Maria, glanced up with a furrowed brow as they entered the kitchen. Liliana didn't wait for instructions but instead made straight for the sideboard, where the carrots lay uncut. She picked up a knife, taking satisfaction in each clack as it collided with the cutting board, then dropped the carrots into the bubbling pot on the stove. Her mother was humming a tune she couldn't quite place.

"One of your own compositions, Mamma?"

"What?" her mother said, looking puzzled by the distraction. "What are you talking about?"

"The song you were humming."

"I was humming?" She continued cutting the bread, stopping only to stir the stew. The familiar smell of garlic, rosemary, and portobello mushrooms filled the warm air. Maria was silent for thirty seconds or more before she spoke again. "I don't understand it."

"You don't understand what, Mamma?"

"You were upstairs reading one of those books, in English?"

"Yes."

Maria shook her head. "I don't understand why you read that stuff, and in a language almost no one here speaks?"

"There is a world beyond Monte Sole."

Her mother dipped a wooden spoon into the stew, tasted it, and cursed the lack of salt. "There won't be much of a world left if the Germans and the Fascists have their way," she said, "and you have responsibilities to your family. We've spoken of this many times."

"And I've listened to you every time. I will support you the best I can, but surely if I could get some kind of lucrative job—"

"Pipe dreams," her mother said as she took the pot off the heat, the muscles in her forearms bulging. She ladled stew into a waiting line of bowls. "Modern ways aren't always the best. Our family has been on this mountain for hundreds of years."

"Father talks about leaving," Liliana said.

Liliana was surprised that her mother didn't have a retort. She wasn't the type to let things go. Maria handed her two bowls. "Lay these out on the table. Make yourself useful while you're searching for your purpose in life."

Liliana brought the steaming bowls of rabbit stew to the table, making several trips before she'd laid out all thirteen. Liliana knew each bowl, knew the chips and cracks by heart, each as familiar as the patchwork stone of the wall, or the gray stains on the ceiling. The walls were bare, save for a few pictures of Christ and the Virgin Mary. An altar dedicated to Mary and the baby Jesus sat in the corner, illuminated by a candle sitting in front of it. Mary and baby Jesus always had candles, yet the girls only had three for their entire room. *I'm not getting into an argument about this with Mamma. Pointless.* The smell of salted herring drifted out of the kitchen.

"Smell that," Lena said to Liliana and Martina quietly so their mother couldn't hear. "Salted herring again. One day I'll be rich and never have to eat salted herring or rabbit, or wild mushrooms, ever again."

"Make sure you invite me over for dinner," Liliana said.

"What's wrong with wild mushrooms?" Martina said.

Liliana went to the outhouse. It was still just light enough that she needn't bring a candle and still warm enough that she didn't need a coat. The thought of another winter going to the bathroom out here was almost more than she could bear. She never used to think like this. Living with Mrs. Chilcott in the warm comfort of that city apartment had changed her, but she knew to keep unwanted comments about the state of the house to herself. No sense in riling her mother—that wouldn't move the toilet indoors. She returned inside as the crowd was gathering for dinner. Her father, Virginio, greeted her with a smile as he took his seat at the head of the table. Lena and Martina sat down at the children's table with their four cousins who lived next door. Aunt Tania and Uncle Vito took their seats and began to pour and pass the wine.

"Hello, Nonna. Hello, Nonno," Liliana said as her grandparents sat down at the end of the table. She picked up the glass in front of her and sipped the sweet red wine her father made. Nothing tasted more like home.

Virginio waited until they were all seated to speak. "I've got one for you. Maria, you'll like this," he said to his wife.

"There are children present," Maria warned.

"It's fine, they'll enjoy it too." He turned to face his two daughters, two nieces, and two nephews at the children's table, his weathered cheeks spread back in a wide grin. "Kids, did you hear that old Mr. Bonucci's truffle dog has learned how to sniff out Fascists?"

"No, I didn't hear that," Lena said, already laughing.

"Yeah, it's easy to tell—every time he finds one, he vomits!"

"You should watch what you say," Nonna said.

"Of course, because holy Mussolini is everywhere! He hears all!"

"Maybe we should be lighting a candle to him," Uncle Vito said.

"Better off leaving a piece of lard in front of his shrine—that fat swine would appreciate that more!"

"Virginio, please," Maria said.

"I've heard some things lately," Aunt Tania said as she dug into her bowl of stew.

"What kinds of things?" Maria said.

"Terrible things the Germans did in a small town near Florence, and in other places around Tuscany."

"Not in front of the children, Tania."

"All those things happened two hundred kilometers away, not here," Virginio said.

"All reprisals for partisan activity," Tania said, "and the Stella Rossa won't stop, no matter who they put in danger."

"I've told you once," Maria said, pointing a fork like she intended to use it. "We won't have this conversation at the dinner table."

Uncle Vito broke the awkward silence. "So, Liliana, what are your plans now? Are you back for good this time?"

Liliana put her fork down, could feel her mother's glare. "I don't think so."

"She's too good for life on the mountain, and thinks she's better than this."

"And why not?" Virginio said. "She's smarter than any of us. I can barely read, but my daughter reads full novels in three languages!"

"Just two, Babbo."

"That's two more than anyone around here."

"You should settle down and find a man," said Nonna. "What age are you now, twenty? I was married to your grandfather when I was your age, already with child." Her grandmother looked much older than her sixty-three years. A lifetime on the mountain had taken its toll. Liliana's grandfather stayed silent beside her, as he always did.

Liliana felt the weight of everyone's eyes on her. It had only been a few weeks since her parents had sent for her, had insisted that she return home.

"I haven't found a man interesting enough to spend the rest of my life with. Not yet."

"What about that Fabrizio?" her mother said. "He seems like a nice boy. Good family." Fabrizio was never going to snare her like those dead rabbits he skinned and hung on hooks in his father's store. Her mother knew that.

"His father owns the store in San Martino," her grandmother said as if everyone didn't already know.

Liliana could see Lena and Martina laughing at the children's table and couldn't help but wish she were sitting there with them.

"He has bad breath, and I'd get better conversation out of one of the cypress trees in the garden."

Maria pushed back from the table, dropping her knife and fork. "There are dozens of boys on the mountain who'd give you children, who'd provide for your future."

"Perhaps I want more than to give a man children, to toil in the fields on land that's not my own." No one answered. The children looked away, focusing on the food in front of them. The seconds slowed. "I don't mean that . . ."

Virginio reached over and took her hand. "We know what you mean, my sweet girl. Some people are meant for greater things. Just be sure to come back and visit us when you take over the world, when the madness of this war is over."

Her mother didn't speak. She just stood up from the table and started clearing plates, continuing the never-ending cycle of labor that constituted her existence.

Liliana stood in front of the mirror and ran a brush through her long chestnut-brown hair.

"Who are you trying to impress at the dance, then?" Martina said.

"Just because I care about my appearance doesn't mean that I'm trying to impress anyone."

"Lupo. I heard Lupo likes her," Lena said and burst out laughing.

"I'm sure Lupo has better things to think about than me, like scuttling around the mountains and shooting at the Germans." Aunt Tania's words at the dinner table came back to her. In a place with few newspapers, rumors always held sway. Most of the official news they got was censored. Reliable information from the outside was sketchy and rare.

"I think he's handsome and brave," Martina said.

"I think it must be weeks since he last had a bath. He probably smells like a haystack after heavy rain," Liliana replied.

"You can always dance with Fabrizio, bad breath and all, or else you could try one of the cypress trees in the woods outside," Lena said.

"Ha!" Liliana said, giving her sister a playful shove. She noticed her arm was bare. "I think I dropped my bracelet outside," she said. "Be ready when I get back. I don't feel like hanging around for you two all night."

The house was quiet as she made her way down the stairs. The dinner table was cleared and clean. Virginio and his brother were in the living room, smoking.

"Where's Mamma?" Liliana asked.

"Outside, I think," her father answered.

Liliana hoped her mother had found the bracelet when she was cleaning up earlier. Liliana looked in the washroom, the shed, and on the courtyard, but neither the bracelet nor Maria were anywhere to be found. She was about to give up her search when she heard whispering from behind the house. Knowing she shouldn't, she moved toward the sound, stopping around the corner when she made out her mother's and Tania's voices.

"How could you say that in front of the children? They won't sleep a wink tonight."

"I didn't know when else to bring it up. I can't stop thinking about it."

"So," said Maria, "now we're alone. Tell me what you heard."

"I heard about a village called Sant'Anna, and a reprisal at another village called Padule di Fucecchio. Because two Germans were wounded by the rebels there."

"They killed the men?"

"I don't know. I don't know many details. I heard a rumor about women and children."

"How could that be?" Maria said. "Why would they shoot women and children? They're not rebels. That can't be right."

"Even so. We need to be careful—for our men's sakes."

Liliana had never heard Tania talk like this. She was usually so happy, so full of life.

"The Germans are scared," Maria said.

"They're animals. And you know what animals do when they're cornered, don't you?"

"I've had this conversation with Virginio. We've discussed leaving."

"Have you said anything to the girls? To Liliana?"

"Of course not. What good would that do?" Her mother's words hurt. "Virginio is going to the land commissioner in a few days to try to arrange the suspension of our lease on the land."

"So we can leave?"

"Temporarily."

Liliana couldn't believe what she was hearing. Her mother hadn't left Monte Sole in years and regularly said she never would again.

"When were you going to tell me this?" Tania said.

"Tomorrow. Before Virginio left, anyway. I'm trying to keep everyone calm. It's just a precaution."

Liliana walked away, determined not to tell her sisters. Mamma and Babbo would handle it. It was probably nothing. People came to Monte Sole to get *away* from the war. That's why she'd come back—upon her parents' insistence. She made her way back into the house, trying to regulate her breathing. Her skin felt cold.

She went back upstairs and put on one of the floral dresses Mrs. Chilcott had loaned her with a wink when Liliana had left Bologna. It was faded, but compared to her other drab gray and black dresses that fit her like a potato sack, it was fit for a princess. New clothes were a memory now, not that many women on the mountain cared. Clothes were for working. The boys at the dance would be dressed in lumpy old trousers, work boots pulverized from countless hours of labor in the fields, vests, and dirty shirts. Some would even be wearing the narrow-brimmed hats their fathers passed down to them, ringed with sweat. The girls' clothes were usually dull, faded black and gray dresses that showed little of their femininity, but those on the prowl for a husband would break out garish blue socks, red skirts, or purple scarves in the hopes of catching a man's eye at the dance.

Liliana glanced at herself one more time in the mirror, pausing to run her finger along the crack in an upper corner, before turning to join her sisters at the top of the stairs. Their mother waited at the bottom.

"Have these girls back here by midnight," she told Liliana.

"Midnight? Thank you, Mamma."

"Are you serious?" Martina asked.

"You're sixteen now, Martina, and Lena, you're fifteen . . . and with the war going on . . . Get going before I change my mind. You make sure they get back here, Liliana, and don't do anything stupid."

"Of course."

Liliana looked at her mother. There was something different in her eyes. Usually they would have had to be back by ten if they were allowed to go at all. Something had changed.

They each kissed their mother on the cheek before setting out. Though the ground was still sodden from the rains that morning, the air was clean, and breathing it in was like taking a sip from a cool mountain stream. Dark clouds loomed above their heads as they walked a few kilometers along the rough-hewn pathway to the next village. They didn't worry about German patrols, not at night, and in a place where crime was almost nonexistent; they traveled without fear.

"How did you get Mamma to allow you to come out, and so late?" Liliana asked her sisters.

"I don't know," Lena said. "I was sure she'd say no. Maybe it's because the front line is so close."

"She asked me to keep an eye on you, and to make sure we brought you home!" Martina said.

"That makes sense. She asked the same of me, about you two."

"Safety in numbers," Lena said.

"The herd mentality. We'll pretend we're deaf or blind if any boys come near us."

"Or at least say we did," Martina said, laughing.

~

The night was like a swamp, thick around him. His uniform was dry now. How long had he been walking and hiding? Twelve hours today, and almost the entire night before? It was hard to know how much ground he'd covered, easier to feel the hunger pangs stabbing at his insides, the blisters on his feet. He tried to think of some point of reference from his past for this experience, to make it more bearable, to keep him going forward and not concede to the overarching desire within him to lie down and curl into a ball on the ground. The terror infesting him brought him back to his teenage years, and for the first time in his life, he felt some tiny sliver of gratitude toward his father for making these feelings at least familiar.

He made his way down a hill, careful to step over jagged stones that littered his path. The sanctuary of the trees was gone now. His limbs were shaking as he continued toward the next tree line fifty meters ahead. A noise from behind sent him running before he realized he'd made the decision to do so, and he felt his foot connect with a rock jutting out from the ground. He came down hard, knocking the wind out of himself. He rolled over onto his back, waiting for the agonizing pain of a broken leg that would end all of this. But it never came. He plunged fingers into the cold dirt and peered up at the dark of the clouds above his head. He longed for the moon to reemerge, to not feel so goddamn alone.

James raised himself up on his elbows, turning his head back toward the noise that had caused him to run. Nothing. All quiet now. No Germans. No Italian partisans. No fellow POWs come to escape with him. *Where am I even going? To the partisans? What the hell do I know about them?* Teddy was the one who'd heard about them, the one who knew the name of the local partisan unit at least—the Stella Rossa. Where was he now?

James thought back to the scene in his mind that was painfully incomplete. What had happened to Teddy, and Pete and Albert? Were they dead? No. They had just run the other way. There had been no time to look back when the bullets were pelting the water all around him. There had been nothing to do but run, and hope. Somehow, he'd made it—this far anyway, but what next? There had been no plan to escape, just a torn-open train car after that bomber dropped its payload onto a train full of Allied prisoners. *What had that pilot been thinking, bombing an Allied POW train? Who knows how many prisoners that idiot killed?* James got up onto his haunches, wondering about his friends again. Perhaps they'd been caught already, and he was the only one who'd gotten away. Anything was possible—even making it out of this alive.

"They made it out," he whispered, unsure of whether to believe his own words. "But you won't unless you get your ass moving."

The next tree line and the comfort that it offered was twenty meters away, and he crouched down as he made his way toward it. No more noise and the welcome sight of the dark foliage above his head renewed his confidence. He used the trees to steady himself as he went, all the time listening out for the Germans and their dogs that he was amazed hadn't caught him already. Perhaps they'd gone in a different direction—after the others.

He had to get to the partisans. They were his only chance. He wasn't going to be able to survive alone out here. The Germans or the Fascists would catch up with him if he didn't starve to death first. He couldn't count on anyone else to hide him long enough for the Allies to arrive. It was impossible to know when this area would be liberated, but he knew they were coming. Everyone in the POW camp knew. That was why the Nazis had moved them by train. The Allied lines were close. The sound of the bombing and the artillery had grown more intense these past few weeks, and the men in the camp had talked about little else since the end of the summer. Rumors had abounded, of course. The official line from their German captors was that the Allies were being hurled back into the Mediterranean, but their eyes told a different story. They were coming, and with them an end to all this. He just had to survive long enough to see it.

The forest elicited a quiet comfort, and the fear within him subsided enough that his legs stopped shaking. His mother had always said everything happened for a reason. What was the reason for this? Or for what had happened to her? He tried to remember his mother's voice, tried to feel her with him, but he couldn't. The sound of her voice had faded within him over these past seven years. Had it been that long? Chief Brody's voice came into his consciousness now, as it usually did in the wake of thoughts of his mother. He thought of what the old man would say—"Stand tall, take pride in yourself, and drive on." So he did.

The trees were ending. The Stella Rossa wouldn't have a headquarters marked with a sign inviting applicants to apply. James would never find them alone. He was going to need help from the locals. Who? How could he know they wouldn't turn him in? His strong guess was that most of the populace in this remote, mountainous region he somehow found himself in were antagonistic to the Nazi occupying forces. The partisans would not be able to exist if the people felt otherwise. Surely the Stella Rossa were largely made up of men from the local population. He was in trouble if they weren't. If this was a stronghold of support for the Nazis or the Fascists they worked in tandem with, he'd find himself in a jail cell soon.

He put a hand on a tree to steady himself. His eyes were used to the dark, but there was so little light. Where were the houses? The local authorities had likely enforced the blackout rules here as in the city, but why would the people adhere to them so stringently? What was there to bomb out here, and who would know if they lit a candle in the dark at night?

He moved along the tree line, peering down at the valley that stretched out below. Some lights were visible now. One house stood out, just visible as a slightly lighter shade of gray against the black all around it. James sat down and tried to study it, tried to imagine the people who lived inside it in this dark, remote place where he'd never dreamed he'd be.

Ten minutes passed as he stared down at the house. It had to be now. The dawn would reveal things he didn't want his pursuers to discover. He stood up and made his way down the hill.

~

The music grew stronger, louder as the sisters approached. They knocked on the red door of the old brick house their friends had decorated for the dance. Liliana's friend Sofia answered the door and greeted the girls with hugs before leading them inside. Several couples were dancing already, their arms tucked by their sides, their legs rising and moving with the music, skipping back and forth. A fiddler sat alongside an accordion player in the corner, a hat on the floor in front of them. Liliana made her way over to them, throwing in a few lire. They smiled and continued playing as she crossed the room to get a glass of red wine. The boys stood on the other side of the room. Liliana could feel their eyes stuck on her like limpets. She turned around with a glass of wine in hand. Fabrizio was in front of her before she could take a sip. He reached his hand to her. "I'd be delighted," she said and knocked most of the wine back before they took the three steps out onto the dance floor. The music flowed around them, and Liliana let herself be swept away by it, the hard soles of her shoes clacking on the stone floor. The song ended, and another boy came, and soon all three of the Nicoletti sisters were on the dance floor. No one else seemed worried about what the future might bring. Liliana tried not to be either, focusing on her dance steps, on the sweet wine on her tongue, on each boy she saw in front of her.

An hour or more had passed when she came off the dance floor. Her sisters were still there, laughing with the boys opposite them. Liliana remembered their collective promise to their mother as Fabrizio came to her again.

"I think it's time I joined the rebels," he announced.

"Why do you feel the need to do that? Just because the other boys have? Your father needs your help with the business. The rebels steal his goods, and you talk of joining them?"

"I can't stay down here and do nothing while most of my friends are risking their lives daily in the fight against the Germans."

"Not everyone was meant to fight or to spend their nights sleeping in barns or in the dirt. Your focus should be on your family."

"What's your focus?"

"I'm trying to find that out."

"Would you think about dancing with me again?"

"Are you sure you don't want to ask someone else?"

"I'm very sure."

"All right, then."

Liliana kept an eye on her watch. She didn't want to push her luck, even with her mother's new leniency. When the song ended, she called the girls off the dance floor, their brows sweaty, their mouths pushed back in broad smiles before she broke the bad news to them—it was time to go home. The boys let them go with promises that they'd see them next time and would save them a dance. Liliana took one last sip of wine before saying goodbye and pushing the door open. The sisters walked out into the night again. They had only gone a few steps when Liliana heard the voice from behind her.

"Liliana. Liliana Nicoletti."

She turned to see the figure emerge from the shadows. A handsome man with thick stubble and a red bandanna tied around his neck, a pistol holstered at his side, walked toward her.

"Lupo," Lena said. "Go ahead, girls. I'll catch up."

"I'll make sure she gets home," Lupo said. The girls rushed off, laughing and whispering to each other.

"To what do I owe this pleasure—the company of the head of the Stella Rossa partisan brigade?"

"Don't be like that."

The conversation her mother had with Tania came to her. This man might be able to do something to avert the disaster that had befallen those communities in Tuscany. If it was a matter of the rebels going too far, what if they took a step back?

"Did you hear about the massacres in Tuscany these past few weeks?"

"Ah, yes. Unfortunately, I did. The Germans are animals. There's only one way to deal with rabid dogs like them."

"More violence?"

"What do you suggest? We stop? We're the only ones in a position to punish them for their crimes."

"Where does it end? What if your actions bring them here, and we end up as the next place they come for revenge?"

"We'll melt away. They'll never find us."

"What if they retaliate against the men of the villages, against my father and my uncle?"

"The Germans know better than to come here. We'd pick them off one by one."

"Just be mindful of the people you're fighting for. Why not just lie low until the Allies come? Everyone says it'll be soon."

"I didn't come here to discuss our operations. We're not perfect, but we're trying every day." He held out a rough hand covered in cuts. "Will you walk with me awhile?"

Liliana stood a few seconds before she felt her feet moving.

"I need to get home."

"As do I, or at least back to the barn I'm staying in tonight. We're leaving before sunrise to go back up the mountain."

"You said you didn't come here to talk about what you do, so what did you come here for?"

"To mix with people who don't smell like pigs. To see people like you. To feel like a part of this community."

"Many reasons, then. So, what's next for the famous partisan leader, Lupo?"

"Join the Allies when they come. Carry on the fight."

Liliana looked up the path for her sisters, but they were too far ahead.

"Good luck, but don't forget about the people you're fighting for."

"I'm sure you need to hurry home. Your mamma is not one to be trifled with."

"You do know me a little, then."

"Until next time, signorina."

Liliana stood there for thirty seconds as Lupo faded into the darkness. She turned and paced down the path, hoping that her sisters would have the good sense to wait for her before they reached home. Thoughts swirled in her mind. Fabrizio. Lupo. Her parents. Her grandmother. Mrs. Chilcott. All brightness faded as she paced along the stony dirt trail. The trees on each side seemed to lunge at her with bony fingers, but she wasn't scared. There was nothing to be frightened of.

Lena's panicked voice cut through the dark. Liliana ran toward the sound as her sister appeared around the corner, panting.

"Come quickly."

"What is it?"

"Just come on. We need you." She turned to run back toward the house. Liliana followed her, her thoughts turning to her grandparents and when Nonna had fallen a few weeks before.

"Is everyone all right?"

"Everyone's fine, come on. You'll see."

Liliana tried to catch her little sister, to shake the truth out of her, but Lena was too fast. They ran. They reached the courtyard outside the old stone houses passed down through their family. Everything seemed normal, save the flickering light coming from the barn. Lena led her toward it.

"What's going on?"

But Lena didn't answer, just held a finger to her mouth. They pushed through the door. The pigs were asleep, their gentle snoring discernible against the silence of the night. Her father sat with Martina in the empty stall where the cow had been. They'd been forced to sell her a few months before. He turned to Liliana, the light of the candle illuminating every line on his weathered face. She opened her mouth to ask what was going on, but as her father moved back, she saw the man beside him. He was covered in dirt, the whites of his eyes like pearls in the puddle of mud that constituted his face. He looked up at her like a child, his mouth full of food, a plate of leftover bread and herring in front of him. He stuffed another piece into his mouth with filthy hands. He wore a uniform, but this was no German.

"I heard a sound behind the house. I almost ran the pitchfork through him. He doesn't have more than a few words of Italian. We thought . . ."

Liliana approached him and bent down to rest on her haunches in front of him. He glanced up at her and then back at the food.

"What's your name?" she said in English.

The man's head jutted up as if on a string. He took a second to chew before he answered. "Sergeant James Foley. Thank you. Thank you so much."

CHAPTER 2

Liliana's father listened as she translated for him. He introduced himself to Sergeant Foley, shaking his grubby hand. Foley greeted him with a few mispronounced words in Italian before bringing his focus back to the food in front of him. Liliana and Virginio spoke as he attacked it, barely chewing before he swallowed each mouthful.

"He doesn't seem hurt—nothing more than a few bruises and scratches," Virginio said.

"Was he alone?"

"Completely. I searched around the house after I brought him in here, but there's nothing."

"Does Mamma know?"

"No. She's asleep. I was up having a glass of wine and a smoke—waiting for you girls to come home." He turned to his younger daughters. "It's time for bed now, girls. Our guest will be with us overnight. Not a word about this to anyone, and leave your mother to me."

"Of course," the sisters said, almost in unison, and disappeared out of the barn.

Foley finished the food and gulped down a cup of water. Tiny rivulets ran down his chin, darkening the dried mud. Liliana pulled over a small bale of hay to sit on, facing the man.

"Where did you come from? How did you end up here?"

"I was in a camp south of here, only a few miles from the Allied front lines. They moved us out by train, bound for Germany. I escaped."

"How did you get off the train?"

"An Allied bomber dropped his payload on the train—blew the side of the carriage off. A few of us jumped out over a river."

"Did any of your friends escape?"

"I don't know." The man put down the cup, held it between shaking hands. "I don't know what happened to the others . . . I just kept running."

She gave him a moment to recover his composure, tried to imagine what he must have been thinking. She let him begin the conversation again.

"I'd heard about the partisans in the mountains here. I figured joining up with them was my best chance."

"Why didn't you try to get back across the lines to the Allies, if they were so close?"

"I figured we'd gone about twenty kilometers north, and I couldn't see how I was going to make it all the way back through German lines alone. I thought I could lie low with the partisans until the cavalry arrived. I don't have any other choice."

"We can't hide you for long." Liliana wondered what Lupo and his men would make of this American.

"I know that. I'm grateful for what you're doing. I was wandering through the hills, hiding from German patrols for the last couple of days until your father found me in the field behind your house."

"What were you doing back there? He almost killed you."

"Just looking for someone willing to take me in and point me in the direction of the partisans. Seems like I got lucky."

He reached out and shook Virginio's hand again as Liliana translated what they'd said. "My father wants you to know that we're helping you because we're committed to the Allies' cause, but if you're a German spy, he'll kill you himself."

Foley took the Italian's calloused hand again. "Tell your father thank you, and he has nothing to worry about."

Virginio stood up, motioning for his daughter to follow him as he walked toward the door.

"He needs a bath. I've never seen a pig as dirty as him. Go get a bathtub, and bring some water."

Liliana took her father by the arm. The American peered up at them as she led Virginio outside. "How do we know he is who he says he is?"

"What do you mean? He's American."

"I've heard stories about infiltrators, about German spies worming their way into the rebels, pretending to be Italian deserters, or even escaped prisoners of war."

Virginio paused and took off his hat. "Try to talk to him. Make sure his story adds up. I don't want to draw the wrath of the rebels. Let's presume we can trust him for now, though. Go and get the water for him."

Liliana went to the house, where Lena and Martina waited by the door. "Babbo's going to kill you if he finds you still up."

"Is he an American?" Lena said.

"Yes."

"Is he rich and handsome?" Martina said.

"He didn't show me his bank statement, and it's a little hard to tell how handsome he is considering he's caked in mud. Come on, help me get some water together so he can have a bath. Perhaps the water will reveal his beauty or his gold teeth."

The three sisters spent the next twenty minutes or so getting warm water together in jugs. Liliana brought each of them out to the barn so Babbo wouldn't catch the girls up. When she'd brought enough, she carried the small bathtub she had bathed in as a child. Her father and the American were in deep conversation—gestures interspersed with a few Italian words—when she sat back down with them.

"Thank you, signorina. What's your name?"

"Liliana Nicoletti."

"It's a pleasure to meet you."

"We'll give you some time to wash yourself off before you settle in for the night."

"Can you get me to the partisans?"

"Yes, but wash first, and we'll come up with a plan later."

Liliana and her father walked back into the house and sat down at the living room table. The girls had gone to bed. She got a cup of water for her father and one for herself.

"I spoke to Lupo only an hour ago."

"He was at the dance?"

"Not quite. He approached me as I was leaving."

"So they're here. Did he say where he was staying? We could get our houseguest over to him now. It'll be too dangerous for him to move during the daytime. If he runs into a patrol, or if the Germans find him here . . ."

"He didn't mention anything other than the fact they were in a barn, and they were leaving early in the morning," she said.

"We could go out looking for them," her father said, "but is the sergeant in any fit state to move? He seemed close to exhaustion when I found him. I had to almost carry him into the barn."

"What if he's a Fascist infiltrator?"

"I don't think—"

"Do you want to risk it? The rebels will burn out the barn if we deliver them an infiltrator. Or worse," Liliana said. Her father seemed to agree with her reasoning. She didn't really think he was an infiltrator, of course. Was it selfish that she wanted to speak to him longer? *There's good reason for him to stay—we can't wander around searching for the Stella Rossa in the middle of the night.*

"OK. Let's keep him here overnight." Virginio reached into his pocket and took out a cigarette. The sweet smell of tobacco smoke swirled around them, dissipating into the night before he spoke again. "I'm going to get him some fresh clothes. You can speak to him again once he's dressed. Be careful—don't let on we suspect anything. If anything happens—if he makes some kind of improper move, call out, and I'll be over with the pitchfork before you know it."

"I don't doubt it."

Liliana waited until the sounds of water sloshing ended. The light still flickered in the barn. It was after one in the morning, but adrenaline dispelled any of the tiredness she should have been feeling. At last her father gave her the thumbs-up and she reentered the barn. The man whirled around but seemed to relax as he recognized her.

He wore her father's old clothes. The trousers were too short and didn't reach his ankles. He looked different from the men around here. He was taller, perhaps two meters or more, while few around here approached that height. His skin was lightly freckled under his eyes, not beaten by the sun until it resembled old leather. The light of the candle flickered across his blue eyes.

"My father has a pitchfork."

Virginio glared at their guest.

"That's quite the opening to any conversation. I'll keep my hands to myself."

"Are you comfortable now?" Liliana asked.

"I was until I heard about the pitchfork." He sat down as she did, less than a few meters away from her. The water in the bathtub was the same muddy color he'd been minutes before. "Best bath I ever had. Best meal too."

"You like salted herring? That's original."

She reached into her mind for questions she could ask this man to test him, to learn his knowledge of a place she'd never been.

"What's your favorite baseball team?" she asked.

"What?"

"You know baseball?"

"Of course," he spluttered. "The Phillies, the Philadelphia Phillies."

Liliana wondered what a horse had to do with baseball, but she knew nothing of the sport and didn't want to look stupid. She pressed on. This time she'd ask something she knew something about.

"Who wrote *The Grapes of Wrath*?"

"John Steinbeck."

"*For Whom the Bell Tolls*? Who wrote that one?"

"Hemingway. Did I pass? I'm an American."

She looked at her father sitting in the darkened corner of the barn, although she knew he couldn't understand what they were saying. He leaned forward and nodded before retreating into the shadows once more.

The man seemed genuine, or was a great actor. She had done what she could. The rebels would vet him themselves. And God help him if he was a spy. She hoped he wasn't. He had a kind demeanor about him, firm yet gentle. The thought of him being kicked to death by the rebels wasn't one that she wanted to contemplate.

"Is it safe here? Will the Germans come?" Foley said.

"Not at night. They never bother us at night."

"What about in the morning? Will they come searching?"

"I don't see why. We haven't heard anything about them looking for escaped prisoners."

"You think they'd tell you?"

"Please try not to worry, Sergeant Foley. We can hide you. We don't want to get caught with you here any more than you do. We'll get you to the Stella Rossa tomorrow night. The German patrols come during the day. It's rare we get raided, but it's too dangerous to be out in daylight."

Liliana sat in silence for a moment, then said, "So you want to join the Stella Rossa?"

"For a while," he said.

"Just be careful. I know the head of the local rebel band personally. He's obsessed with weeding out infiltrators."

"I hope so. He's got nothing to worry about with me."

She imagined them questioning him, tried to imitate them in her mind. "What unit were you with? How were you captured?"

"I'm with the Third Infantry. We landed at Anzio in January. We were stuck there a few weeks, the Germans all around us. My captain ordered me to scout ahead of our lines, looking for some mortars that were lobbing bombs down on us. We got cut off." The man stood up and walked over to the window. It was a black mirror, and she could see his reflection as he stared into it.

"What happened then?"

"They came in to mop up and got me. I surrendered."

Liliana thought to question him on the details of the day he was captured, but thought better of it.

"Tell me about where you're from in America."

He turned around to face her again. "It's a little fishing town, down at the tip of New Jersey. You know what New Jersey looks like?" Liliana shook her head. "It's long and thin, and there's a little peninsula down at the tip. The town's called Cape May. It seems a million miles away from here. It's a quiet place, not a lot going on, at least in the wintertime. Summer's a different story. There's a beach we used to go to when we were kids, on sunny days."

"Is your family still there?"

"No. My sister lives in Philadelphia now, and my parents are gone. How many people live in this house? I met your sister—how old is she?"

"The one who fed you? That was Martina. She's sixteen. My other sister, Lena, who ran to get me, is a year younger. My mother's asleep. She doesn't know you're here. My grandparents live with us too, and my uncle and aunt and four cousins live in the house next door."

"How are you able to speak English so well?"

"I studied English in university. Spanish too. I had to come back here because of the war—classes were all suspended."

The interrogation wasn't going as she'd envisaged it. He seemed to be getting more out of her than she was out of him. She stood up, offering him some more water, surprised that he hadn't shown any apparent sign of wanting to go to sleep yet. Her father was dozing in a chair and startled when she approached.

"How is it going?" he asked.

"Well, I think. I believe him. He seems authentic."

"Talk to him a bit more, then we should let him sleep."

The American gulped down the water she'd brought him in seconds.

"You should have told me you were thirsty," she said.

"I will next time. What can you tell me about the rebels?"

Liliana sipped from her own cup of water, contemplating his question.

"Are they communists?" he asked.

"No. The name means 'red star,' but they've no particular political affiliation. They stand for the destruction of the Fascists and the Germans. Not much else. Their leader goes by the name of Lupo."

"The wolf?"

"I thought you didn't speak Italian."

"Just the important words and phrases."

"I saw Lupo only a few hours ago." One of the pigs snorted, and the American jumped, sliding on the gritty floor in the process. "It's OK," she laughed. "It's just a pig. Prunella won't hurt you, will you, girl?"

"Big brave soldier, eh?" Foley said with a smile as he sat back down. "What were you saying about the Stella Rossa?"

"Lupo and his men have become the law on Monte Sole, for better or worse. They run things now. The Germans might own the day, but Lupo owns the night."

The American raised his hand to cover a yawn. His body was slouching over as he sat now.

"You can stay here tonight, and we'll figure out where to put you tomorrow morning. You must be tired."

"I am. Thank you, Liliana."

"You're welcome, Sergeant Foley."

"James."

"You're welcome, James."

He extinguished the candle as they left, and the dark of night enveloped him.

James woke with the dawn. He felt the fear first. He felt it before he knew where he was or what had happened, even before he had opened his eyes. His heart hammered in his chest. His breath felt stilted, and he coughed, trying to draw more oxygen into his lungs. He raised his head; a piece of hay stuck to the side of his face. The snorting of pigs mixed with the low whispers in Italian outside the door. The mother pig was on her side, feeding the piglets. There must have been eight or nine of them sucking on her teats.

"Morning, Prunella. Seems like you have your hands full there," he said.

He raised himself to his feet, brushing the straw off the old pants the father had given him the night before. Everything ached. He longed to lie back down, to sleep for days, but hunger drove him on. The Germans came during the day. If they found him, all he'd endured would have been for nothing, and this family who had taken him in would be in danger. He wouldn't allow that to happen. He'd die first.

The daughter, the beautiful girl who'd gently interrogated him the night before, came in with bread and water.

"Did you sleep?" she said as she handed the food to him.

"I did. Let me tell you again how much I appreciate everything you and your family have done for me."

"We're glad to help. It's nice to have someone to practice my English with too. It's been a while."

"You'd never know," he said. "You speak English better than most Americans I know." James ripped the bread in half and stuffed it into his mouth, aware of her eyes on him as he ate; he put a hand over his mouth.

Liliana's father and another man came into the barn.

"This is my father's brother, Vito. He lives in the house next door. We thought it only fair to tell him," Liliana said. "If the Germans find you here, they won't differentiate between his family and ours."

"I understand. I don't want to get you in trouble. You've done so much for me already."

"I spoke with my father and my uncle. They have a hiding place for you. Then we leave tonight," Liliana said.

He shook both men's hands once more, thanking them. A middle-aged woman dressed in a faded, plain black dress came in behind them, looking James up and down, speaking in Italian.

"I'm Sergeant James Foley of the US Army. Pleasure to meet you, ma'am." James extended a hand to her. She took the ends of his fingers in her hand.

"This is my mother, Maria."

"Please tell her how grateful I am that she's allowed me to stay here. I'm sure I owe my life to you all."

Liliana began to translate, but her mother threw her hands in the air and walked out before she could finish.

"Mamma's pleased to meet you too."

James finished the last of his breakfast before Virginio led him out to the courtyard. The morning sun sprinkled through the leaves of the tall trees surrounding the three-story houses. James walked in silence behind the two men, Liliana by his side. The children playing in the courtyard stopped to whisper as he passed.

"Hello," one said in English—he thought this must be Lena. She looked ready to burst with the sheer excitement of this American in the courtyard of her family home.

He thought to say hello back to her but was all too aware of her father in front of him, so he nodded instead. He heard her laughing from behind him as Virginio led him into the house. He motioned for James to sit at the table and to help himself to the cheese and rabbit meat laid out for him. James did his best to restrain himself from attacking the food.

"Are there any German patrols around?" he asked Liliana.

Virginio sat down beside his brother as Liliana translated the question. Virginio answered him—making it plain whom he was to address.

"My father said that there are lookouts in place, just in case. If any Germans come, we'll get plenty of advance warning. We've washed your uniform. We'll bring it to you when it's ready. My father and uncle have designed a space for you to hide. It won't be comfortable, but it's too risky to leave you in the barn."

"I'm sure it will be fine."

"My father is going to go out with Vito to find the rebels. It could take a while."

"How often do the Germans come?"

"Hard to say, perhaps every week or so. The Fascists come too, more to push us around, trying to collect taxes they likely pocket themselves. Either is bad news."

Virginio took James to the outhouse, then led him up a staircase to where Vito and Liliana waited. There were three beds in the room, one messy and unmade. Virginio spoke in Italian, then Liliana translated.

"My father wanted me to tell you that you will need to be gone from here by nightfall, no matter what the circumstance. He also wanted me to tell you that this is the bedroom I share with my sisters."

"I understand. *Grazie mille*, signore."

Virginio handed him two bottles for his time in the wardrobe—one empty and one full of water. They removed the clothes, laying them on the bed before taking out the board to reveal the space James would spend the rest of the day crammed into.

It was just tall enough. James inhaled the clean air of the bedroom one last time as they placed the board a few centimeters in front of him. The two men slid the board into grooves along the bottom and side of the wardrobe. It fit perfectly, and James slipped into darkness once more. He heard them speaking, the sound of the door shutting, and then he was alone.

There was just enough space that if he cranked out his elbows, he could raise his arms. He pressed his fingers against the wood in front of him. His mind receded back to his childhood, bound in the closet, watching the tortures outside.

Liliana tried to put James out of her mind. Surely there was somewhere else they could have hidden him? He'd hardly be able to breathe in there. But she knew when to argue with her parents, and this was not one of those times. It was almost one in the afternoon now. He had been in there for hours. The children were still camped up on the hill outside, reveling in their role as lookouts. Lena had been up there with them for the morning, to supervise, but had come back down to work in the kitchen with Martina, Liliana, and their mother.

"Did you see how handsome he was?" Martina said.

"Stop that talk immediately," her mother said. "You put that man out of your mind."

"Can you imagine if he took us back to America with him, back to his big house? He could take us for rides in his automobile every day. We could eat pork and pasta and beef and all the fruit we could carry."

"The American will be leaving us in a few hours, and that will be the end of it." No one spoke. All four concentrated on kneading the dough for tomorrow's bread.

"He was handsome, though, wasn't he?" Lena whispered. Liliana tried to contain her laughter in front of her mother.

She ate lunch with her mother and sisters. The men still had not returned from their search for Lupo and the rebels. After they had finished, Martina and her mother began to prepare the evening meal before tackling some other chores.

"I'm going to go back up and keep watch. Trusting our lives to a bunch of kids doesn't seem wise to me," Lena said.

"So we'll trust our lives to you, a fifteen-year-old, instead," her mother said as she scrubbed the vegetables.

Lena chose not to answer and disappeared out the door. Liliana went out to the barn to make sure he hadn't left any trace. Ten minutes later she decided to check up on her cousins keeping guard. They were fifty meters up the path on the hill, just where it bent around, watching. She climbed up to them. Eleven-year-old Dino, and Mario, his ten-year-old brother, greeted her with whispers, putting fingers over their mouths.

"Where is Lena?"

"She was up here this morning, but we haven't seen her since."

"I think I can guess where she is," Liliana said. She fought back the anger within her—anything not to be her mother.

James opened his eyes as he heard the door to the bedroom open. The sound of a light footfall followed, and then the clothes in the wardrobe were taken out. He held his breath. The sunlight poured in, blinding him before Lena's smiling face appeared. She said something in Italian, motioning for him to come out. A plate of food and a glass of water sat on the bedside table. He knew he shouldn't, but he still clambered out of the space and sat on the bed. She nodded approval as he ate the bread. *Christ, if the father catches me up here, he'll tear my balls off.* More footsteps up the stairs and the door opened. Liliana looked angry and whispered something through gritted teeth. They seemed to be arguing about what their parents would say if they caught either of them in here alone with him. He continued eating. Liliana shooed her sister out of the room. Lena waved a solemn goodbye to him as she shut the door behind her.

"You shouldn't be out here."

"I know. I saw the food your sister brought. I was famished, I couldn't resist."

"I think you'd rather face the Germans than my mother if she caught you in here with her fifteen-year-old daughter."

"Noted. I didn't mean any disrespect. Can I just stay here for a few minutes? And finish the food she brought me at least?"

"If anyone comes . . ."

"I know. I'll get back into the wardrobe quicker than you can say Jack Robinson." His eyes drifted over to the window and the books underneath. "*Mrs. Dalloway*? You're reading that, in English?"

"Have you read it?"

"No." He finished chewing and then took a few seconds before he continued. "My mother was a voracious reader. I remember seeing the book when I was growing up. She had hundreds piled all over the house. I read a few, but never that one . . . What other books do you have?"

She got up and went to the bookshelf beside her bed. She came back holding a few and placed them beside him.

"*The Grapes of Wrath*. I read this one." He put it down and picked up the thick, dog-eared paperback underneath it. "*Gone with the Wind*. This was one of my mother's favorites." His hands were shaking. He handed the books back to her. "I started it, but never quite got to finishing."

"Why? Didn't you like it?" she asked.

"We moved. I moved. I went to live somewhere else. I couldn't bring much stuff with me."

"I finished it. Would you like to try and read it again?"

"There's not much light in that wardrobe to read by, and barely enough space to hold it out in front of me if there were."

"Another time, perhaps."

A cacophony of cowbells tore through the air. Liliana jumped up. "What is it?"

"The Germans. That's the signal from the lookouts. A German patrol."

James stood up and made for the wardrobe, Liliana for the window. "How many?" he whispered.

"One officer and six soldiers. I think they're SS."

She ran back to the wardrobe. James stood in place and she tried to position the board, but it slipped, the dull sound ringing out through the house. She picked up the false front again and slipped it back into place. The Germans were in the house now. He could hear them talking to the mother downstairs with harsh, rasping accents. Darkness overtook him once more.

Liliana took a few seconds to calm down as she finished hanging the clothes, reassuring herself that they would never know. The sound of jackboots on stone came up the stairs. She left the bedroom and closed the door behind her. A young German soldier was standing on the stairs below her, his brown eyes trained on her, his rifle down. He didn't look more than twenty-one.

"Go downstairs," he said in Italian.

She thought to say something, to ward him away from the bedroom, to somehow protect the American in the wardrobe, but what could she say? Best not to arouse more suspicion.

"I'm going," she said and continued down.

The young soldier remained still as she moved past him but moved up the stairs seconds after.

It took her ten seconds to descend to the kitchen. Three other soldiers were at the table with her mother, eating bread still warm from the oven. The officer she'd seen in the courtyard appeared in the doorway.

"Do you mind if we ask you to wait outside while my men undertake a cursory search of your house? We won't be more than a few minutes," he said in perfect Italian.

"Of course," her mother said. "Girls, let's go sit in the courtyard. It's a beautiful day, and we could use a break."

She led her three daughters outside. Lena was almost in tears. Her mother put an arm around her as they sat down on the ancient tree stumps that served as stools at the courtyard's edge. Liliana and Martina sat in silence, listening to the soldiers searching the house. Liliana waited for the sounds from the bedroom, shouting, and a rifle shot. Then what? Run? Could she leave her mother? She stiffened her posture, biting down on her lip.

The officer appeared at the front door of the house, ten meters from where they sat. He took off his hat, using his forearm to rub sweat off his brow, then began to walk toward them.

"Do you mind?" he asked. "I haven't had a chance to rest all day." He took his hat in his hand as he sat down next to Liliana. He was wiry and fit. His face was lined like that of an older man, though she guessed he wasn't more than thirty-five. Light-brown stubble dotted his weathered face. He wore the Iron Cross on his gray uniform, and the death's head adorned the hat resting in his lap.

"This is rather more pleasant than Russia," he said. Liliana's blood froze. "The sunshine, the beautiful scenery, the wine, the food. This is far more agreeable. What's your name, young lady?"

"Liliana Nicoletti."

"You have nothing to fear, Liliana. We're just here to find partisans. Are you a partisan?"

"No."

"Exactly as I thought. Do you know where I can find them?"

"No."

"Everyone says the same thing, but they hit the German supply lines to the front almost every day. Somebody's lying." He turned his icy-blue eyes on her. "My name is Hauptsturmführer Werner Brack of the SS. You have heard of the SS?"

"I have."

"Then you'll know that we are the *Führer's* crack troops, sent to do the job the regular Wehrmacht cannot. Can you guess what we're here to do, Liliana? You seem like a clever girl, I'm sure you can."

"I couldn't say."

"Oh, come now, don't be shy. What do you think the superiors in Berlin sent me here for? Why do you think they took my elite men from the meat grinder in Russia and brought us here?"

Liliana saw an SS man through the window of her bedroom on the third floor. If she were going to run . . .

"You're here to find the rebels."

"I knew you were clever. You look it. You're not quite correct, though. We're here to find and destroy the partisan scum that is so cowardly attacking our supply lines to the front. And you know what, Liliana? We need your help. Because without your help, they'll scuttle back to their rat holes, and we'll all be in danger. Do you understand?"

"I think so."

"I'm not sure you do. Is this your mother, and these are your sisters?"

"They are."

"And these other children, the ones on the hill, who warned you we were coming? Are they related to you also?"

"They're my cousins, Hauptsturmführer Brack."

"You want to keep them safe, don't you?"

"Yes."

"The only way to do that is to rid the area of the partisan filth who are draining your resources and focusing the anger of the Reich on your peaceful little community." He shuffled his hat from one hand to the other. "They're bringing death and destruction when we only want peace. Now, I ask you again, do you have anything to tell me?"

His eyes seemed to bore through her. Would they spare her family if she told? What about if she told them about Lupo and the rebels? Could she betray them, or the man in the wardrobe in her bedroom? Her mother and sisters were sitting a meter away, helpless.

A voice called out from the house in German. Brack stood up. "It seems our work is done here." He tipped his hat to her mother and sisters before turning around to face Liliana again. "You never answered my question, Liliana."

"I'll keep an eye out for anything out of the ordinary, and be sure to report it."

Brack walked back toward the house. The soldiers who'd searched the house were all outside now. Liliana could follow the gist of their conversation. They hadn't found anything in either of the houses. It was time to move on. Brack walked back to where Maria was sitting.

"So sorry about the mess, signora." He turned and walked away, the soldiers in tow.

CHAPTER 3

They waited until dinner was over to let James out of the wardrobe. He groaned, stretching out his tired limbs as Liliana translated for Virginio and Vito once more.

James asked, "Did they search any of the neighbors' houses?"

"Yes," she said after her father spoke.

"It seems like a big coincidence. Have you noticed more activity from the Germans lately? More troops, more operations?"

"Maybe. We've been searched twice in the last three weeks now, but never by an officer before. People say there are more troops than there used to be, but it's hard to tell. We keep to ourselves here." Liliana answered him directly this time, translating what she'd said back to her father, who seemed to concur.

"I need to get away from your house."

"No one's going to argue with that," she said. "Some rebels are staying in a barn about three kilometers away. We'll take you to them after you've eaten and changed back into your uniform." The mother brought a plate of food—leftovers from their dinner. He thanked her again before he inhaled it in seconds. He had never known hunger like this before, not even in the POW camp. Now he was to be a partisan, living and fighting in the mountains. For how long? How long would it take for the Allies to arrive? They were only twenty kilometers away, but the war was slow, and winter was coming. Those twenty kilometers might as well have been hundreds.

The night was crisp, a sweet, woody smell in the air. They moved in silence with Virginio at the front. Vito stood at the back of their tiny convoy with Liliana walking beside James in the middle.

"There's little chance of us running into any Germans at night," she said, "but my father didn't want to take any chances. If we see anyone, we're getting off the road. You run as fast as you can."

"Got it."

He wished he'd taken her up on the offer of the book. He wished he didn't have to do this and that he could go home.

Twenty minutes later a patch of houses came into view.

"This is it," Liliana said. "We'll wait here while my father goes to make sure everything's in order." They stood still, waiting in silence as Virginio walked toward a large barn. They watched him push through the door and go inside. James wanted to tell her how much this meant to him, and how he could never repay what she and her family had done. He wanted to tell her how scared he was and for her to reassure him that everything was going to be all right, but her uncle was glaring at him, so he kept quiet.

Virginio emerged and waved them the fifty meters or so to the barn. Vito pushed the door open, holding it for James and Liliana. Perhaps a dozen men lounged on the hay in the stalls. Several looked younger than James's twenty-three years—little more than teenagers. They all looked up as he entered, before dropping their heads in disinterest. A man in his thirties stood up and introduced himself as Gianluca. He shook James's hand and started talking. Liliana translated.

"You can stay the night here with these men, and then in the morning they'll bring you up the mountain to see if you're fit to join the Stella Rossa."

"Fit to join?"

"I'm sure it'll only be a formality for you."

Gianluca pointed to a man lying alone in the corner. "You can stay with Antonio, the other new man over there. Get some sleep—you're going to need it."

The partisan returned to the card game he had been playing. James turned to Virginio and Vito, shook their hands one last time, thanking them. They slapped him on the back and went to the door.

"Goodbye, Liliana. Thank you. Perhaps we'll see each other once again while I'm here. I don't know where I'll be."

"I'll be at the dance at the Laffis' old barn in Poggio on Thursday nights. I've seen members of the Stella Rossa there before. Perhaps if you're ever close by . . ."

"Liliana," Virginio said from the door.

"I have to go. Good luck, James."

Her father took her by the hand, and the door closed behind them. None of the other men paid him any mind. He went to the new man in the corner, but he couldn't speak English. James lay back on the hay, foreign and alone. He tried to think of Liliana's face. It was the only thing that blocked out the dread. He closed his eyes, but sleep was hours in coming.

The veil of night hadn't yet lifted when a rough hand awakened James. The other rebels were packed and ready to go. He and Antonio were the last to be told. They didn't have weapons, weren't trusted with them yet, and were forced to carry bags of supplies instead. Lanterns were extinguished, and the rebels slipped out the barn door. The early morning was still, cool, and damp. The clouds above were lightening, the sun coming in an hour or so. They moved out in silence. James and Antonio walked toward the back of the formation and were guided up the hill behind the barn. James was impressed by the discipline these men showed. Perhaps the image he had in his mind of a disorganized rabble was wrong. Each man carried a weapon that seemed clean and new—an assortment of Sten, Breda, and Browning machine guns and rifles. One hauled a mortar. Their uniforms betrayed the random nature of their backgrounds, however. Most wore the plain clothes of the men of Monte Sole, but several sported Italian Army uniforms. One man wore British Army fatigues.

The formation trudged up the mountain in silence. The sun rose behind them, an orange ball of flame lifting over the horizon. The line of men stopped. The partisan leading James and Antonio said something, reached into the satchel he was carrying, and removed two blindfolds, tying them around the new men's eyes. James thought to protest but realized the futility of it. He felt a partisan take him by the sleeve, leading him up. It was hard to tell how long they kept on for, perhaps an hour or more. James stumbled several times and had to be hauled back to his feet by the man assigned to lead him. He didn't speak, just kept on. He heard voices and smelled the smoke from a fire. They stopped. The blindfolds were taken off.

Several dozen men lounged around, their weapons beside them in the dirt. A fire burned in the middle of the clearing they had settled in, a cauldron of soup or stew cooking over it. A few of the rebels glanced over at him, but most continued to snooze or chat or play cards.

A handsome man, with tight curly black hair and several days' stubble, approached him, speaking Italian to the men who'd guided them up here before focusing on James.

"You're an American?" he said in English.

"James Foley of the Third Infantry Division."

"And you want to be James Foley of the Stella Rossa," he said.

"I'd be honored if you'd take me."

The man barked something in Italian, and the rebels who'd brought the two men poked them with the barrels of their rifles, urging them forward, away from the camp.

James knew better than to ask questions. Antonio chirped like a bird, however, and the handsome partisan growled at him to be quiet. They walked a hundred meters through the brush to another open space. Two shovels lay on the ground.

"Dig," the partisan said.

The two men did as they were ordered and sunk the shovels into the cold, stony Monte Sole dirt. The partisan directed Antonio to join digging the hole James had begun, and soon they'd dug a trench two meters long and one meter deep. Antonio was panicking, barely able to hold the shovel. James felt his own body shaking. Was there any escape from this? They couldn't mean to kill him, could they? He was an American soldier.

"I don't know what's going on here," he said. "I'm an American soldier. I want to join you to fight the Germans."

"Get out of the hole."

He stepped up and out of the hole. Antonio did the same but pushed into James, knocking him over as he made a break for the cover of the woods that surrounded them. The sound of machine-gun fire rang out, and his back spouted crimson as he fell to the ground in a heap.

"We just had to be sure," the handsome partisan said. "We had word that he might have been an infiltrator sent by the Fascists. We know now." He helped James to his feet. "I am Lupo, the leader of the Stella Rossa." Another rebel walked over, the barrel of his gun still smoking. "This is Gianni, my oldest friend, and second in command here."

"We're pleased to have you," Gianni said. "There are several other escaped prisoners here, although I think you might be the only American."

Gianni led James back to the camp as Antonio's body was dumped into the grave he had helped dig. James was introduced to a cluster of men. One introduced himself in English as Jock.

"Nice to meet you," Jock said in a thick Scottish accent. "Always nice to have a new guy around."

"How long have you been up here?"

"I've been with Lupo for almost six months now, putting my time in until we're liberated. It's been quite the ride, though. I dunno if I'd want to introduce him to my dear sister back in Aberdeen, but he's a leader, and that's what we need." He slung his rifle over his shoulder. "We'll have to decide what to call you next."

"Foley. My name is James Fo—"

"You think my name's Jock? We all take new names. All the locals cut themselves off from their families. I don't know most of these lads' real names or who they are, but I'd die for any of them."

He turned to the other men and said something James couldn't understand in Italian. One of them looked at him and came out with "Baseball." The other men laughed.

"Looks like your name's Baseball now."

"I can live with that."

James moved with the group as they shuffled over to where Lupo stood on a stool. A hundred or more men waited, hushed, and he began to speak. Jock stood beside James to translate for him.

"This is our land," Lupo said. The rebels deliberately restrained their approval, nodding instead of clapping. "This is our land. No one's going to take it from us. Not the Germans. Not the Fascists. No one! It's ours."

"It's not mine," Jock said before repeating himself in Italian to the amusement of the other men.

"No, but we thank you and our other Allied friends for all you do to defeat our common enemy," Lupo said before getting back into his speech. "Our parents and grandparents and their parents and grandparents have worked this land for hundreds of years. We were here before the Germans and the Fascists, and we'll be here after we throw them off our land." Several men applauded, making sure not to make too much noise. "The Allies are close, but our jobs are far from over."

He unslung the rifle from his shoulder and handed it to Gianni. "We must prove to the Allies that we are their equals in vanquishing the menace of the Germans. I've dealt with the British and Americans on the radio—you all know that. We've benefited from their supply drops, but I know this much about them—we're going to have to earn their respect. If we lie down now and wait for the Allies to sweep through, they won't recognize anything we've done here. Too many of our men have sacrificed themselves for me to allow that to happen. We will be recognized and we will be incorporated into the Allied forces that will liberate all of Italy."

Twenty minutes later James's squad was ready to move out. He was issued a Sten gun, five magazines, and two grenades. He was to be in the company led by Lupo himself.

"Welcome to the Stella Rossa," Jock said.

Liliana walked to the store alone. She tried to brush the thoughts of the American from her mind. Why had she told him about the dance on Thursday night? She'd never see him again. He would be on the mountain, then he would disappear forever. He had drifted in and out of her life like pollen in the spring breeze.

The sound of a plane overhead brought her back into the moment, and she ran to take cover. Once she realized it was too high to strafe the ground, she relaxed enough to peer up and try to make out the markings. It was German. She continued on as leaflets began drifting down on the wind, blanketing the path in front of her. She bent down to pick one up. It was a cutting from the Bologna newspaper, *Il Resto del Carlino*. It was a statement from Generalfeldmarschall Albert Kesselring, the commander of the Axis forces in Italy, dated that day, the seventeenth of September.

The actions of partisans can no longer be tolerated. From this moment on they will be acted upon immediately and in the most severe manner possible. The entire Italian population must carry out this battle, without quarter, for the destruction of banditry and delinquency. Whoever knows where a band of rebels is in hiding and does not immediately inform the German army will be shot. Whoever gives food or shelter to a band or to individual rebels will be shot. Every house that has harbored a rebel will be burned to the ground.

Liliana was panting by the time she made it past her parents' house to where her father and uncle were working in the field.

"Have you seen this?" she said.

The two men took the paper from Liliana's hand. She knew how much faster it would have been to read it out to them but stood back and waited.

"Bluster," Vito said. "They make so many threats. We should have all died five times already."

"Not like this," Liliana's father said. "Never as explicitly as this." He handed the paper back to his daughter. "Is your mother in?"

"As far as I know, she's out with Martina checking the rabbit traps and picking mushrooms."

"Excellent. Vito, if she asks, tell her I've gone to Marzabotto."

"What are you going there for?"

"To try to reason with a Fascist."

"Better to try and reason with a lion while your head's in its mouth."

"Just tell her. Come with me, Liliana."

They left her uncle and started walking down toward the next village. They could reach the town of Marzabotto, the municipal hub of the area, in less than two hours on foot, but her father had another idea—Luigi Torricelli. He went into town several times a week, so they hitched a ride on the back of his cart, sitting among the eggs, milk, and corn. Liliana sat beside her father, looking out at the rugged, uneven beauty of the land.

Less than an hour later they arrived at the office of the local land commissioner, a bureaucrat who had been a greengrocer before the Fascists came to power. Now he sat behind a desk in a gray suit. His door was open, and they could see that he was alone, yet he made them wait more than twenty minutes. Liliana studied the Fascist propaganda posters on the wall warning against the perils of the Allied forces and how ratting out your neighbors was patriotic.

The bureaucrat called them in at last, not standing as they entered, not looking up from the papers he was reading until they sat down.

"Signore Fabbro," her father said. The man put the papers down on his messy desk. Portraits of Hitler and Mussolini stared down at them from the wall behind him. "I want to discuss the possibility of breaking the lease on my farm holding and moving my family away."

It was incredible for Liliana to hear him say those words. Her mother agreeing with the decision was beyond her comprehension. War made the unthinkable routine.

"I applied a few weeks ago," he continued.

"Oh really," Fabbro said.

"Yes, I sat in this very office when you denied my application."

"Let me see," Fabbro said. He got up to go to the filing cabinet in the corner. Liliana stayed quiet. "What was your name again?"

"Nicoletti."

"Oh, here you are." He made his way back to the desk, opened the file, and closed it again. "You were rejected. What can I do for you?"

"I want to file an emergency petition to break my lease. The war is closing in. The front lines could be on my doorstep any day and the rebels—"

The man sat forward. "You have information about the rebels?"

"Not other than that they're putting my family in danger. The Germans published an article in the newspaper this morning."

"I'm aware, Signore Nicoletti, but the law is the law. If you leave, you forfeit the lease and will have to pay the balance on it. If you don't have the money, your house could be seized."

"I don't. I can barely feed my family. I'm asking you, as an Italian, to let us go. Fill out your forms, but let us go."

"You farmers—stubborn until the end. The law applies to all of us. You can fill out another application, but there is a six-month waiting list now."

"Six months? We might not have six days."

Liliana looked out the open window. A truck full of German soldiers arrived in the courtyard outside. They jumped onto the rough cobbled yard. Their camouflaged uniforms were different than what she'd seen before. Each soldier bore the mark of the SS on his lapels.

Her father was silent as they left the office. They met Luigi again and climbed on the back of his now-empty cart as he made his way back toward the mountain.

"I can't believe Mamma agreed to this," she said after twenty minutes of silence.

"They'll only come for the men," her father said under his breath. "They won't touch the women and children."

James had passed three cold nights sleeping outdoors. There was little food. The stores were almost empty, and the shopkeepers in the valley had grown wise to the rebels' ways. There was hardly even anywhere to steal from now. They had bullied a poor farmer to give up his bread, milk, and eggs the night before, despite his pleas that it was all he had. James had eaten what he'd taken. It was the only morsel he'd had all day. Lupo left the farmer an IOU, as he always did. How he intended to pay all these farmers and shopkeepers back when the war ended was beyond the understanding of any of them, if any cared to think about it.

James rubbed his hands together in some vain attempt to clean them. He was filthy and tired and scared. They spent most of their days hiding out in the thick scrub or on top of one of the mountains, but they could stroll around with some impunity after the sun went down. The rebels didn't seem overly worried about a German assault. It seemed that they'd evaded the Germans so many times as to become masters of it. James just hoped their confidence was justified.

He rested under a tree, and Jock came to him. He, like everyone else here, was escaping something. He was a fellow prisoner of war, just like his friend Karoton, a Russian who'd jumped a train just as James had. Karoton didn't speak much English and not more than a smattering of Italian, but the notches on the stock of his rifle for the Germans he'd killed made his intentions for joining the Stella Rossa clear as the mountain streams.

"Enjoying your holiday in the Italian countryside?" the Scot said.

"Very much. The food's not quite what I'd hoped for, but the company more than makes up for that."

"And the bathing facilities?"

"Mud baths are excellent for the complexion."

"Christ, I'd kill for a cigarette." Jock took the rifle off his shoulder and sat down beside James. "You OK?"

"Other than the fact that I'd eat my own arm off and I smell like a pigsty assaulted by a company of racoons? Yes. I'm alive."

"More than we could say for many," Jock said. "A few of the men have been talking. They reckon we're pushing too far."

"How so?"

"Mauro got a letter from his cousin yesterday when he was in town. Cousin lives, or lived, in a place called Sant'Anna. A small place in Tuscany, a couple hundred kilometers from here, almost at the coast. Seems that the Germans came through a few weeks ago, killed everyone.

51

Women, children. Everyone. Hundreds. The bastards came in and wiped everyone out and burned the bodies with wood taken from the church."

James thought of Liliana and her family. "You think that could happen here?"

"Who the hell knows? Who knows if Mauro's cousin is telling the truth at all? Or even if Mauro has a cousin. Lupo won't hear a word of it. Says we have to press on," Jock said as he pushed his fist up into the air with faux histrionics.

"Even if we're endangering the lives of the people we're meant to be fighting for?"

"Apparently so." Jock spat in the dirt before standing up. "Lupo's gotten us this far . . ."

Both men looked up as a man called Dieci—a nickname he'd gotten because he'd killed ten Germans—approached them. He said something in Italian to them and walked away.

"Looks like Lupo intends to see how far he can push this. Get your gun. Something big is going down. Right now."

James jumped up to follow Jock. They ran through the brush until they saw the others from their squad. Lupo was directing, as always. They gathered around him.

"I just got a signal that there's a car coming along this road with some officers. We're going to take them out."

James had never killed a man before, had never even engaged an enemy in combat. Lupo put his hand on James's shoulder. "Are you with me, Baseball?"

James knew there was only one thing to say. "Every step of the way, Lupo."

"Well then, let's go."

They walked for ten minutes. Lupo led them out of the brush to a hill overlooking a winding, hedge-sided road. He directed them in silence, ordering Jock and James to the other side of the road. They'd be exposed—isolated from the rest of the group—if they didn't kill every German coming. Lupo gave the signal, and Jock ran, keeping his body low to the ground. James cursed under his breath as he followed. The Scot took a position behind a boulder by the side of the road. James lay in a thick bush, in front of where the ambush was to take place. He would have a clear view of the oncoming car. The rest of the squad was hidden up on the hill.

He settled down, trying to get comfortable. The barrel of the Sten gun was wet where he held it. This was a different kind of fear than the one he knew, and somehow there was a comfort in that. Jock was about five meters away, lying on his front, the barrel of his Sten gun pointed out from behind the rock.

The minutes trickled by until the car came into view. It was a convertible, the top down. There were four men—a driver and what looked like three officers. James closed his eyes, drawing breath deep into his lungs as he brought his finger to the trigger. The car slowed as it came to the corner where Jock was lying, and the sound of gunfire ripped through the air. James got to his knees, taking aim at the driver, unleashing a hail of bullets that chewed up the hood of the car, striking the windshield and then the man himself. Blood spurted on broken glass. The firing went on, bullets pummeling the car and the now lifeless bodies inside. The gun stopped as the ammunition in his magazine ran out, but his finger remained on the trigger, every cell in his body focused on squeezing it.

A voice from the hill called out and the firing ended. James retreated behind the bush as Lupo emerged from the brush on the hill, the others following. The men in the car looked like they'd been shredded by wild animals, their eyes open, their faces streaked with blood. The rebels smiled, slapping each other on the back, slinging their machine guns over their shoulders as they strolled down the hill.

James felt like his body was made of stone. His hands were still shaking. Jock waved to him, and he managed to walk toward the car.

He tried to trace the path of the bullets he'd fired. The driver's face was gone. He tried to figure if the bullets that had killed the driver were from his gun. Had he killed this man? Did it matter? The other rebels were gathered around the car. Lupo was happy. He searched the corpses in the car, handing out cigarettes from a broken cigarette case, and checking their ID papers. He reached down for a leather satchel by a dead man's feet and said something in Italian.

"Baseball," he said. "Have a look." It was a detailed map of the German front line and the troops deployed there. "You think your generals would be interested in this?"

"I know they would, but how do we get it to them?"

"Have a little faith, my friend. We have ways—"

The noise of a truck cut him off. The smile melted from his face. One of the rebels ran to the first bend in the road and called back, the panic evident in his voice. The squad scattered, running through the bushes and back up the hill. James looked back and saw two trucks, both spewing German soldiers onto the road behind them. The bullets followed seconds later. One of the rebels was hit, calling out as two others put their arms around him, dragging him on. James ran behind Jock. The cover of the trees was only a hundred meters away, but the German soldiers were advancing up the hill behind them now, taking to their knees to fire before getting up to run. More men were hit. James almost tripped on the body of a seventeen-year-old boy they called Baby Face, a ragged wound blooming red in the middle of his chest. James reached down to him, but Jock dragged him on.

"He's gone. Keep moving. We're all dead if we don't make the trees."

Lupo ran ahead of them, the leather satchel in his hand. Another rebel went down, clutching his chest, and then another. James's breath burned in his lungs. He could hear bullets whistling past his head, chewing the dirt around him. Three of the rebels had reached the trees and were laying down suppressing fire. The Germans below them took cover. James made the trees, with Jock just behind him.

"There's still six of our men down there," James said. "They might not all be dead."

"We have to assume they are, or else we all will be," Lupo said.

The Germans had stopped fifty meters or so down the hill and were setting up mortar positions. James saw Ming, one of the rebels they'd left, still moving, writhing in pain in the dirt, the Germans only meters away from him.

"Lupo, Ming is still alive. The Germans are almost on him," James said.

"I see him."

He reached across to one of the other rebels and took the hunting rifle he was carrying. He raised it, resting it on a branch, taking aim through the scope as the other men continued to fire. The Germans were around Ming now, one lifting him by the lapels. Lupo fired, and Ming's head sprayed red.

"What?" James said.

"Better that than they torture him to death. I've seen it too many times."

The soldier who was holding him let his body flop to the ground. Lupo fired another shot, putting the German down.

"Time to go," he said.

What remained of the squad turned and ran through the forest. They kept going up, the woods ever thicker. The crumps of mortar rounds landing were audible at the tree line behind them, but they were long gone.

They reached the temporary camp a few hours later, just as night was drawing in. Few spoke. Lupo sat down with James to go over the map. James made a quick drawing of it, stowing it in his pocket before handing the original back to Lupo.

"Your OSS will be most interested in this," Lupo said. He dispatched it to a messenger who would get it to an Allied agent in Bologna that night.

"Was it worth it?" James asked.

Lupo got up and went to his tent. James stood back, the adrenaline of the chase fading out as exhaustion came in its stead. After deliberating for thirty seconds, he decided to follow him.

"You never answered my question," James said.

Lupo laughed. "You think I have to answer to you?"

"Is the Stella Rossa going too far? Are we endangering the local population now?"

"This is war, Baseball."

"I know where we are and what we're doing. I also know the Allies are coming soon . . ."

"And you think that means we should just let the Germans go about their business?"

"Did you hear about the massacre at Sant'Anna? All those women and children? Hundreds, I heard."

"Rumors, just rumors. No one knows what happened, or even if anything happened. I read the newspapers. They didn't report anything of the kind."

"Mauro's cousin—"

"Mauro's cousin," Lupo laughed. "Listen to yourself. Do you really expect me to change the course of our fight against the Germans because of a letter Mauro got from his cousin? The man's a drunk."

"What if he's telling the truth? What if the Germans did murder hundreds of women and children because of what the rebels did there—the same things we do every day?"

Lupo stepped forward, so close to James that their noses almost touched. "Then we'll make them pay. We'll drink the blood of every Nazi bastard from here to Berlin."

"At what cost? What about the people here? They're defenseless. Are we going to stand up to a full Nazi assault if they come for the people here?"

"We've heard this a hundred times. How long have you been here, a week? It's not going to come to that."

"How do you know?"

"Because I know, all right? This is my land. And if you're not with us, you can leave. This is my brigade, and we're going to do everything we can to kill every Nazi on this mountain between now and when the Allies get here."

James walked away.

CHAPTER 4

They were all thinner. The government rations weren't enough, and it had been a miserable harvest season. Grandparents reminisced upon the harvests of their youth as they sat staring into the fire, flames dancing in their eyes. The people of Monte Sole assured anyone who would listen that they would recover their way of life once the war ended. The halcyon days of their youth would return. Liliana didn't have the heart to argue with them.

Most of Liliana's family had taken Vito's view that the latest German threats were nothing more than empty words, the last gasps of a dying regime. The Allies were coming, and with them liberation. Her father didn't mention his concerns again.

The burning cat was screaming—that was how Lupo had phrased it. They'd all heard innumerable warnings about German offensives before. This one came from a local Fascist boss, Lorenzo Mingardi, who warned any Fascist refugees in the area to vacate Monte Sole because the Germans were going to destroy it. An order had come through to excise the partisans from Monte Sole with no delay. Everyone was to be killed. There were to be no exceptions. Mingardi had fled to Bologna with his family after delivering his message.

Lupo was confident that nothing was going to happen but didn't leave anything to chance. Messengers were sent scurrying all over the mountain to warn other rebels of a possible attack. But they determined they would not tell the people of the mountain community—to avoid creating a panic. The rebels were to be even more watchful, even more paranoid than usual, and were to be ready to slip away at the first sign of trouble.

The process of passing the message took almost a full day. The rebels were split into squads and distributed in nearly every barn and hayloft across Monte Sole. There were thirty or forty men at a barn in Possatore, another fifty in the haylofts in Steccola, forty in the headquarters at Cadotto, a well-armed force in the churchyard at San Martino, and smaller units dotted all over. The Germans had put the squeeze on the Allied airdrops that kept the Stella Rossa supplied, and their ammunition was dwindling, but morale was still high. Most were convinced that the end of the war was weeks away. If the Germans did come, they'd slip away as they always did. They'd suffered losses, but the Germans had never caught up with them. They disappeared into the ether every time the Germans got close, and they would do so again if the need arose.

James sat in the barn at Cadotto with Jock and Karoton. James placed his weapon down, pointing to the notches along the wooden stock of the Russian's rifle, fudging to find the words in their common language of Italian.

"How many notches now?"

"Twenty-two."

"Nothing this man enjoys more than killing Germans. Nothing in this world," Jock said. James's weapon was caked with mud, and he set to cleaning it after he'd finished the paltry serving of soup and bread that constituted that night's dinner. Lupo and Gianni were studying the copy of the map of the front line that James had drawn. The radio played beside them, the upper-crust English broadcaster just about audible from where James sat. Few in the barn were talking above a whisper, but Lupo shushed them as he zeroed in on the announcer's message.

"That's it," he said. "The signal—the Allies received the map we sent them!" A hushed cheer went up around the barn. Lupo and Gianni embraced one another. Several men offered their congratulations.

"Nothing Lupo likes more than to look good in front of the generals in London," Jock said so only James could hear.

James gave a thumbs-up to Lupo and went back to cleaning his gun, thinking about the abstract idea of home, thinking about the girl he'd met in the barn. He ran a cloth along the barrel of his weapon, staining the fabric with the mud that came off. "What about that warning from that local Fascist? Mingardi?" he said to Jock, who was pretending to smoke a cigarette through empty fingers.

"If that man told me water was wet, I'd ask for a second opinion." Jock reached over and put a hand on James's shoulder. "We don't know if the rumors about any massacres are true, and Mingardi is hardly trustworthy. I understand where you're coming from and I'm nervous too, but what would you have Lupo do? You're new here. We've all heard warnings like this before."

"But women and children? We can't defend the people of the mountain against an assault. We're not built for that."

"No, we cannot. The Germans would scythe through us. We just have to hope Lupo's right."

"Why are we playing games with the lives of the locals? Why don't we warn them?"

"Because it's probably not true. Because most of them wouldn't and couldn't leave anyway." He pointed a finger at James. "You're still thinking about that girl you told me about."

James threw the rag down. "If we warned them . . ."

"You don't think these guys are concerned about the people here? We're outsiders, buddy, but most of these men have been here all their lives. Their mothers and fathers and sisters are still at home. You don't think they want to protect them? We have to follow orders. It's just like being in the regular army—we aren't paid to make those decisions. We have to let it go."

"We're being paid? Where's my money?"

"I saw a rainbow yesterday; I think it was at the end of that."

It was hard to argue with what Jock had said. This place would be a memory to him in a few weeks. Most of the other men would be here the rest of their lives. Protecting this place was tantamount to walking a tightrope—do too little and the Germans never leave, do too much and reap the whirlwind they'd bring.

"I *was* thinking about that girl."

Jock laughed. "How'd I know?"

"You have a girl back home?"

"Aye, a wife in Aberdeen. A wee bairn too—my son, Hamish. He's three now. I think about him pretty much all the time. I doubt he'd know who I was if he fell over me on the street."

"We'll just have to make sure you get back to him soon."

"Aye, and I'm looking forward to the process of making him a new brother or sister, let me tell you." They both laughed. "You have anyone back home?"

"Just a sister. I think about her all the time. Is that pathetic?"

"Not even a little bit."

James got up and went to a trough, plunging a cup into it and taking a drink of what tasted like the best water he'd ever had.

"She's only seventeen, still in high school. We're close. We had to be, growing up. It was a tough house. She went off to live with our aunt in Philadelphia when things fell apart."

"We all need someone to keep us going over here, someone to come home to."

"It's ridiculous. I don't even know her plans for next year—if she wants to go to college. I miss her letters."

"We'll get you back to her. Put your trust in Lupo. He hasn't steered us wrong yet."

"I hope you're right," James said and lay back on the pile of straw behind him that was to serve as that night's bed.

CHAPTER 5

Virginio burst into the room just after dawn. Liliana jolted upright. The other two girls were still asleep. "Wake up! Girls! Wake up! The Germans are burning houses. It's not safe here." Martina and Lena opened their eyes, weary and uncomprehending. "Get dressed. We have to leave." He ran back down the stone stairs. Liliana bounded out of bed. It was slate-gray outside, the rain spitting down through the half-light of the early morning. The distant sound of a machine gun firing cut through the air. The Germans had come for the revenge they had promised.

"Get up," Liliana said, trying to contain herself, trying to be the adult in front of her little sisters. "Father says we have to leave." Three minutes later, they had all dressed and run down to the kitchen, where their mother waited.

"What's going on?" Lena asked.

"I don't know, but we have to leave."

Their mother embraced each one of them. She gave them a piece of yesterday's bread, and they drank from the cups she'd laid out. Uncle Vito and Aunt Tania appeared with their four children, who clung to their parents like they were life rafts adrift in a storm.

"Get out into the courtyard," Vito said. "You're going to the church at Casaglia. You'll be safe there."

"I'll get Nonna and Nonno," Maria offered. "We'll catch up."

"What about you and Father?" Martina asked Vito.

"It'll be the men they're after. They won't bother women and children. We'll go up the mountain and hide with the others there."

Her father entered, the wet of the rain glistening on his clothes. He went to his nephews and nieces and then his wife, embracing each of them in turn, and then his younger daughters and finally Liliana. "Be safe," he whispered. "This will pass. Everything passes." Her father and uncle left to join the other men in the scrub of the mountain above them. Aunt Tania led the group outside. The rain thickened as they walked toward the church. Liliana could see smoke billowing from several houses in the distance. The sound of gunfire rang out through the valley like bones snapping.

Gunshots wrenched James from his sleep. The light of dawn was just breaking through the night, but James could see rebels scattering through the barn. Jock extinguished the lantern beside him, casting the barn into a murky half-light. Men called out inside and outside the barn. Two rebels shoved the door open and were cut in half by German bullets. Men scrambled to firing positions, grabbing for weapons and ammunition.

Lupo gathered them around. "We get out," he said. "We do not engage the enemy. This is a fight we cannot win."

Gianni went to the back door, his girlfriend, who had been visiting for the night, beside him. She was hit several times in the chest and fell down in a crumpled heap. He bent down over her.

Jock peered out a front window. "They're all over the perimeter."

James crept to a window at the back of the barn, where he saw several SS troops in camouflage running through the rain. "More over here," he called out.

Lupo tugged at Gianni's arm, telling him to leave his girlfriend. Another rebel went down, clutching at his neck before going still.

"We've got to get out," James said.

Karoton was by the front door, doing his best to lay down covering fire. The noise of the guns stopped for a few seconds before the sound of a heavy machine gun cut through the air. Tracer bullets flew through the barn, setting the hay alight.

"Time to go," Lupo said, dragging his best friend beside him. Karoton got up, inching backward as he fired. Several rebels tried to get out the side door but were cut down in seconds. The fire spread through the barn, the tracer bullets still slicing through the air. Two more rebels went down. Lupo led Jock, Karoton, Gianni, and James up to the loft. They went to a window. Dozens of SS troops were approaching from almost every direction.

Gianni seemed to snap back into life. "We're dead if we stay here. We have to make it to the woods and then to Ca' Termine," he said in English.

"Agreed. Let's go," Lupo said. The SS entered the barn below. Karoton opened up on them, killing three men. They climbed through a window and then across the top of the barn, afforded some cover by the darkness and light fog of the early morning. Then they jumped down into the stable and burst through a door. Lupo was first and a waiting SS man raised his rifle, but Gianni was faster. He killed the German with a shot to the throat. Gunshots and German voices sang around them. The men jumped into a wet ditch in front of the stable and squelched through the ankle-high water. The scrub was two hundred meters away, and each man hauled himself out of the ditch and ran toward it across a fallow field. Gianni was at the front, with Lupo covering the rear as they ran. The German fire came again, raking across the field around them. Gianni was hit, a bullet striking the back of his thigh, sending a puff of crimson into the air. He fell onto the sodden ground. Lupo stopped beside him.

"Keep going!" Jock shouted, pulling at James's arm. Karoton took the wounded man across his massive shoulders, and they ran. The muddy ground sucked at their feet, dragging them back toward the pursuing SS. They reached the scrub. The Russian still had Gianni on his back.

"Where's Lupo?" James shouted.

"What? Where is he? We can't leave without him," Gianni said.

Dozens of SS were in the field behind them, taking firing positions.

"We have to go right now," Jock said.

"No. We can't leave him," Gianni screamed. But they started running again, the SS bullets tearing bark off the trees around them.

"Where are we going?" James said.

"To our emergency zone—on top of Monte Sole."

"There is no safer place in the world than a church," Nonna said as she shuffled along the path toward the church at Casaglia. Liliana had her arm, and Martina had Nonno in hers. Their family had joined together with several others to form a caravan of women, children, and elderly making their way toward the perceived safety of the church. They could hear the gunfire, the sounds of grenades exploding, and the screams of animals left to die in burning barns. Few spoke. They just kept on through the rain. The group reached the church at about eight, and each family took their usual seats in the pews facing the altar. Liliana sat between her two sisters, holding hands. The young priest, Don Ubaldo, greeted them as they sat. They joined him in saying the Rosary in Latin. Soon the little church was full.

A few minutes passed before machine-gun fire outside rattled the windows. Several women called out. The young priest raised his arms to calm them, but his hands were shaking.

"Have courage. The saints will protect you," he said. "This is the house of God."

They heard jackboots on stony ground and German shouts. Then the doors burst open. Several people screamed as the SS appeared. The

Boni family left their usual place by the second door and made a break for the field outside. Liliana's sisters gripped her wet hands tighter. Machine-gun fire rang out from the meadow.

The Germans were shouting something, and Don Ubaldo made his way down the aisle toward them. The SS soldiers began directing the people in the church out the door, ignoring Don Ubaldo's inquiries as to their intentions. Liliana and her family stood up and joined the line of people now forced to leave the small church. The soldiers herded the terrified members of the congregation to the courtyard outside. The rain had stopped and a dull sun peered through gray clouds. Seven SS men stood with their weapons pointed at the crowd. The dead bodies of the Boni family were strewn in the field a few meters away.

"We should try to make a run for it," Martina said under her breath to her sisters.

"How can we leave Mamma, and the little cousins, and Nonno and Nonna?" Liliana said.

Aunt Tania was beside them, her four children huddled around her. Maria was with her parents, her arm around her mother. It was true. Even if she and the other girls somehow got away, they would shoot her mother and grandparents as punishment. Another man walked around from behind the church, eyeing the cringing crowd. Liliana recognized him immediately. It was the officer who'd come to their house. He'd seemed like a reasonable man. Surely, she could talk to him, find the way out of this madness?

"Herr Hauptsturmführer Brack," she said. "Excuse me, what is going on?"

But the officer kept walking. Don Ubaldo was last to leave the church and went to him. Liliana was close enough that she could hear their conversation.

"What's going on here? These are women and children," the priest said. "What could you possibly want with them?"

"I need you to move your flock to the farmhouse where the Sixteenth Waffen-SS has set up a temporary headquarters."

"Who has given these orders? What need is there to bring women and old men and children—"

"I am the one who issued the orders, Don Ubaldo."

"What about the people who escaped the church? They were gunned down?"

"Only a partisan would run like that, and they were treated as thus. If you and your people cooperate, we can avoid any further unfortunate incidents."

"I'm not going to be party to such a ridiculous action."

"Have it your way," Brack said. The German officer stood back and drew his pistol, pointing it at the priest's face. Several women screamed, but the young priest didn't flinch.

He turned to the crowd. "You are to be processed at the local SS headquarters. Stay calm. This will all be over soon."

Brack replaced his pistol in his holster. Don Ubaldo walked to the front of the crowd, his sandals hissing on the stony path. He moved the crowd down the road as the SS officer had ordered. The pack moved slowly, dithering with every step. The SS men surrounding them were dressed for combat. Each carried a machine gun and several grenades. All their helmets were festooned with leaves and twigs. Brack led the way, with Don Ubaldo beside him. Soon, another squad of perhaps a dozen SS men joined them. All around them the sounds of explosions and gunfire grew louder.

It took them over an hour to go three hundred meters—to reach the old cemetery that served the church. Her mother glared at the nearest German soldier but didn't speak. The soldier deflected her glare, paying no attention. The German officer, Brack, and the priest argued at the head of the column, but Liliana couldn't make out their words. The group stopped as the men shouted at each other. Brack stood back, his arms folded, as the young priest gesticulated. A few seconds later two soldiers took Don Ubaldo back toward the church. He didn't speak to the crowd as he passed them. The SS officer followed. The crowd stood. No one dared to speak. Thirty minutes passed before the soldiers who'd taken Don Ubaldo returned without him. Liliana could feel her sisters shaking in her arms, and most of the little children were crying. Aunt Tania carried one of her children, then another, in her arms, but she was growing weary and could only hold them for a few seconds.

The German officer gestured toward the cemetery, and one of his men used the butt of his rifle to strike the lock off the chain around the doors of the gate. The Germans seemed suddenly in a hurry. They shouted and used the flats of their gunstocks to herd the group through the gate. The walled-off cemetery was little larger than a tennis court. The SS officer appeared again. He ordered the people to line up in rows against the wall of the tiny burial chapel that served the cemetery. The crowd twisted and surged like a single living being.

Gianni cried silent tears as they reached the rendezvous point. It seemed over. The Germans were surging up the mountain behind them, and almost all the surviving men had already broken for the Allied lines. Those who remained had done so to see Lupo. James walked through the brush to the edge of the tree line. The valley was on fire below. He stopped counting at two dozen flaming farmhouses. He raised binoculars to his eyes. He saw the SS marauding through the valley and, just below him, a group of maybe a hundred woman and children being herded into a small cemetery like cattle, perhaps a hundred meters down the mountain. A dozen SS men guarded them, prodding them with their rifles as they lined them up against a wall. Jock joined him.

"What are you looking at?"

"They're rounding up civilians now." Terror overtook him as he recognized faces in the crowd. Liliana clutched her sisters, and the SS men were setting up a heavy machine gun on a cart outside the gate.

"It's the family that hid me. The girl I told you about—she's down there. They have her."

"There's nothing we can do for them," Jock said. "The Stella Rossa is finished. We have to get out of here while we still can." The small crowd of rebels left had gathered around Gianni. "They'll lead us through the Allied lines. We'll never make it without them. There's nothing more we can do here. I'm sorry."

"You go."

Liliana held both of her sisters tight to her chest. The SS officer strolled past as if on a promenade on a Sunday morning. Silence descended for a few seconds before he waved his finger toward the entrance and a heavy machine gun on a cart was wheeled in. The screaming began. Liliana heard her grandparents praying behind her, and she turned to her mother. She had never seen her cry before.

"I love you," she said and reached forward to stroke her daughter's hair. The children were crying at the front. An old lady burst out of the crowd, throwing herself on the nearest German soldier. Liliana recognized her as a refugee from Bologna, a tall, elegant woman with an expensive silk scarf around her neck. The woman pulled at the SS man for a few seconds.

"I need to see my daughter. I need to see her. She's pregnant. Please!"

The SS man shrugged her off. Another soldier threw her into the mud and fired a bullet into her chest. A hush fell on the cemetery. Mothers held their hands over children's mouths as the gunner inserted a belt of ammunition into the machine gun. He knelt and cranked something as Liliana's mother grabbed her from behind, swinging her body around as the cacophony of the machine-gun fire began. Bullets slammed into the wall behind them, showering the crowd with plaster as bodies began to fall all around her. An SS soldier ran forward and lobbed a grenade into the mass of people, and Liliana felt herself raised into the air as if picked up by a giant hand and then the thud of her body as she fell back down onto the ground. More bodies fell on and around her. She was trapped below someone. Who was it? Where was her mother? Her sisters? Screams filled the air, drowned out only by the hammering of the machine gun as it spat more and more bullets into the crowd. Liliana couldn't speak, almost felt mute, only capable of wondering where her family was. A tangle of arms and legs descended on her, and wet blood spread all over her body. She tried to make out the faces but couldn't see anyone. *This isn't my blood. This is other people's blood.* Everything went black.

James watched in horror as the machine gun in the cemetery opened up, and the crowd collapsed like dominoes, bodies flailing on top of one another.

"Oh no," Gianni said. "The women and children." Tears flowed down his face. "Lupo . . ." The name of his best friend came as a whimper from shuddering lips.

"Oh, my good God," Jock said. "I never . . ."

"We have to get down there. Some of them are probably still alive," James said.

"There's nothing we can do. They're killing everyone. We can't stand up to them," Gianni said.

"We can't just leave. We can't just do nothing," James answered.

"That's exactly what we're doing," Gianni said, wiping the wet from his face.

"Those are your people. You can't just abandon them."

"Is it better we die too? Someone has to be left to fight the Germans, to get revenge for what we've seen today."

"We brought this on them."

"This is war. We can't bear the blame for the Germans' crimes. We have to go. And, Baseball, it's too late."

"I'd rather die than not try. I have to try." His mother appeared in front of him. He heard her screams from the crowd below. This time it would be different. *These people took me in, risked their lives for me. For what? So I could watch their slaughter?* Some things were worth dying for. The machine gun still spat bullets into the crowd. None in the shuddering mass were standing now. The other SS men leaned against the walls, smoking, chatting with each other. James picked up his Sten gun. The barrel was shaking. *I don't think I can do this, but how do I live with myself afterward if I don't?*

The machine gun stopped, and Liliana heard her mother's voice beside her.

"My love, are you still alive?" The voice came through a tangle of bodies. Liliana couldn't see where she was, only the bodies that lay on top of her, pinning her to the cold ground.

"Yes, I'm unhurt," she whispered, incredulous at how she had somehow not been hit. "Where are the girls?"

"They're gone. They're beside me." Liliana began sobbing under the mass of corpses covering her. "Oh no, Liliana, please be quiet. The Germans are still here."

She heard the Germans call out and then the sounds of more grenades being thrown into the mass of dead. Several minutes passed. She heard a strong, operatic voice. *Am I dead?* One of the SS men was singing. She recognized the aria. And she was back in Mrs. Chilcott's apartment listening to the phonograph, could remember her playing the record. It was "Largo al factotum," from *The Barber of Seville.*

Maria called out for each member of her family. Only Aunt Tania answered through the mound of corpses, her voice weak and distant.

"My children are dead, Maria, and I am shot. I'm so tired . . . I have to—" A gunshot rang out, and Tania's voice was gone.

Liliana forced herself to be quiet. The SS man finished his aria to the applause of his fellow soldiers. She waited a few minutes until the noise of the Germans receded. "Oh, Mamma, they are all dead."

"I'm shot . . . my darling girl . . ."

"No. Please."

More shots rang out. Liliana tried to raise herself—saw the SS officer, his pistol drawn, finishing off those still alive. She collapsed back down.

"Mamma, everyone's dead."

"You're not. You can get out. If anyone can, it's you—"

A pistol roared. Liliana held her free hand over her mouth to quiet herself. She heard the Germans dragging some bodies out, even talking to one of the wounded, telling her that they'd look after her. She thought about Martina and Lena and how they'd danced. More shots. She held her breath, waiting for death or silence or both.

Several minutes passed. She began to push the corpses off her, squeezing her body free. She could see her mother a meter away, a bloody hole in her forehead, her eyes imploring. Lena was beside her, lying on top of Martina and Cousin Dino. They could have been asleep.

She tried to dismiss the horror, to focus on escape, on somehow staying alive. She could hear breathing in the pile of bodies. Several people were still alive. It was impossible to know exactly who or where they were in the tangle of limbs all around her. How long before the Germans came back and finished them all off? Two Germans were in the corner, facing away from the crowd. The officer was bent over a wounded girl, telling her how much she looked like his wife back in Austria. There was no one by the gate. It was only three meters away. The Germans would come with their pistols again. This would be her only chance. She shoved a body off her and ran for the gate. The SS officer turned at the sound, and as she looked back, she saw that he had sent two men after her. A shot struck the gate just as she reached it, but she kept running.

James stood still, the binoculars stuck to his eyes. Jock tugged at his shoulder again.

"We have to go right now."

"We're leaving," Gianni said in English. "We're the last. The Germans are coming. We're all going to die if we don't get out now."

James kept his binoculars on the cemetery. A body rose from the heap of corpses—a woman, even. But it couldn't be her. Couldn't *possibly* be her.

"It's her."

"Who?"

"Liliana."

"We're going. Right now. Don't make me leave you behind, Baseball," Jock said. "I'm sorry about those people, but I have to get home to my son. Think of your sister."

The Germans saw her and fired a shot, but she kept on. Two SS men jogged after her, seemingly bored at the thought of it all.

"I'm not going anywhere."

"I won't let you die for nothing." Gianni said, "Grab him," and Karoton clamped his hands on James like a vise. The Russian dragged him back.

"Let me go. I have to do this."

"Go," Karoton said, releasing him.

James didn't hesitate. He clutched his Sten gun and ran down the hill. Looking back was useless. The rebels were already gone. He skidded on the trail, stones scattering in his wake as he sprinted down. *What am I doing? What am I doing? I'm all alone.*

Liliana was covered in blood, her clothes wet and sticking to her skin. She was trying to run as fast as she could, but her body felt heavy, as if the dead were still on top of her. She could hear the two SS men behind her, could see the shots from their rifles chewing up the ground on either side. She kept running, her legs turning into concrete, her energy waning. She reached a river at the end of the road, the Germans perhaps fifty meters behind her. If she could just get across—her cousins lived a few kilometers away. She waded into the river, lifting her legs as she went, but her dress was too tight, too heavy with water and blood. The SS men arrived at the bank behind her. A shot hit the water, and she heard one of them call out in perfect Italian.

"Enough running. We've had our exercise for today." She turned around to face them, her arms above her head, and saw the faces of her would-be murderers. "You had a little accident, I see," one of them said, and they both laughed. "How about you pull down your dress, and we might let you live."

"I'd rather die."

"All right, have it your way, then," the SS man said and raised his rifle to take aim at her. He closed one eye and moved his finger around the trigger. Liliana thought to speak, but what was there to say now? She let her hands drop to feel the water between her fingers, closed her eyes. The sound of a machine gun tore through the air. The side of the SS soldier's head exploded in crimson blood. His body fell sideways to the ground. The other SS man turned toward the sound and was hit in the chest. He collapsed on the muddy riverbank. He clutched his wound, writhing in pain. A figure appeared behind him, a Sten gun in his hand.

"Liliana," James said. "We have to get out of here now. There's SS all over." He held his hand out to her, five meters from where she stood frozen in the river. "Let's go."

She moved toward him, taking his hand as he helped her onto the bank. The SS man was still moving at his feet. James put a bullet in his head. "Get his rifle. You're going to need it."

CHAPTER 6

Liliana reached down for the rifle. The two SS soldiers were still, their blood draining down the riverbank and into the water. James raised a finger to his lips and knelt to survey the road that led from the cemetery. It was clear. She wiped the mixture of mud, water, and blood away from her face and shouldered the rifle. She hadn't fired one in a few years—not since her father had shown her how. James was saying something to her now, but his speech came as a blur, as if he were talking underwater. He repeated it, his words coming into focus.

"Where should we go?" he said. She felt his hand on her shoulder. They were hiding behind a bush. "I need you," he said. "I'm dead without you. The rebels are gone."

"My mother," she managed, her voice coming as a whisper. "My sisters. They're shot."

"I'm so sorry. I saw what happened. We were on the mountain looking down. I came back for you."

"My father escaped with my uncle."

"Where are they? Can we go to them? The SS heard those shots. They're going to realize something's amiss when these two don't come back."

"I don't know. They're on the mountain somewhere."

"Do you have any idea where they might be? I was up there. The rebels have fled for the Allied lines. The entire area is crawling with SS."

Liliana tried to think. The myriad hunting cabins and hidden lodges dug into the mountain cycled through her memory. She remembered the trees in the woods beyond her house and how she had hidden under the mass of roots in an old foxhole as a child, but that was an hour or more away. She felt James's hand on hers, warmth against frozen skin.

"The Stella Rossa's emergency meeting point is only a few hundred meters back up the mountain. We can hide out there until we figure out how to find your father."

She couldn't find any words, just tapped him on the arm instead.

"Let's go," he said and moved out low to the ground. The air crackled with gunshots, interspersed by the low thump of grenades exploding in the distance. She held the rifle in her hands. It felt foreign, ugly—smeared with mud and blood. They made their way along the river for fifty meters or so, stopping at a ditch to look out. She saw them first and pointed—thirty or so SS soldiers making their way up the mountain, spread out in single file, two hundred meters on their right.

"Oh no. No! They're making for where I came from—the only place I knew to go."

"My uncle and aunt live about ten minutes away."

"Lead on. We can't go up the mountain now."

They made their way back along the riverbank. The cemetery was only a few hundred meters away. What would become of her family's bodies and the hundreds of others littering the mountain? She felt a hand on her shoulder, and they ducked down behind an old wall she'd walked past dozens of times. James pointed up the path that led toward the cemetery. Two SS men were coming, a hundred meters up the road. The two dead SS were on the riverbank only a few meters away from their hiding place. They had a minute or less. Once the men found the bodies, the whole area would be swarming with soldiers.

"We have to get across the river now. Keep running once we hit the other side. We have to get as far away from those bodies as we can. I'll need you to lead. Go now."

Liliana slipped down the riverbank, feeling the cold shock of the water once more. She raised her dress to run through the waist-deep water and heard James slip in behind her. They reached the other bank, about eight meters away. They started running across a road and into the woods, their legs pumping. Another path lay in front. Liliana stopped to check it out, looking up and down, before sprinting across it and into the trees on the other side. They ran like this for ten minutes or more, until she had to stop. She bent her body over, her hands on her thighs, gasping for breath.

"I think we're safe," James said. "We're far enough away. They'll think that some of the last partisans killed them."

"Is that not what we are?"

"What?"

"The last of the partisans?"

"We have to get to your aunt and uncle's house. We're dead out here."

They stayed in the woods, moving parallel to the road. Liliana was aware of every sound she made, from the crunching of her feet in the leaves underfoot to the swishing of her wet hair and dress. She stayed behind the American for a minute or two before he turned to her. She had heard it too—footsteps on the road. They took cover in the roots of a large tree as an old man stumbled into view, crying out. Six SS soldiers were entertaining themselves chasing him down. She could hear their voices as they called after him. They were only a meter or so behind him. They came to where she and James were hiding. She put a hand on her rifle. James put his hand on hers, shaking his head. The old man fell onto the road, holding his hands up, begging for mercy. The SS men shot him in the chest and head. Liliana felt her body tense. The only justice would be to make them pay for what they'd done. James's grip on her hand grew tighter. The SS men shouldered their rifles, leaving the body of the old man in the middle of the road.

They waited several minutes to be sure there was no one coming, then stood up again.

"I didn't want that vermin to get away any more than you, but we can't engage every German we see, no matter how much we want to."

"My aunt and uncle's house is this way," Liliana said, and she began through the fallen leaves again.

More SS soldiers came down the road, but they seemed uninterested in searching through the woods that ran alongside it. Liliana and James hid until they had passed and resumed walking.

The sight of the smoke came first. Uncle Giorgio and Aunt Claudia lived in a small village that Liliana had visited dozens of times. Several of those farmhouses, hundreds of years old, were ablaze. They watched from the trees for a few minutes. The SS were gone, but the destruction remained. No signs of life were visible.

They darted from the trees to the hulk of a charred house.

"My aunt and uncle's house is at the end of this row. Some of the houses are still intact, but where are the people?"

"They must have taken them away."

What about her uncle and aunt and their three children? They had nowhere to go now but to the house. Liliana and James made their way through the back of the garden behind the first house and into the second, past a burning barn and a wall riddled with bullet holes. No blood, just bullet holes. The houses were empty; the only sound the shrill cries of the livestock and the crackling of the fires. They moved in silence, taking several minutes to walk a hundred meters or less. Uncle Giorgio and Aunt Claudia's house was the last, built above a gully that extended down thirty meters to a stream below. Liliana had raced her cousins down to the water and back up the steep hill as a child. The house was intact, but silent. Liliana thought of her cousins, how they might be the only family she had left now. The hope that they would open the back door for her, welcoming her inside, lit a tiny spark in her.

James motioned for her to stay behind and made his way to the garden behind the house, where the vines and bushes had been torn to pieces as if by a hurricane. The fence over the gully was gone. He went to it and almost dropped his submachine gun. He turned around and paced back to her, his face pure white.

"What is it?" she said.

"It's nothing. We should get out of here."

"No, there's something . . ." She tried to push past him. He took her arms, but she shook loose and went to the gap where the fence had been. The gully was full of the dead. The people of the houses, her uncle, aunt, and cousins among them, lay at the bottom, their bodies shredded by bullets, lying at ungainly angles where they'd fallen. Her uncle lay to the side, his face distorted in horror. His sixteen-year-old son Marco, whom he'd barred from joining the Stella Rossa, lay dead beside him, his eyes open, staring into nothing. There must have been forty or fifty. She felt James's hands on her again, dragging her away.

"Wait, did you hear something?" James said.

The sound of German voices from down the road drove a spike of fear into her. They were trapped by the gully.

"They're coming."

"There's nowhere to go," James said. "Into the house. Now."

She felt her limbs give way as he dragged her to the door.

"Is there an attic? Somewhere to hide?"

The urgency in his voice jolted her back out of the daze that had overtaken her. Her life didn't matter anymore. Saving his was all that mattered now. She led him inside the old house. The breakfast dishes were still on the table. James reached over to grab some bread, stuffing it into his pocket as they hurried past. They ran up the stairs to the second floor. The front door opened, and the sound of German being spoken came again. They stopped still against the wall of the second-floor hallway. They could hear SS men taking off their backpacks, pulling up chairs in the kitchen.

"We have to keep going," James whispered.

She took his hand and led him onward. There seemed to be several different voices in the kitchen, and she heard wooden chairs being dragged out from the table across the cold stone floor. The attic had a trapdoor, nearly three meters off the ground at the top of the stairs. The ladder was gone. She put the rifle over her shoulder as James boosted her up. The door gave way as she pushed against it, and she pulled herself inside. He jumped up to grab her outstretched hand. She thought he might pull her down until he used his other hand to pull himself up. She replaced the trapdoor, and they fell back.

James was on his back on the other side of the trapdoor, his hand over his mouth. Two small windows at either end of the attic illuminated their drab surroundings. James stood up as the German voices on the bottom floor grew louder. He inched to the window. She raised herself to her haunches, placing the rifle on the wooden floor like it was a newborn baby. He motioned her to come to the window, about four meters away. The attic was shaped like the triangular roof, and she had to go to the middle to stand up straight, walking past dusty tools, covered furniture, and boxes of old toys that she had played with as a child.

"Don't put your head up too far," he whispered into her ear. "Stay hidden."

She did as she was told, kneeling down at the edge of the window frame. Hauptsturmführer Brack sat in the courtyard in front of the house with two other officers. His men had brought out a table, and the three officers sat on kitchen chairs, drinking wine. A dozen or so SS soldiers were lined up to attention as a junior officer barked orders at them. Two men wearing the clothes of locals entered her sight. *It can't be. It's him.* It was her father, bent over, helping to carry a case of ammunition. She recognized the other man as Antonio Baggio, a farmer who lived about five minutes' walk from their house. The two men set down the heavy box and went back for another.

"That's him—that's my father."

James didn't reply. He had his back to the wall, the Sten gun between his legs as he sat.

"I don't see Uncle Vito, but that's my father. We have to get him away from here."

"How?"

"We have weapons. We could . . ." She trailed off, aware of how ridiculous she sounded.

"There must be thirty SS, and they're only the ones I've seen."

"I recognize that officer." She felt a surge of hatred. "He was the one at the cemetery."

He sat still, rocking the Sten gun back and forth in his hands. "It seems like they've set up their headquarters here temporarily."

"What do we do if they check the attic?"

"Shoot."

They went silent for another minute or so. Liliana watched as her father went back for another case of ammunition.

A tear fell onto the dusty wooden floor. She hadn't realized she'd been crying. They sat there, waiting for the footsteps up the stairs. Shouting and cheering from the courtyard below roused her attention, and they both raised themselves up to peek out the window. A dozen SS men marched into the square, their weapons pointed at seven bloodied members of the Stella Rossa.

"Do you know them?"

"No," he replied.

The officers stood up to inspect the prisoners. A rebel spat in one of their faces, and the younger officer stood back, drew his pistol, and shot the man in the chest. Brack shouted at the SS officer, ripping the gun out of his hand. He directed the prisoners around the house and into the backyard. Liliana went to the back window. Shots rang out and the rebels tumbled into the gully.

She watched her father load ammunition for another hour. Then he disappeared down the road with several SS.

"If they wanted him dead, they would have killed him already," James said.

"They pick up men every so often to be Todt workers," she said. "My friend's father was taken last year. They never heard from him again."

"He seems as tough as they come. He can survive."

"He's as good as dead unless I can get to him somehow." She picked up a piece of wood from the floor and examined it in her hand. "The rumors about the other villages were true. The Germans were killing women and children. No one believed it."

"We heard the rumors too, the warnings."

"And they fled, like cowards," Liliana said.

"They weren't equipped to stand up to a frontal assault. They had no choice."

"You chose differently."

He didn't know what to say, what to think. How could he possibly comfort her?

"This is not the Stella Rossa's fault. Anything they did was for the good of the war effort. No one bears responsibility for this but the Germans."

"I saw Lupo myself two weeks ago . . . Now my family are dead," she said. Her head dropped and she said nothing more. He knew this wasn't the time to debate the whys of this situation.

"I'm so sorry. I don't know what to say. I don't even know how we're going to get out of this alive."

She didn't answer.

The day faded. James was too afraid to talk, look out the window, or even move. They had been in the attic for hours. The gunfire and explosions in the distance had not abated. The German officers were gone now, replaced by regular troops who seemed to be using the house to rest or eat before heading back out to murder and pillage. Liliana had sat in stunned silence most of the afternoon. He had tried to offer her some semblance of comfort, had tried to put his arm around her, but she'd shoved him away, saying she wanted to be alone. He'd tried to give her space by sitting at the other side of the attic. But it was better to be close if the Germans did come. Better she die quickly at his hands than be captured by the SS. He had been waiting for them to come and kill him all day. He'd expected his twenty-three years to end at any minute, in this dusty attic beside this girl who'd experienced things he could only imagine. But they hadn't come. And now, for the first time, he was beginning to believe that they might not die in the next five minutes.

The noise from downstairs had settled to a murmur. He stood up, wiping the memories of his youth away from his mind. They came on thicker and stronger as the light of the sun dissipated into night, so much so that he almost had to swat them away like mosquitoes. He thought of his mother, tried to draw strength from her. He had tried praying earlier but didn't have the heart for it, or the conviction that it would do any good. He'd seen religious pictures and statues in every house he'd been in on Monte Sole, plastered everywhere. But where was their God now?

For reasons he couldn't comprehend, his mind drifted to his high school girlfriend. Maybe he should have married Martha Goodwin when they turned eighteen like she had wanted. But he hadn't. He had left. Martha had married George Barkley instead and had three kids, one after the other, before she was twenty-one.

"They must have checked the attic before we came up," he whispered. She didn't raise her head. "Is there any way out of here?" He waited thirty seconds before he asked the question again. She didn't answer. He reached across to her, touched her shoulder. "I don't pretend to know what you're going through, but I need you. I'm dead without you." He placed the Sten gun on the wooden floor and moved to her, almost close enough that they were touching. Her head was still rooted between her legs. "When we met, I told you I was born in a tourist town, a little spot at the end of the line. People would come every summer and have their time at the beach and leave us behind when the sun faded. You've seen those movies about ghost towns?"

Liliana raised her head.

"Maybe not. My father was a fisherman. He was out at sea a lot. Those were the good days—when he was gone. I asked my uncle Ted about him once, whether he started drinking before or after the war in France. Ted said he always had it in him, like a dormant volcano, I guess." The sound of gunfire close by cut across him.

A few seconds passed before he began again. "He'd wake up in the night screaming or get up covered in sweat, with tears running down his face. He talked about his friends—guys who he'd seen killed twenty years before—as if he'd just talked to them that day. It got worse as time went on. He was a mean drunk. He'd be out at sea or sometimes just out, for days at a time, and he'd come back looking to take it out on someone."

"Did he beat your sister?" she said.

"Once, but I never let him do it again. I took the beatings for her."

And he was back in the house again, coming home from school as his father held Penny's long hair in one hand, stuffing a rigid finger in her bloodied face with the other. James picked up the heaviest thing he could find—a copy of the Bible sitting on a grubby coffee table. He swung it at him, and he dropped her. That was one of the worst beatings, but worth it.

"What's her name?"

"Penelope. Penny. She's almost eighteen now."

"Did he beat your mother?"

"Oh yeah. Everyone knew us around town, walking around with fresh bruises blotched across our faces. I dreamed of running away. Me and Penny talked about it almost every day."

"What about your mother?"

"Why didn't she leave? I don't know. She was afraid. My father used to say he'd find her wherever she went, and that she'd never get by without him. We were poor. The old man didn't make much, and whatever he did make he spent on booze. We never saw much of it. Mom left school at fourteen and didn't think she could support us, I suppose. She was always so concerned with what everyone else thought, with what the neighbors would say. And I don't suppose she ever realized just how bad it would get. My pop was all right sometimes—when he was sober, and he'd tell her he was gonna change, or that he had a plan or whatever, but it never came to anything."

The sound of footsteps downstairs interrupted him, and he snatched the Sten gun off the floor again. It must have been ten o'clock now, and the gunfire around the mountain had finally faded out. The SS were celebrating. The sound of chairs being dragged across the floor screeched out. The marching songs followed. James and Liliana sat silent for a few minutes, frozen.

"Did your father change?" she asked through the dark.

"Only for the worse. I remember the smell most of all. The fish smell. It stuck to him; no matter how many times he'd scrub himself down, it was always there, lingering." Was that why James could never go back to the marina? The smell? The invocation was too much. He fought back the memories overwhelming him before continuing. "I'd arrive home, and she'd be lying on the couch, groaning in pain." Dish towels full of ice, melting on the floor, that she'd used to dull the pain. She'd hold her hand out to him as he tried to stifle the anger he felt. She had never wanted to hear that—just to hear him say how much he loved her and that he and Penny were going to be all right. He gripped the Sten gun, leaving a residue of sweat from his palms on the cold barrel.

"It all came to a head on September twenty-sixth, 1937 . . . I was sixteen. I had basketball practice after school, and I got home after, in my sports uniform. I got a glass of water and heard something out in the living room—a rustling or something. I walked out and got hit in the face with something hard. I went down and felt hands dragging me, and then a rope being tied around my wrists. I came to a few minutes later, my head throbbing. I was used to pain, but this was something else. My dad was there, standing over me, a metal rod about two feet long in his hand."

James had been able to tell immediately how drunk his father was. He knew the different levels by the look in his eye—he'd seen them all so many times. His father started yelling, something about trying to undermine him in his own house and that he was the boss. James tried to speak but got a slap across the face. His hands were tied behind his back, and as he tried to stand up, he realized his father had tied them to a hook in the back of the closet. He tried to stand, felt winter coats ruffle against his hair, but fell back down in a daze. His mother came home a few minutes later. The groceries fell out of her hands, apples rolling across the wooden floor. He said he'd show James who the man of the house was, and that his son was going to learn a lesson. "He took the iron rod in his hand and beat my mother with it. She went down, and I thought that would be it. I screamed at him to stop, but he didn't. I couldn't move. He tied me up and stuck me in the closet, but left the door open so I could see. He kept on hitting her. The cops came in. They took him, still shouting and flailing, kicking his legs. I felt hands on me, untying my arms, and someone led me out."

Liliana reached across and took his hand.

"They took my sister away—she was only ten. She went to live with our aunt in Philadelphia. I went to a foster home. Aunt Katie didn't have enough room for me too. I was glad that Penny got to go to a good home, and I saw her pretty often."

"How was the foster home?"

"I didn't last long."

"Where is your father now?"

"Serving life. They moved him last year to a place in Trenton. He tried to write to me, but I returned the letters. Penny's a senior in high school now. A straight-A student. She's so smart. I miss her."

The singing and laughter downstairs were still going on.

"How were you able to live with that? How did you not curl up in a ball, rob a bank, kill yourself?" Her demeanor was changing. She was holding her head up now, looking him in the eyes. The tears had dried.

"Is that what you're feeling now?"

"How did you get through? What happened to you?"

"It wasn't what, it was who."

"Who?"

"Chief Bill Brody. He was there the day my mom died. I was still in Cape May awhile after that—in a foster home. I didn't like it much. I wanted to get out, so I took to burgling houses."

"I can't imagine you doing that."

"Then you won't be surprised to hear that I wasn't much good at it. I got caught, but Chief Brody made sure the charges got dropped. He fixed up a room for me and took me in. I stayed there almost two years, started writing in a journal every day."

"He adopted you?"

"I don't know what you'd call what he did, but he saved me. I know I'd be dead or in jail if it wasn't for him. He's the hero of my life."

"We're going to get out of here," Liliana said. "We're not giving up." She stood up, making her way across the attic to the back window. James lost her in the darkness, unable to get up until he heard her whisper, "Come over here."

He raised himself up to a crouch, agonizing over every step, aware that any noise would be the end of them. The semicircular back window was about a meter in diameter and about half that high. It was caked in dust. She wiped it clean with a rag she'd taken from the floor and tapped on the old glass with her finger.

"How quietly could you break that? There's a ledge just below."

The ledge led around the house to the stable roof. The drop was four meters or less, and from there another three to the ground. The trees lay five meters beyond, across soft ground.

"How do we know there aren't any SS keeping guard out there?" he said.

"We don't, but we do know one thing—if we stay here, we're dead. It's only a matter of time."

James reached into his pocket for the bread he'd taken from the table downstairs. He tore it in half. They finished it in seconds. It did little to satiate his voracious hunger, and nothing to wet his dry throat.

The singing stopped. They both stood still, waiting, before it resumed a few seconds later. James went to the corner and pulled up a dusty sheet that had been covering an old armchair. He waited until the dust settled before placing the sheet against the glass. "Can you hold this in place?" He folded the sheet so that the layer of fabric was a few centimeters thick. Then he went for the Sten gun. He poked at the glass with the barrel of the submachine gun, aware of every sound. The glass didn't break. He brought the barrel back farther, propelled it into the glass, and held his breath when it crunched. The singing stopped again. They looked at each other through the darkness. Footsteps sounded on the stairs. James turned toward the trapdoor, aiming his gun at where they'd be coming through. They stood still for a minute or more, but the singing began again.

"Try again," she said.

He brought back the gun and the glass shattered. Tiny shards cascaded down into the garden where her cousins and their neighbors had been shot. Liliana brought the sheet back. A round hole in the middle of the glass let the fresh night air in. She handed him some sheets, and they covered their hands as they picked the remaining glass out of the frame. Ten minutes later the glass was gone and wrapped up in sheets at their feet. Liliana went back for her rifle, stowing it on her shoulder. James poked his head through the window. The ledge was there—barely a third of a meter wide, but there. It led along the side of the house until it stopped at the angle of the roof. The stable was below. Jumping onto the old roof would make quite a din if they made it that far, but she was right—this was the only way.

"You go first," he said. "I'll help you out until you get your balance on the ledge."

"Who's going to help you?"

"I'll figure it out."

He took the armchair, placing it in front of the window. She climbed through the window, whirling her legs around so they dangled out onto the ledge. He held her hands as she gained her balance.

"I'm OK," she said and moved along the ledge and out of his sight. He climbed up on the chair and swung his legs up through the gap, turning his body to lower himself down onto the ledge. She was already a meter or so ahead of him. He looked down at the garden, illuminated by the light from inside. A sentry was smoking a cigarette. He would hear them if they jumped to the stable, but what choice did they have now? James inched along the wall, the ledge seeming to get narrower as he went. He wondered how the sentry hadn't looked up. Each footstep was a miracle, each puff of dust that came off the ledge as they went a potential death sentence. Liliana reached the end of the ledge, her body still pressed against the wall. He knew he would have to be fast, that the sentry would look up as soon as she jumped. He tried to signal to her, but she didn't notice. She jumped down. He jumped after her. She came down on the terra-cotta tile. He landed beside her. The sentry shouted as Liliana helped James to his feet, and the sound of a rifle shot cut through the air.

"Run. Now."

She jumped to the ground first. He followed her. The door to the outhouse flew open a meter or so from where they landed, and a young SS man came out buttoning up his pants. James raised the Sten gun and stitched three rounds across his chest. More shots rang out as they ran through the darkness. They made the tree line. She was ahead of him, somehow able to see the fallen branches that he stumbled over. James didn't dare look back. He knew they were coming.

CHAPTER 7

Liliana remembered these woods from her youth, running with her cousins and her sisters. She dodged past the trees, somehow managing to vault over rocks in her path. Her face, her hair, her dress were still smeared with blood and mud and dirt. The SS bullets were still coming. She didn't stop, didn't look back. The American was behind her. She could hear his footsteps between shots. *They're drunk. They can't follow us for long—not through this.* She tried to determine where they were running to, up a hill, up the mountain. Her lungs were on fire, her legs beginning to seize up. The incline was becoming steeper, the trees more sparse. She heard his voice behind her.

"Stop running. We made it. They're not coming after us anymore."

He bent over double, his submachine gun in his hands. The clouds had parted above, and the moon shone down, illuminating the scrub in ghostly white. Silence settled over the mountain once more.

"We'd be dead if they weren't all drunk out of their minds," he said.

"We have to go back for my father."

"What?"

"I can't leave him."

"We have no idea where they're even keeping him. We can't just go down there and start asking around."

"Do you suggest we just leave, slip through the lines like the gallant Stella Rossa?"

James sat down on a rock, trying to catch his breath. "The orders were not to engage the enemy in a battle they couldn't possibly win."

"And where is Lupo? I assume he escaped through the lines with the rest of them." Liliana squatted down on her haunches, took the rifle off her shoulder.

"Dead. I didn't see him, but he was with us, and then he wasn't. The SS were behind us. He went down. Gianni and my friends Jock and Karoton got away."

"Lupo was a good man. I know he never meant for any of this to happen. He was just doing what he thought was right, but you never answered my question: Am I meant to just leave my father?"

"What would you have us do? We can't go down there guns blazing. They'd cut us to pieces. I'm so sorry about . . . everything, but we can't get to your father. It's just not possible."

"I have to try. I won't leave without at least trying to get to him."

James stood up. A breeze swept through the trees, rustling the leaves above their heads.

"Liliana . . ."

"No. I won't. I won't go. Help me get my father, and I'll lead you to the lines. I swear I will."

"You're asking me to do the impossible. There are hundreds, maybe thousands of SS soldiers swarming the mountain, murdering anything that moves."

"I know that, and I know how insane it is, but I can't leave him. I can't do it." She turned to leave. "I realize that it's not fair to ask you to risk your life, so I'll go alone."

He reached out a hand to her. "Wait. Just wait a goddamn minute. We need to get away from here and find somewhere we can rest for the night. I think I recognize where we are. There's an old Stella Rossa camp a few minutes up the mountain. We can talk about your father in the morning."

He walked on. She followed him a few seconds later. They moved in silence. The valley smoldered below, the fires dying, the smoke still visible against the night sky. They walked for twenty minutes in silence, the ghosts of her family all around her. She tried to concentrate on putting one foot in front of the other or the physical pain in her feet and legs, but the trauma of the day infected her like a virus.

"What am I going to do without them? Who am I going to be?" she said out loud.

He turned to her. "You have to survive this. We can't give up."

"Everyone that defined who I am is dead—except him. You have to understand why I can't just let him go."

James didn't answer, and they trudged on.

They arrived at the deserted camp a few minutes later, and she wondered why they had made for it. It was little more than a fire pit with a few trenches dug around it that the rebels might have used for sleeping in, or as firing positions. There was no food, no water, and no shelter.

"There's a stream over here," he said, and she followed him through the dark to the rushing water behind the camp. She dipped her hands in, cupping the cool water to her mouth, rubbing it over her skin. The dried blood and mud were running down her face, and she dipped her head into the water. She came up gasping.

"We need sleep. I know this place doesn't seem like much, but it's safe. Try to rest. We're going to need every ounce of energy. Come beside me. We can keep each other warm." He saw her wavering. "Please, this is no time to worry about the morality of the situation." He held out his hand. She climbed down into the trench and lay beside him. He seemed to fall asleep in seconds. The stars loomed above her head as the minutes stretched into hours.

The sound of gunfire in the valley below them came like distant rain. James felt like his head was a concrete block. She was awake beside him. He wondered if she had slept at all. He raised himself up without speaking. It was probably seven in the morning, and the killing in the valley had begun again. Fresh smoke surged into the sky from dozens of new fires.

James sat down on a rock and checked his gun. It was clean. He had half a magazine and one spare left. He checked Liliana's rifle—a standard-issue Gewehr 43 with five rounds in the clip—and handed it back to her.

"How do we get to the Allied lines from here?"

"I'm not going without my father, or without at least trying to find him."

"We've been through this. We can't—"

"I'm not going to ask you to make some mad death charge. I know what I'm asking. I'm not a fool. All I ask is that we take a look. You have binoculars on your belt, maybe we could use them, just to look, and then we can see from there."

"We need food. There's nothing here. We're going to have to make our way down into the valley to get it and to get out of here. If we see your father or anyone who might know where the Germans took him . . . I don't know."

Liliana sat up, wiping the dirt off her dress. "All I ask is that we look. I'm not going to waste our lives. You have my word on that. I thought about what you said last night as I lay in that hole. I need to survive this. It's what my father would want."

"He's a good man. I owe him for taking me in. I'll help if I can, but the important thing now is to move. We can't stay in any one place for too long, and we're going to run out of energy if we don't eat soon."

He led her away from the camp, wary of every step. The SS still hadn't come all the way up the mountain, but it was daytime now, and surely they'd be coming to mop up whatever remained of the Stella Rossa soon. There were only so many civilians they could murder before they came for the partisans again.

They walked for almost an hour before the smoke from a charred farmhouse came into view. They kept on until the trees ended and then crawled on their bellies the last three hundred meters. Two calves stood untethered in the front yard. Pigs rooted around, and the chickens ran loose and pecked at flowers in the garden. They stood up, making their way past the liberated animals. The house was a hulking wreck. The ground floor appeared to be gutted, so James got a ladder and set it against the outside wall. She held the ladder, keeping an eye out for SS as he climbed up into a bedroom. The beds were black and smoking, the windows cracked. Two coats hung in the wardrobe. He put one on and went to the window to throw the other down to Liliana. The stone stairs were hot as he made his way to the small kitchen on the first floor. The kitchen was untouched by the fire that had engulfed the back of the house where he'd entered. A pot of soup sat on the countertop. He spooned some into his mouth, taking a ladle to dole out the rest into a bowl for Liliana. There was meat on the sideboard, and he ate some before pocketing the rest. He was walking out to her when he noticed the blood spattered on the wall in the living room. He tried not to look and kept on out the door, the bowl of soup for Liliana in his hand.

"Did you see anyone in there?" she asked. She was wearing the coat he'd thrown down.

"No. Nothing." He handed her the soup and some of the meat. She ate it in less than a minute. "We need to get out of here."

"To where?"

"To the one place we saw your father, I suppose—the SS headquarters we escaped from last night."

"Thank you."

"Is there somewhere we can observe the house from? Somewhere close enough that if we do see him, we can do something about it?"

"I think I know where."

The food seemed to reinvigorate her, and she led him away from the ruins of the farmhouse and back up the mountain. He stopped her when they reached the tree line, and they crouched down to listen. There was nothing close, though the gunshots in the valley continued. They entered the trees, and she led him along a path that he didn't see until they were on it. He wondered what would satisfy her. *Will seeing her father be enough? What if we can't find him?* Would she continue the search until the SS inevitably caught up to them? He thought about the Allied lines. *Can I make it without her?* Did he want to leave her? He would go along with her for a few hours. If they stayed undercover, they might even survive the morning. And then all they had to do was make it through the German positions on the front lines and the thousands of troops stationed there.

They reached a hill close to her aunt and uncle's house. The gully full of corpses was visible below, and no matter how he tried, his eyes were drawn to the festering mass of death. The house was fifty meters or so below them but obscured by foliage.

They sat for a while before she came up with the idea of climbing a tree. It took them a few minutes to find one with footholds that would support them. She was a meter off the ground when she heard a murmur, and then the leaves fluttered above her head. She climbed to the first branch, a large, thick limb, and peered up. Two boys, not more than ten years old, sat above her, shivering, their arms wrapped around each other. James motioned for her to go up to them, and she climbed up to the branch they sat on. They cringed when she held out her hand.

"Don't be afraid. I'm not going to hurt you."

The boys didn't move. She glanced through the leaves at the houses below. Nothing was moving. She didn't see a single SS man.

"How long have you been up here?" she said. James was beside her now. The boys moved farther away, the branch swaying slightly. "Please, don't go any farther. Where are your parents?"

"They're down there," the younger of the boys said.

"Where?"

"Down there," he said, pointing at the gully.

Liliana stayed silent a few seconds, struggling to get out the words. "How long have you been up here?"

"Since yesterday morning," the younger boy said.

The older boy turned his head. "Go away, this is our hiding place."

"My name is Liliana, and this is James. He's an American. What are your names?"

A gust of wind blew through the trees, and a loud explosion sounded in the distance. The younger boy let go of his brother.

"My name is Luca Vialli. This is my brother, Luciano. I'm eight, and he's ten."

"It's so good to meet you. Have you had anything to eat?"

"No."

"Give him some of the meat."

James held out the scraps of chicken he'd taken. Luca looked at it a few seconds before snatching it out of his hand. He began to devour it without giving his brother a scrap. Luciano elbowed him, but he didn't seem to care.

"Give your brother the rest of it." Luciano finished the remaining food in seconds. "Where are the soldiers?"

"They left this morning. It's quiet down there now."

"Did you see any local men with them? Carrying ammunition, maybe? They have my father. We were here yesterday, stuck in the attic of the house in the corner."

"The Pasellis' house?" Luca said.

"Yes. They were my cousins."

"I'm sorry."

Hearing those words from him almost led her to break down. "Thank you."

"They did have some local men with them," Luca said. "I think I've seen your father around, Signore Nicoletti?"

"You've seen him?"

"I think so. He was with the SS this morning, but they left a few hours ago."

She turned to James to translate.

"That's all very well," he said, "but we have no idea where they might have taken him, or even if he's still alive."

"Why would they kill him now? They can't get their trucks and their half-tracks through the narrow roads up here. They need slave labor to move their supplies. The SS is still here." As she finished, a burst of heavy machine-gun fire tore through the air about a kilometer away.

"What about these two?" James said. "We can't just leave them here."

"No, we can't." She spoke to the boys in Italian again. "Will you come with us? Do you have family somewhere we could bring you to?"

"We have—"

"Don't tell them," Luciano said.

"You can trust us. We're not Germans. He's an American soldier. Look at his uniform." She switched to English. "Show them your uniform." James did as he was told, sticking out his chest and holding his arms out wide. She spoke to the boys again. "You can't stay here. The SS will come. We can protect you."

"We have cousins in Rioveggio, our aunt and uncle live there."

"We can get you to your aunt and uncle, but you have to trust us."

The two boys whispered to each other for a few seconds, arguing over what to do.

"Can you get us more food?" Luca said.

"If you come with us. We can find some together. We gave you the last of what we had. How did you get away from the SS?"

"We were playing up here when the SS came. Our father already told us not to come down if they ever raided the house. We've hidden up here before when the Germans came, although it was never this long. It was never like this."

"No, it wasn't," she said. "Will you come with us? We can't stay here."

"OK."

"They have family in Rioveggio," she told James once they'd all come down from the tree.

"How far is that?"

"Only a few kilometers through the valley and over the mountain. We could walk them over there and come back."

"For your father? We're going to get off the mountain, and then come back?"

"You can leave. You can do whatever you want, but I can't leave these boys to die. Those SS devils don't make any distinction between Stella Rossa and women and children. They lined the children up in front at the cemetery so they would have clear sight of them with their machine guns. These boys will die without us."

"I know that. I want to get them out of here. It's just that coming back to get your father—it seems like suicide."

"We'll track him," Liliana said. "People are hiding all over the mountain, just like these boys. We'll find them, and then they'll tell us where to find him. He's still alive—I can feel it."

"This argument is pointless. We probably won't make it to Rioveggio alive anyway," James said. "Let's try, though. Let's try and get these boys back to their family."

"Boys, stay with us, but most of all stay silent. If the Germans find us—" She cut herself off.

A few seconds passed before Luca spoke. "They'll shoot us all."

"Yes, they will. Let's go."

They made their way southeast toward Rioveggio. Liliana walked in front, with the two boys in the middle. They went a few hundred meters before Liliana spotted an SS platoon in the valley below, loung-ing outside a burning farmhouse, bodies of the freshly killed littering the ground. She took James's binoculars, scanning the horrific scene for any sign of her father.

"He's not there," she said and handed the binoculars back. He folded them up and put them on his belt.

Somehow, Liliana felt calm and purposeful. What else could she do? What other choice did she have? James, and the boys, were relying on her. They went on, low to the ground, aware of every sound around them. They came into a clearing surrounded by a ring of trees. There was no sound except the intermittent rattle of SS gunfire in the valley below. Death seemed to be closing in.

Liliana heard the whisper of her name and stopped. She motioned to James, who was oblivious. The boys held their arms up in puzzlement. She heard it again and remembered her grandmother telling her to listen when she heard her name being called because it was her guardian angel looking out for her.

"Liliana, it's me, Fabrizio," said the voice. It was coming from a pile of leaves about three meters away.

"Fabrizio?" she said as he pushed back the camouflaged cover of the hole. Several other voices whispered besides his.

"She's a friend of mine—it's Liliana Nicoletti." Fabrizio climbed out of the hole. "She's not going to give us away," he said. Fabrizio's face was lined with dirt, his hands filthy. His mother appeared behind him. Liliana was just able to make out the black shawl over her head and her angry eyes.

"You're alive!" Liliana said.

"I've been hiding here since it all began, with my parents and my sisters." He looked at James and the two boys. "Where are your—"

Liliana shook her head.

"I'm sorry . . . but your father's alive. I saw him not two hours ago."

The words hit her like a bolt of lightning. "What? Where?"

"I was out fetching water at a stream a few hundred meters south of here. I saw him carrying supplies for the SS with another man."

A flood of hope surged through her. "My uncle Vito?"

"I don't think so, but it was your father—I'm sure of that much."

"Was he with a tall, thin officer with gray hair, Hauptsturmführer Brack?"

"I don't know. I got out of there when I saw the Germans."

"Are there many others hidden up here?"

"Some, I haven't seen many. We've been here since dawn yesterday. My father dug this hole months ago as an air-raid shelter. What's it like in the valleys?"

"Like nothing I could ever have imagined. Everyone. They're killing everyone. The Stella Rossa is gone."

Fabrizio's father appeared from out of the hole, his face streaked with mud and dirt.

"What about him?" he said, pointing at James.

"He came back for me. I need you to take the boys." She gestured to Luca and Luciano, who stepped forward.

"We can't, there's no space."

Fabrizio's mother stuck her head out of the hole. It was strange to see her like this—someone who'd always cared for her appearance—so caked in dirt. "I'm so sorry, Liliana, but we don't have any more room."

"Signora Brasi, we would only be leaving them a short while. We're taking them to Rioveggio."

"With Germans all over? Are you insane?"

"We have nowhere to hide. They have family there, but in the meantime, I need to find my father. The SS have him, and now we know where."

"No. They can't stay here," Fabrizio's mother said.

"How about I stop asking?" She pulled back the bolt on the rifle. She brought it to her shoulder and pointed the barrel at Signora Brasi. "We need this small favor. Nothing more," she said. "It won't take long. We can't take the boys with us. We'll be back for them. Don't force me to do something I don't want to."

"What are you doing?" Signora Brasi said.

"Liliana," James said.

"TAKE THE CHILDREN."

"OK, OK, we'll take them," Signore Brasi said. His wife started to protest, but he shut her down. "No, Maria. We'll take them. You'll be back within a few hours?"

"Yes," Liliana said and turned to the brothers. "Come over here, boys. These people are going to look after you for a while."

"No," Luciano said.

Liliana went to them, taking their hands as she crouched in front of them. "We have to find someone, but we'll come right back. I promise."

She brought them back to the hole. Signore Brasi helped them in as his wife stood back with her arms folded.

"I saw your father down the hill from Caprara," Fabrizio said, "loading ammunition. I was a hundred meters away, but I'm sure it was him. That was about an hour ago, but it seemed there was a lot of work to do. I'm sure he's still there."

"Thank you."

"Remind me not to mess with you," James said as they left. "You weren't going to pull the trigger, were you?"

Liliana shrugged. "I never did like her."

They made their way back down the mountain, and the burned-out hulks of houses and barns came into view. Wherever there were houses, there were bodies scattered on the ground outside. They heard German voices below them and took cover in a bush. Liliana reached for the binoculars. Several dozen SS men milled around some houses in full combat dress, their rifles and submachine guns slung over their shoulders. She ignored the murderers, scanning for their supplies. A few seconds later she saw her father, sitting down on a patch of grass beside another man. Her heart jumped.

"There he is," she said and handed the binoculars to James. "What do we do now? There must be fifty SS soldiers down there."

"We wait until they move him, but not too long. We're not safe here, and we promised we'd be back for the boys."

She said nothing but lay down next to her rifle, studying the scene through the sight at the end of the barrel.

"Be patient," he said.

"But not too patient."

Now it was his turn not to answer.

An hour passed. Her father hadn't moved. He still sat on the patch of grass, his head down as the SS walked around him. James was leaning back against a tree, struggling to keep his eyes open, when she nudged him.

"They're moving!"

Two SS men forced her father to his feet and prodded at him to walk. The three men disappeared as the charred wreck of a house got in her line of view. A few seconds passed before she saw them again. Her father and Antonio were carrying a large crate of ammunition. She handed the binoculars to James.

"This is the only chance we're going to get," he said. "Where does that road lead to?"

"The next hamlet, a few minutes' walk away."

"How many minutes?"

"Ten, maybe twelve."

"If we take the guards out with guns, we're going to bring every SS man for miles. We'd never make it back to the boys alive." He unsheathed the knife on his belt.

"But there are two of them," she said.

"I'm working on it. The first thing we have to do is get ahead of them. They're leaving."

Liliana took the binoculars again. "We have to go."

She led him out of the bush and past the houses where the SS had congregated. They stayed parallel to the road, keeping it on their right as they hurried through the brush. They were both panting when they stopped. They were a hundred meters in front of her father and the SS men, halfway between two groups of houses. The road was empty. They had clear sight fifty meters in either direction.

"How are we going to do this?" he said.

"I can create a distraction," Liliana said.

"They'll shoot you."

"I'll make sure they don't. I'll be on the other side of the road. You come behind them. My father will react too."

"Good luck. Don't do anything stupid."

"You too."

She tore across the road to the brush, five meters away. She heard the SS men talking a few seconds later, and then the footsteps before they appeared around the corner. She undid the buttons on her dress to expose the skin on her chest. She used the sweat on her palms to wipe the dirt off and took a deep breath. They were coming, her father and Antonio carrying the box of ammunition with the SS men behind. She took a handful of soil, keeping it hidden behind her back as she stood up.

"Excuse me," she said.

The SS men raised their guns and then laughed as they saw her.

"Are you lost, little girl?" one of the Germans said.

Her father almost dropped the ammunition crate. She saw James stand up on the other side of the road, his knife glinting.

"I have information on the whereabouts of the Stella Rossa."

"Do you?" one of the SS men said.

"Yes, in exchange for my safe passage."

The SS men stopped. "So? Where are they?"

Liliana threw the soil in the nearest SS man's face and jumped at him. James was on the other man before he had a chance to raise his weapon. He wrapped a hand around the German's face and drove the knife into his back. He pulled his hand back and drove the knife in again. The SS man fell. The other soldier threw Liliana down, but Virginio was on him in seconds. He grabbed the German's arms before he had a chance to fire. The submachine gun spilled onto the road. James stabbed him in the throat, his hand coming back saturated in sticky crimson. The German gurgled and went down. The other man wasn't dead and went to reach for his gun beside him on the ground. He was crawling toward it when Antonio picked it up. He used the butt end to finish the SS man off. Then everything went quiet.

Liliana wrapped her arms around her father, kissing him on the cheek. "I thought I'd lost you."

"Where are the others? Your mother and the girls?"

"They didn't make it." She was glad they didn't have time to dwell on those words she had to say.

"What happened?"

"We need to go. Now," James said.

Antonio was already making his way off the road into the brush.

"Antonio, where are you going?" her father said.

"I have to see my family," he said as he disappeared down the hill.

"Let him go," James said. "They're coming." He rifled through the SS men's magazine pouches for spare ammunition.

"What happened to Maria . . . and the girls?"

"The SS came for us, I barely got away. I'd be dead too if it weren't for our American friend."

"Nonna and Nonno?"

"They're all gone, Babbo." She took her father's hand, leading him toward the brush. "Why didn't the SS shoot you? Why are you still alive?"

"They found four of us hiding on the mountain. They killed Vito and Roberto but spared us because they needed two men to carry ammunition. I suppose they were going to kill us later, or send us back as slaves—until you came." He motioned toward the two dead SS men. "Should we move the bodies?"

"There's no time. We have to collect the boys and get out of here." James handed the SS man's submachine gun to Virginio. She translated to her father, telling him about the boys as they crossed into the brush on the other side of the road. They reached the clearing a few minutes later and lifted off the top of the camouflaged opening to reveal the hole beneath. Signore Brasi passed the boys out in turn.

"How dare you point a gun at me, Liliana Nicoletti," Signora Brasi said. "Virginio, do you have any idea what your daughter did?"

"If we survive this, you can send me a strongly worded letter. How about that?" Liliana said.

"Who's this?" Luciano said.

"I'm Virginio Nicoletti, Liliana's father."

James was on the edge of the clearing, peering down through the binoculars. "Cover the hole—dozens of SS are coming. We have to go. NOW." James scooped Luca up in his arms, shouldering his Sten gun as he ran up the mountain. Signore Brasi closed the hole and was invisible again.

CHAPTER 8

James cursed under his breath, struggling beneath Luca's weight. He put him down. The others were behind them, running. A mortar round exploded twenty meters to the left, sending dirt and slivers of wood flying through the air. "Come on," he shouted to the boy, even though he knew he couldn't understand him. He thought to turn around, to hold off the SS for even a few minutes to give the others a chance to escape but knew it wouldn't do any good. They'd swamp him in seconds. His sacrifice would be for nothing. There wasn't anything to do but keep running. Another mortar round landed, closer this time, and shook the ground around them. Virginio was struggling to keep up, and Liliana had her arm around him as they stumbled over dead branches. The brush grew thicker as James dodged through the trees. He heard a gasping behind him. Luciano had fallen. He went back for the boy, helping him to his feet as another mortar round boomed behind them. The others caught up, red faced and panting. James dropped to his knees and whipped out the binoculars. He had to move several times to get a clear view through the trees. The SS were still advancing, perhaps two hundred meters behind them.

"Are they chasing us?" Liliana asked. "Or are we in their path?"

"Hard to say. They might not have found the bodies yet. Maybe they're done murdering women and children in the valley and decided to see who they can find on the mountaintop instead." Another mortar round exploded, this time fifty meters below them. "We still have to get down the other side of the mountain to get to Rioveggio, or anywhere. We need to keep on."

He replaced the binoculars and took Luca's hand, leading him up the mountain and only looking back when they neared the summit. Dozens of fires dotted the valley below them, needles of black smoke ascending into the blue sky. Machine-gun fire still sounded. It was hard to believe there was anyone left to kill. The trees parted, and they were in the open. A man about the same age as Virginio sat fifty meters in front of them at the summit. He paid them no mind. James drew the binoculars again to look down the other side of the mountain. Lines of smoke filled the horizon, and dead bodies lay everywhere. Nothing was moving, and in the distance, across the river, he could see a town—Rioveggio.

Liliana didn't recognize the man at the summit, his head down.

"What are you doing here?" her father asked.

The man glanced out at the burning horizon before letting his head drop again.

"Are there any Stella Rossa here? Is there anywhere to go?"

"What reason is there to go on?" the man replied.

"What?"

"Death is coming. I'm ready."

"We have two children here. We need to get them to Rioveggio," Liliana said.

"You won't make it. The mountain is swarming with Germans. German sentries, German riflemen, and German machine gunners— the whole mountain's turned German in the space of a day."

"They're coming up behind us. Is there anywhere to hide?"

"I'm finished with all this . . . *civilization*." He said it like a dirty word. "What did it ever do for us? It provided me with a job, working sixteen-hour days as a porter for twenty-five years, a bare patch of land you couldn't plant weeds on, and a bare pittance to support my wife and my uncle and my brother and my seven children. My family was all that made life bearable, but they're all gone now. All dead."

Another mortar round landed behind them.

"Leave him," Virginio said. "The SS will be here in a few minutes. I wish you luck, my friend."

"Go hide in the ruined house down there," he said, pointing toward a clump of trees below them. "The SS have been there already. There's no one left there to kill."

As they left him, he brought his head up to face the horizon.

Liliana ran to James, who was already moving down the east face of the mountain.

"Follow me," she said. The boys were by her side, her father just behind her as they ran down across the scrub. The old farmhouse came into view through the thicket of trees, still smoking, the roof collapsed, the stone walls blackened from the flames. Dozens of bodies lay crumpled and torn outside, collapsed on top of each other from where the SS had lined them up, the blood staining their clothes still wet. A shot rang out from on top of the mountain. The mortar rounds had stopped. They reached the farmhouse, an old two-story building that had probably stood for two hundred years before the SS arrived that day.

"We can't stay here," she said.

"They're coming behind us now. They're on top of the mountain, and there are more of them coming from below." James handed her the binoculars and dragged her around the side of the house. She saw the SS advancing up the mountain toward them. He led her back around to the front of the house, where her father and the boys waited. "We've got one chance." He dragged her to the pile of bodies and reached his hand down. It came back red, and he smeared the blood on his uniform. "Do the same for your father and the boys. We play dead." He took his gun and hid it under the pile of dead and lay facedown. He moved the body of an elderly woman over his and went still. Liliana spread scarlet blood on each of the boys.

"You have to be brave. The bad men are coming, and if we make a sound, we'll all die. Close your eyes and count to a thousand." The boys closed their eyes and nodded, their lips tight together, their limbs shaking.

"We can do this," Luca said and directed his brother to lie down at the front of the pile of corpses.

Her father put his hands on her shoulders. "I love you, my darling. I couldn't be more proud of who you are."

"We'll get through this, Babbo. Just be silent. They won't be expecting anyone to be alive here. I think they swept through here an hour or two ago."

She lay down beside her father on top of the pile of rigid bodies. He squeezed her hand once and then let go. They lay still for several minutes before the footsteps came, before they heard German being spoken. She kept her eyes closed. It was difficult trying not to breathe, trying not to balk at the feeling of dead flesh pressed against hers. The memories of the cemetery came. Martina's and Lena's faces flickered through her brain, and she felt her mother's hands on her and could hear the sickening thud of bullets striking flesh.

The sounds passed, the tree branches swishing and twigs breaking underfoot as the SS moved by. She heard two voices, and the footsteps stopped. Two SS men stood maybe a meter from her, in front of the pile of bodies. Liliana could smell their cigarette smoke. They began chatting. Liliana felt her body begin to cramp, her back tightening. She held her breath, fighting the pressure as it turned to pain. The SS men were still talking, though she couldn't hear them now. She longed to get up, knowing that the simple act of standing would end the pain building in her back. She stayed still, biting down on her lip. The other SS had moved on, seemingly having secured the area to their satisfaction.

One of the men said something, and she heard a cigarette being stubbed out and then footsteps as they left. She counted to thirty before she dared move. The mere act of shifting her body provided enough relief for her to lie there another few minutes, but soon the pain came again. She turned her body a few centimeters, listening. She lay like that for hours. None of them moved, not until darkness fell.

It was James who spoke first.

"Is everybody OK?"

"I think so," she said as she reached out to her father. The bodies below them were cold now. She tried not to look at their faces.

Her father closed the eyes of the woman he'd been lying on, making the sign of the cross on her forehead.

"I'm sorry," he whispered.

Liliana got off the pile of corpses, brushed herself off, and embraced each of the boys in turn. Seeing the murdered had become perversely normal. She hadn't even looked at the bodies as she climbed off. "You did it. You were so good. I didn't hear a sound." The boys didn't answer, and she could see Luciano was crying. She hugged him again. Her father patted the American on the shoulder, trying to tell him how grateful he was. James embraced him back.

"Is that Rioveggio down there?" James said.

"Yes," she answered, "about two kilometers down the mountain."

"We should stay here awhile. The SS party should be beginning soon. Let's wait until they're good and drunk to try to make it past them."

He flopped back against the wall, his eyes screwed closed as he held the barrel of his Sten gun. She put a hand on his shoulder.

"Go to your father. I'll be fine. We move out in three hours."

She went to her father, who was with the two boys on an old bench at the back of the house. The dark of the night was all around them now.

"Why did the Germans do this?" Luciano asked. "Why did they kill everyone?"

"I don't know what makes men capable of such things," her father said. "We thought they were coming for the rebels, not our families, not our children." He seemed to be in a daze.

"Mamma saved me," Liliana said, sitting beside them. "When the firing began—she threw her body in front of mine."

A single tear streaked down Virginio's rough, weather-beaten face. "And the girls?"

Why wasn't she crying? What was this numbness she felt? Had her feelings died with her mother and sisters in the cemetery?

"They died . . . I made a break for it. James found me, and we've been running ever since."

"Did you see your grandparents and your cousins?"

"I left them there in the cemetery. I think there were a few still alive in the pile of bodies, but not from our family."

No one spoke for a minute or more.

"I could never have imagined anything like this."

He put his arm around her, embracing her. "We have each other now. You have to promise me that you'll survive this, no matter what should occur."

"We both will, and James and the boys too."

"Just promise me you'll do whatever it takes to live through this. I can't lose all my children. I'd rather die myself than have that happen."

"Stop talking like that. No one else is going to die. We'll all see each other through this."

"We need food and water," her father said. "Help me check the house."

She followed him into the burned-out wreck. There was no food to be found. The best they could muster was some water, which they brought out in chipped mugs. She brought some to James.

"What if the boys' uncle and aunt are dead too?" she asked him. "How do we know they didn't level Rioveggio and kill everyone there?"

"It seems pretty much intact from what I can see through the binoculars," James said. "I didn't see bodies on the ground either. It seems that the SS were focusing their efforts on the mountain itself, and every human being on it."

"How much longer is this going to go on?"

"The SS will keep on until they consider the Stella Rossa completely eradicated," he said. "We can't wait around to find out."

"James, I never had the chance to say—"

"We're far from safe. Maybe there'll be time for thanks at the end, but for now go to your father. You need each other now."

He settled back to his position, the only sound the distant refrain of SS marching songs.

James waited three more hours, until the last of the fires had died on the mountain, and went to the others. The boys were asleep, passed out on the dirt. Liliana and her father were in each other's arms when he approached. It felt wrong to interrupt them, but he had no choice.

"We have to go now," he said. "It seems quiet. This could be our only chance."

Virginio understood without his daughter translating and stood up to go to the boys. Luca woke in a few seconds, but his brother took longer, and she had to kneel down, whispering in his ear before he opened his eyes. She told them what was going on and stood ready.

"Do you know this area?" James said.

"We do," she answered. "We should stay away from the houses, wherever the SS might be."

"Hopefully most of them are in a stupor."

"We'll soon find out."

James led, with Virginio just behind him. He could hear the boys whispering to each other about two meters back, and he stopped to tell them to be quiet. Liliana translated, and they moved again. They kept to the trees, avoiding the meadows and tilled fields torn up by countless SS boots and the hooves of livestock set free. Clouds had crept across the moon and stars, and it was hard to see more than a few meters. They all caught their feet on fallen branches, the boys tripping several times, and the pace slowed to a crawl. James heard a rustling in front of them and held out a hand for the group to freeze. They heard snorting, and a massive pig waddled past them, seemingly oblivious to their presence. They waited until it had passed before making their way again.

They slinked between the lights of the houses, the sound of SS singing drifting out into the night. Their songs varied from raucous war songs to sad laments, with loud laughter and hollering in between. James thought about the Allies and how close they were, the frustration rippling through him.

They walked for another hour in absolute silence, giving wide berth to houses crammed with SS, creeping past sentries who kept watch while slugging from bottles of whisky. They were almost upon Rioveggio before they realized it. It was blacked out to guard against Allied air raids, and the leveled house on the edge of town across a river, a hundred meters in front of them, was evidence of the dangers of stray bombs.

James squatted, and the others gathered around him, just short of the river. It was about six meters wide.

"The boys can lead us to the house from here," Liliana said. "It's on the other side of the village."

"We just need to negotiate the river now. The bridge is far too risky—it'll be crawling with Germans."

She muttered to the boys in Italian for a few seconds.

"The boys know an easier place to cross. It's deep here, and the Germans might be along."

"Come," Luciano said in English.

They kept close to the ground while they moved, aware of every footstep, every breath. An SS sentry lit a cigarette on the other side of the river, illuminating his face for the briefest of seconds. The only light they could see was the glowing red ember on the end as he dragged the smoke into his lungs. They stayed still as the night itself, watching the man smoking. A few minutes passed before he moved on in the opposite direction.

They crept downriver. The three hundred meters they covered took them almost an hour. They didn't see any more guards. They sat in silence and waited another twenty minutes to cross. Better to be careful than dead. James went first, wading waist deep through the frigid water. His teeth were chattering as he reached the other side. He gave the signal for the others to follow. He kept watch, looking for the glowing embers of cigarettes in the night. The boys crossed, followed by Liliana and her father.

"So where to?"

"Luca will go in front. He said it's only a kilometer or so away."

"We're going to let the eight-year-old take the lead?"

"Do you know the way?"

He drew his knife and gestured for Luca to come forward. The little boy moved silently and quickly over the rough ground. Luca squatted in front of James and said something in Italian.

"Luca says you need to trust him," Liliana said.

"OK. Lead on."

They kept low, crossing over a quiet road. The sound of bombers on their way to Bologna came overhead, and the searchlights shot up, illuminating the clouds with sabers of light. They waited until the bombers flew past before going again. Luca went about fifty meters at a time, then stopped to listen, only moving again after several minutes of silence. *This kid knows what he's doing,* James thought. An hour later they'd reached the village of Rioveggio. They hid behind a house, shuddering together. The sound of the SS singing came again. All the homes were blacked out except the ones occupied by the Germans.

Could the kids come with us, make it through the front line? James wondered. *No. No. This is their place. They need to be with their family.*

They crept across a dark, deserted street. They crouched down behind an abandoned cart. James put his fingers through the bullet holes in the wooden frame. The boys struggled to contain their excitement now, with the house only a few meters away.

"Tell the boys to go alone. We don't want to scare anyone inside."

Liliana gave them the instructions. "They want us to meet their family, to stay the night with them."

"Just tell them to get inside first."

The boys disappeared across the street and around the corner.

"We're not safe yet—far from it," he said.

"But the boys will be."

"God, I hope so."

Luca appeared around the corner a few minutes later, holding a man's hand. He pointed to where they were hiding. The man came to them, holding out his hand to Liliana, offering profuse gratitude to all of them. He led them back to an old house on a cobbled street and then shut the door behind them. They set down their weapons and collapsed onto the seats the man offered them. He lifted each of the boys in the air to embrace them. A few seconds later the entire family appeared, the mother and three cousins dancing around the two boys, joy lighting their faces.

CHAPTER 9

Liliana had woken from a mercifully dreamless sleep. James was still curled up in the corner, the remnants of the food the boys' aunt and uncle had to spare on the plate in front of him. She was beside her father, their hips touching as they sat together in the dark of the attic Signore Vialli had offered. It would have been far safer to turn them away, even though they had brought the Viallis' two nephews down from the mountain.

Signore Vialli told them that the genocide was confined to the mountain itself. The SS had attacked from Rioveggio but were almost all gone now. The village had been their temporary base, the coming of the rain their cue to attack. She wondered how many had died—seven hundred, a thousand, more? It wasn't a conversation she wanted to have out loud. Visions of the SS in the cemetery came to her in the darkness, their pistols drawn, firing into the heap of bodies. She clutched her father's arm.

"I promised James I'd get him to the Allied lines," she said. "That was before I even knew you were alive."

"You should honor your word. James is a good man. We owe him the chance to get back to his unit."

"What about you, Father? You don't have to come. You could stay here—wait things out."

"You think it's safe here."

"Probably safer than trying to get through the lines."

"And that's why I'm not letting you go without me—I'm going to make sure you get through."

"What about us? Where do we go back to?"

Her father shifted from his sitting position, making his way to the tiny window a meter or so away. He peered out at the hushed street below. "There's nothing here for us now—nothing to keep us from leaving. Everything, everyone we had is gone. In one day."

"Where do we go from here?"

"Monte Sole will never recover from this. The Nazis have destroyed us. And for what? The Allies are still going to come. They'll probably be here in a week, or perhaps two. I'd rather be behind the advance. It's hard to discern soldier from civilian in this horrific war. The Allied advance will finish what's left of what we knew."

He returned to her, putting his arm around her shoulders.

"We have each other," she said.

"Don't let what you've seen here change who you are, my love. Don't let the evil that the SS scum have inflicted imprison you. You will survive this—I'll make sure of that. And when you do, you must live the most wondrous life, beyond any of our simple imaginations. Don't let their hatred live. Leave it behind, and you will have won."

The sound of artillery pounding the mountain woke them. Liliana went to the window, watched the explosions churning up the soil and foliage.

"They're going after what's left of the Stella Rossa," her father said.

"Chasing shadows," she answered.

The sun was high in the sky, and they could hear children playing together downstairs. The trapdoor to the attic opened. Luca popped his head up. "Were you comfortable last night?"

"Of course, my young friend," her father answered.

Luca disappeared, and Signore Vialli climbed up, bearing a tray of bread and water.

"I'm sorry. This is all we can spare."

"This is wonderful," Liliana said as they ate. Vialli sat there, waiting for them to finish before he spoke.

"I hear the Allied lines have moved. They're about ten kilometers away. You should be able to make it there in a day or so, but only at night. Moving during the day would be far too dangerous. The Germans are like ants crawling over the carcass of Monte Sole now. You got off just in time. More and more are arriving."

"How are we going to get across the lines?" Virginio asked.

"Follow the river. Make your way south. I can't be more precise than that without going down there myself. Look for a way through. I'd suspect that the Allies are on one side of the river and the Germans on the other, but I can't say for sure."

"Can we stay here until dark?" Liliana said.

"Of course. You're family to us now, all of you." He shook each of their hands as Liliana translated for James. "The sun will be gone in seven hours, and then you should get going. We'll be praying for your safe passage."

The boys came up to sit and talk with them in the cramped space when their uncle left, with Luca parking himself in James's lap for the duration.

The artillery continued throughout the afternoon, and Liliana felt her nerves rising as the sun faded and disappeared. Signore and Signora Vialli came to the attic to deliver one last meal of soup and bread she'd managed to come up with. It was magnificent, and Liliana thanked them again as they left the confined space.

Night came. It was time to leave. James couldn't remember the last time he'd felt the embrace of another human being. Was it his sister before he shipped out? It was hard to say. But now each member of the Vialli family, the parents, their three children, and Luca and Luciano, took turns.

"Luca wants you to bring him to America," Liliana whispered to him.

"Maybe someday."

They made their way out onto the silent, empty street. The moon in the cloudless sky lit their way.

The SS had put a strict curfew in place, and only a foolish or desperate person would defy them. *Sums us up,* James thought. They followed Signore Vialli's instructions to get out of town and soon walked among the bushes and trees again. They moved in single file, with Virginio at the front and Liliana in the middle. Monte Sole receded behind them. They didn't stop for anything other than the sign of German patrols. They came to roads where Nazi trucks rolled past, carrying troops and armaments to the front, and waited until the sound of the engines had faded into the distance to steal across. *What if we actually survive this? What will become of Liliana and her father?* He knew his future held a reunion with his unit and rejoining the war effort, but what of his companions? A refugee camp? They had no one south of the Allied lines, or even north of them now. He wanted to talk to them, to gauge what their hopes might be, but he didn't. He kept on despite the pain racking his limbs and the hunger in his belly, and the fear that they might not make it after coming this far. He kept on.

Liliana felt the fear awakening within her again. The tiredness that had superseded it had faded into the background, masked by adrenaline. It was well after midnight when they passed the German encampment, crawling on their bellies through dark fields to reach the relative safety of the brush beyond.

James held a finger to his lips. "From now on we'll likely be moving between German positions."

They kept walking. An hour later they came to a long cornfield that sloped down to the river. The sky remained cloudless, and the moon and stars shone silver from above, illuminating the way to the calm gray water. They crouched down together at the edge of the woods to survey the scene.

"This is it—the last few hundred meters. According to Vialli, the Allied positions are across the river. The water isn't moving too quickly. It shouldn't be dangerous. Don't look back once we hit the river."

"Where are the Germans?" she asked.

"I think we've managed to slip through their positions, but they're all over. They're not going to leave their front lines unguarded. Be on the lookout for sentries." He shook Virginio's hand. "Good luck."

Liliana embraced them both. "Be careful," she said.

"Let's go."

They stepped through the brush into the exposed area of the field, walking beside each other, their guns ready. She counted the steps as they went. *One hundred twenty-one, one hundred twenty-two.* The river was fifteen meters in front, and she could see there was a drop of about two meters to the water that had been invisible from the top of the field. James stopped. Virginio kept on.

"Hey," James whispered. "Do you see—"

A loud whooshing sound preceded the flashing of bright light, and suddenly it was like daytime all around them.

"Trip flare!" James shouted as the German fire came. "Keep going." Tracer bullets singed the air around them. Virginio went down on one knee to fire back. He shouted something. Six or seven German soldiers advanced down the cornfield after them.

Bullets were churning the earth, flying over their heads. James fired back, trying to give Liliana and Virginio some cover. Liliana tried to run, to get to a rock about three meters away, but something hit her like an almighty fist in the back of her leg. She reached down to feel it. Her hand came back wet. The pain was like she'd been stabbed with a molten rivet, and she rolled on the grass. She felt James's arms around her. He picked her up. They ran down toward the river, now just a few meters away. Her father ran beside them, tracer bullets zipping red lines through the night. They reached a rock at the end of the field, the Germans thirty meters behind.

"They'll cut us to pieces in the river," her father said. "I have to hold them off."

"No, come with us."

"This is the only way. I told you I would get you through this." He gestured toward the river below. "Take her. Now!"

James dragged Liliana to her feet. They stumbled a few steps and he threw her off the riverbank. Cold water engulfed her. She tried to stand but couldn't. James was beside her now. She felt his arms on her. They waded through the water. She looked back over her shoulder at her father firing the submachine gun at the Germans, halting their progress through the field.

"We can't leave him," she said. The pain was so much she could barely get the words out.

"We have to keep going. He's doing this for us." The water swirled around them, the other side getting ever closer. Liliana looked back one last time as they reached the bank on the other side. Her father was gone. He had been squatting behind the rock, firing, seconds before, but the Germans were there now. *No. No. We can't leave him.* James hauled her up the bank and laid her on her back. He went on one knee, reloading his weapon before firing across the river. Five or more Allied soldiers arrived around them, speaking in British-sounding accents. They shot back at the Germans on the other side of the river, who scattered back up the cornfield. A few seconds passed before the guns stopped. All went silent.

"I'm Sergeant James Foley of the Fifteenth Infantry Regiment, US Army. I'm an escaped POW. She helped me. She took me through the lines."

She wanted to sit up, to tell them they had to go back for her father, but couldn't speak.

"Anyone else with you?" a voice said.

"I don't think he made it," he said and put down his Sten. "She needs a medic."

"You heard the man, boys. Get the little lady back to the medical tent."

She felt hands on her, carrying her up toward their positions. Everyone was speaking in English now, but for some reason, she couldn't make out what they were saying.

She wasn't sure of the dream, just its essence, and she saw her father, his hand out, beckoning her, but she couldn't reach him. She tried, but he was gone and she was back in the river. A jolt surged through her body and her eyes flashed open. The pain in her thigh came first, and she reached down to touch it. James was there by her bedside, white light spilling through the window beside him. She tried to speak, to ask him where her father was, and if this had all been some terrible nightmare, but the words caught in her throat and came as a mumble.

"Don't try to get up," James said. He was out of the wooden chair he'd been in, leaning over her now.

She was in a hospital ward with dozens of wounded lying in orderly beds with white sheets.

"Where am I?"

"In a hospital in Florence. You've been asleep for two days. The doctor says you're going to be just fine."

He was clean, his hair washed, and his heavy stubble gone. He looked like a different man.

"My father?"

He shook his head. "I'm sorry, Liliana." *I'm the last of my family. They're all gone.* "We never would have made it if he hadn't stayed to cover us. I owe him my life."

She knew it—knew that he was gone, but that didn't lessen the shock of hearing it. Tears slid down her cheeks. She wanted James to hold her but couldn't ask. He sat back down in his chair, looking like he didn't know what to say.

"How long have you been here?" she said after thirty seconds of nothing.

"Since we arrived yesterday. They let me stay the night upstairs, and I came back in the morning. But I have to go soon."

"Back to your unit?"

He nodded. Who would she have once he left? She'd be completely alone. No one else knew her, or maybe ever could, like he did.

"It doesn't seem fair . . . ," she began. The words didn't come easily. "After everything you've been through, you have to go back to the front."

"Fairness is strongly discouraged in this man's army." The clouds shifted and sunlight broke through the window. "I wish it didn't have to be this way, but I can't change it."

They were interrupted by the sound of a voice behind him. A doctor appeared. He had streaks of gray through the sides of his sandy-brown hair and the whitest teeth she'd ever seen.

"It's a pleasure to finally meet the young lady who escaped through the lines," he said, holding a tanned hand out to her. James stood to salute his superior officer, but the doctor kept his focus on Liliana. "We're all very impressed by you here."

"Thank you, Doctor."

"I operated on your leg. It's a clean wound. You'll be back on your feet in no time. In the meantime, if you need anything, you ask for me—Major Hawley. I'll be back as soon as I can to check up on you."

"Thank you, Major."

The older man smiled. "Oh, and Sergeant—time's up—you need to report back to your unit. The guard outside will drive you back to where you need to be."

"Yes, sir."

Liliana felt her skin go cold. *No. Please let him stay.* She knew the futility of her feelings. There was nothing to be done. She'd probably never see him again and was going to have to start over, to face everyone she met as a stranger.

"That's my call. My chariot awaits." He stopped talking but didn't make to leave.

"James, I just wanted to say . . ." The words failed her. There was too much to say.

"Me too, Liliana. Me too. What are you going to do now? Do you know anyone here?"

"Yes. I have friends here. I'll stay with them." She wondered if he could tell that she was lying. "Please stay safe."

He paused a few seconds. Perhaps contemplating her lie. "I'd ask for an address where you'll be staying with these friends, but I'm guessing you don't know it."

"I don't."

"I hope we can meet again someday. Maybe we can sit down and have a drink, get something good for dinner, something that we didn't have to scavenge or steal?"

"That would be wonderful." She felt cast into a vortex of loneliness, as if he'd left already. Everyone else already had.

"How will I find you?" he asked.

"I don't know. I wish I could tell you."

"I left the chief's address in Cape May," he said, pointing to a piece of paper by the bed.

"I'll use it."

A soldier called his name from the end of the ward. James turned to wave to him and took her hand. "You'll be fine, Liliana Nicoletti. You're the strongest person I've ever known."

"Thank you."

She embraced him, felt him kiss her on the cheek. She took his face in her hands.

"Stay alive," she said.

"And if I can't, I'll die trying."

She stifled a laugh as he walked down the line of beds. He stopped for one last look back as he reached the door. She waved to him and he was gone.

PART II

CHAPTER 10

May 1948—Lüneberg Heath, northeast Germany

Hauptsturmführer Werner Brack blinked his eyes open, awakened by the noise of the other men climbing out of their bunks. He pushed back the thin blanket and sat up, rubbing the tiredness out of his eyes with a thumb and forefinger. The image of his daughter, Hilda, appeared through the haze of his mind. Today was her ninth birthday. Another year had passed—another year without seeing her. He wanted to look at the last letter his wife had sent, which Hilda had added a note to, showing off her best handwriting, but he felt the other men's eyes on him. *What does she even look like now? Has she forgotten me? Stop it.* There was no room for that here, not in this life that had been thrust upon him.

He rose from the bed, uttered a few words to his bunkmate, Lothar, formerly of the Einsatzgruppen in Russia. Lothar had left family behind too. Most of them had. One of the other men gave a Hitler salute, but what was the point now? The sense of defeat solidified within him. Brack pulled on his pants and slipped his shirt and vest on. He sat with the other men for breakfast. He didn't say much, and no one seemed surprised.

They were all former soldiers, either Wehrmacht or SS. There was no difference now. Losing the war had assigned the same label to each of them. They were "war criminals," and where better to hide out than this place with neither electricity nor a telephone—somewhere the occupying British Army could never find them, even if they cared to look. The nineteen men ate in silence, and Brack's mind wandered back to his daughter. He pictured her skipping home from school, her blond hair in pigtails and a bright smile on her face—the very picture of Aryan vitality. He dropped the fork from his hand. It clanged on his metal plate, drawing the stares of several of the other men, who grunted and then returned their eyes to the food in front of them.

He had tried to purge the thoughts of his wife and daughter from his mind. Was it more painful to remember them or to forget them? It mattered little. Barely an hour passed that he didn't see them as clearly as if they stood in front of him. His wife, Ingrid, had pleaded with him in her last letter to set a date for when they could be reunited. Though he longed to see her and Hilda more than anything in the world, he hadn't replied. It wasn't safe.

The thought of venturing past the local village terrified him. He'd read the stories in the papers of former soldiers and bureaucrats being plucked from their families' arms and thrown into jail or ending up at the end of the hangman's rope. The news of his old friend Rudolf Höss's death had shaken him the previous year, and for what? Trying to eradicate the Jewish menace? He should have been lauded, but they tried him in some kangaroo court and hanged him.

The Allies would never understand what they'd been trying to do. No one wanted to kill, but when the greater good called for it, it was only the most honorable and true Aryan patriots who could step up and get the grisly job done. He'd seen men who'd pulled the trigger too many times, who were haunted by the eyes of the vermin they'd been tasked to eliminate, driven to the bottle or even madness. The men the Allies were executing now as criminals were nothing more than ordinary soldiers trying to fulfill their duty, to follow their orders, and ultimately, to make the world a better, safer place.

Brack finished his breakfast and stood up with the other men. Lothar walked beside him, trying to make small talk. Brack found it difficult to answer, and Lothar soon desisted. The silver dew of early morning covered the trees all around them. The sun shone across the forest, the leaves sparkling like diamonds. Brack slung his ax over his shoulder as the group of men walked together. It was going to be another fine day. He raised the blade of the ax and chopped at the trunk of a tree, the wood coming off in chips at his feet. He thought of his family again and realized that he had to leave here.

The day passed as all the others, and the men trudged back to the campfire to play cards and drink. Brack washed his blackened face in an old munitions barrel filled with rainwater and settled back by the campfire. Someone passed him a bottle of schnapps. He took a deep pull and handed it back with thanks. Cigarette smoke filled the air, and Brack took out a cigarette of his own, asking the man beside him for a match. He stared up at the sky and the gray smoke. He heard the shuffle of a newspaper but didn't look at the headlines, even though newspapers were rare out here. He would eventually read it, even though all the news these days was bad. The halcyon days were gone.

"Hey, Brack," Lothar said. "Did you see this?" He shuffled over to where Brack sat, pointing out a story at the bottom of the front page. "You were in Italy, weren't you? Did you know this man?"

Brack read for a moment, then took a few seconds to form the words stuck in his throat. "Yes, he was my friend." He brought his eyes to the headline again.

FORMER SS OFFICER EXTRADITED TO ITALY TO ANSWER FOR CRIMES

Lothar took back the paper, reading aloud. "Former SS officer Walter Reder has been extradited to Italy to stand trial for his part in what has become known as the Marzabotto Massacre, which occurred in Monte Sole, forty kilometers south of Bologna, between 29 September and 5 October 1944, in which approximately eighteen hundred civilians were murdered by SS troops."

"Murder?" Brack said, despite himself. The eyes of all the men around the fire were on him. He quieted once more. He'd told them nothing of what he'd done in the war. None of them spoke of any specifics of what they did, but all were there for a reason. Lothar stopped reading but pointed out the sentence at the end of the paragraph.

> Authorities in Italy are still seeking Werner Brack in connection with the massacre. As of this time, former SS Hauptsturmführer Brack is at large and will be tried in absentia along with Reder.

Brack settled back onto the tree stump that was his chair, taking a long swig from the bottle of schnapps. Lothar went back to his place. They ate dinner, played cards as the sky darkened above, the trees becoming an impenetrable wall of black around them. The drunken men sang wistful songs about the glory years of the Reich and spoke of their families. Some drifted back toward the cabin. Brack still stared into the fire.

The desire to leave felt like a wild animal trapped inside him, relentless and uncontrollable. He was going to spend the rest of his life in some dingy Italian prison cell. The story only confirmed what he already knew. He, along with Reder, was to be a scapegoat. They were just following orders. "Murder." The term made him laugh. Who was to be held accountable for the murders perpetrated by the partisans? The partisans were held up as heroes, while he and his men, many of whom were dead now, were vilified as monsters and criminals. If he was to be a condemned man, then he should be granted one final wish—his was to see his family one more time, to hold his daughter in his arms again and feel the swish of her hair against his face. He had hidden here long enough.

All the men left, one by one, until only he and Lothar remained.

"You want to leave?" Lothar said.

"Is it that obvious?"

Lothar opened the newspaper to the wanted ads, holding it up so Brack could make out the words by the fading light of the fire. "You see this?" he said, pointing to an ad at the bottom of the page. "This is from Gunther."

"The contact?" Brack thought back to the man who'd arranged jobs for them here after they escaped the Allied prison camp, back in '46.

"The very same."

"What does it say?"

"It took me awhile to work out the code, only using the third letter of each sentence, but I have it now. It says, 'Meet in town Saturday for escape route.'"

Lothar went with him, riding on the back of a logging truck to the outskirts of the town of Celle, almost an hour away. The driver let them off short, and the two men stayed silent as they made their way through the fields toward the beautiful baroque buildings, untouched by Allied bombs, in the center of town. It was night when they arrived, the wide streets still busy with pedestrians. Brack saw the British soldiers first, skulking on the corner, smoking cigarettes, and laughing among themselves. He didn't need to tell Lothar to keep his cool. The two men strolled by. The tavern was at the end of the street, and Brack felt some relief as he shuffled across the wooden floor, kicking sawdust as he went. He took a seat away from the windows at the front. Lothar went to order and came back with two glasses of beer. The two men sat opposite each other at the plain wooden table, speaking little. Smoking. Waiting. They were on their third beer when Gunther sat down beside them. He looked healthy and well fed, not half-washed and gaunt like they were. His black beard was streaked with gray, and he had a deep scar across his forehead, but who didn't have scars now?

"Gentlemen," he said. The two men nodded in reply, and he continued. "I'm glad you got my message. I didn't want to draw attention to your hiding place by visiting. How are you?"

"Still alive," Brack said. "Is there news?"

"There is for those looking to start a new life, far from the prying eyes of the occupying forces."

"I'm listening."

"We've heard of a new opportunity, a new escape route out of Germany, out of Europe."

"To where, exactly?" Lothar asked.

"Argentina."

Brack nodded. He knew of the Argentinean sympathies for the National Socialist cause, but it was somewhere he'd thought of little in his life. He'd hoped somehow to get back to Austria, to live in a cabin in the mountains, his wife and daughter by his side. It was time to stop playing out that impossible fantasy in his mind. Gunther looked back at him, waiting for his reply. His companion beat him to it.

"How?" Lothar said.

"We've established a network of sympathizers, people willing to help us evade the Allies." Gunther stopped talking as the lady of the house came over to take their orders.

"What a lovely dress that is."

"Thank you. What can I get you?"

The men ordered food and waited until she'd gone to begin speaking again.

"The route goes through Genoa."

Brack took a deep drag on his cigarette. "Italy? Is it safe there?" He thought of Reder and the chance that he would be delivering himself to those who'd flay him alive.

"It will be. We've made sure of that. We have safe houses and sympathizers all ready and waiting." Gunther took a swig of his beer. "You'd likely never see Germany again."

"What of our families?" Brack said.

"They'd be free to follow in your wake. No one could stop them. You could start a new life with your loved ones."

"I'm interested."

"Me too," Lothar added. "I'm starting to feel more like a mole than a man, living underground."

"Take some time to think about it. I'll need three hundred marks from each of you, for IDs and expenses."

"I don't need time," Brack said. He pushed the money across the table. It was almost half his savings.

They met Gunther at the back of the tavern a week later. They made idle chitchat for a few minutes, ordering a round of beers before Gunther reached into the satchel he'd brought. He pushed their new papers across the table.

"Harald Berk," Brack said.

"It's close enough to your own name that you'd answer to it."

"From Breslau?"

"It's in Soviet hands now, mostly destroyed. Any parish registers or official records will likely have been destroyed in the bombing." He pushed a list of towns and contacts across the table to each man. "Memorize the names of the towns and the people you'll meet there."

"Father Eduardo Dömöter?"

"Don't waste my time, or yours, with questions. Everything has been arranged, from your passage to Argentina to the visas you'll need to enter the country. Your only concern will be reaching each of your contacts safely. In the meantime, memorize the sheet in your hand. A lot of loyal people will suffer if this list falls into Allied hands."

Brack read through the list three times. "You can take this back now."

"I'll need a little more time than that," Lothar said.

"You have one more minute."

"And what happens at the end of our journey?" Brack said.

"Buenos Aires has a firmly rooted German community, with its own neighborhoods, private clubs, restaurants, schools, and even three major newspapers in German. It's a home away from home, the best you'll ever get." Gunther leaned in, looking around to make sure no one was listening. "You're going to have to split up. Brack—you're first to go. Your train leaves for Munich in the morning."

"No time for goodbyes, then."

"None."

"Where did you serve, Gunther?" Lothar said as he handed his list back.

"That's not even my real name," he said. "Good luck, gentlemen." He stood up and left.

It felt ironic that traveling to the border of his home country would be the most hazardous part of his journey. The train ride to Munich passed without incident. His papers were good enough to fool the lazy eyes of British and American soldiers daydreaming of their sweethearts back home. He doubted the soldiers themselves would deem him a war criminal—a label for bleeding hearts and rabid politicians. They would have known what he knew: that a soldier does his duty. Orders are not given to be questioned—only to be followed. He had been a good soldier. People died in war—he was sure the Allied soldiers would have understood that much. But the border police swarming the town of Mittenwald were not soldiers. They were looking for fugitives.

Brack got off the bus he'd taken from Munich, keeping his eyes to the ground as he went. A border policeman stopped a man a few meters in front of him and was checking through his papers. Brack noted an alley on his left he could escape down. *Stay calm. Just breathe.* The policeman didn't look up from the other man's papers as Brack passed.

He arrived at the hotel. His hands shook as he turned the door handle and approached the woman behind the desk, who greeted him with a smile and led him to his room. The room was simple, but comfortable. He collapsed on the bed, falling asleep in seconds.

A few hours passed before he heard knocking on the door. He held his ear to the wooden panel, listening to the man on the other side breathing.

"Who is it?" Brack said.

"Uncle Wilhelm," the voice said.

Satisfied with the code words, Brack opened the door. A small, portly man with a gray beard shuffled through, carrying a bag.

"Welcome to Mittenwald. I trust you've had a comfortable journey so far."

Brack nodded, knowing his answer didn't matter.

"I think we can dispense with the pleasantries. I've arranged for a hunter to meet you here tomorrow morning. He's an experienced man who'll lead you through the mountains and over the border. Don't leave the hotel room. This town is thick with police. They'd love to get their hands on the likes of you. We had a man caught here last week. He—"

"I won't leave. Although, if I need to go to the bathroom . . ."

"There's one down the hall, but don't go any farther than that." He dropped the bag on the floor. "I've brought you some food and beer to get you through the night. Good luck, and *Heil Hitler.*" The man gave the salute. It felt good to return it, and for the first time in as long as he could remember, he felt alive again.

Brack kept pace with the hunter, stride for stride, along well-worn paths through the woods and into the mountains. His guide didn't speak, even when they stopped for lunch—he just sat staring as he ate the sandwich he had packed, never even letting Brack know when it was time to leave. He just stood up and walked on, stopping to look back until Brack followed. They hiked for several hours until the air grew thinner and the sky seemed to sink toward them. Soon, all signs of human life disappeared. There was comfort in that. There were only the mountains and the sky, blue as Hilda's eyes, hovering just above the white-tipped peaks that sprouted up all around them. Any sadness in leaving Germany, the country he had dedicated his life to, was negated by the return to his homeland. He waited until he was absolutely sure to ask the question. The hunter was a meter in front of him, as he had been the entire way.

"Are we in Austria now?"

"Yes."

They kept on until they reached an old hunting lodge, the only building he'd seen for an hour at least. The hunter pushed through the door, leaving it ajar for him to follow. As night fell, Brack looked back on the German countryside for what he knew would be the last time. He drew the curtain and went to bed.

The next morning the hunter prepared a breakfast of bread and salami, with freshly brewed coffee. They ate together, not speaking until the hunter glanced out the window at a border guard making his way toward them. Brack felt the blood drain from his face.

"Don't worry," the hunter said. "He'll have seen the smoke from the chimney. He likely only wants a cup of coffee."

Brack hid in the wardrobe, listening to the border guard and the hunter chatting and laughing as if they were old friends. How did he know they weren't? He thought of all the searches he'd overseen, and how the wardrobe would have been the first place he looked. He had always been amazed at how stupid people had been hiding from him.

But he knew the border guard wasn't searching like he and his men once had. Half an hour later the stranger was gone, and with him, the hunter's ability to string more than two words together. They trudged deeper into Austria in silence along winding mountain paths, avoiding any patrols.

Brack lay awake that night in the safe house. The next contact was in Innsbruck. It was a place he knew well.

The taxi drove away. Brack slung his bag over his back and examined his shoes. The leather was almost worn through. He looked left and right along the suburban street. Several of the houses were destroyed, charred black from the explosions. He heard children playing in one of the bombed-out ruins but never saw them. His feet carried him up toward the house almost without his consent, and he was knocking on the glass pane of the door before he realized it. An elderly lady answered, the crow's feet around her eyes widening as she recognized him. The door opened. Brack stepped forward and through.

"Hello, Aunt Helga."

"Werner?" the old woman said.

"Yes. I can't stay long. Is she here?"

Aunt Helga's mouth moved but no sound came out.

"I need to see her."

She responded with a nod and led him through the house. The only sound was their footsteps on the thin carpet and the ticking of the old grandfather clock in the hallway. His mother sat at the back window, peering out, wrapped in a blanket despite the warmth of the day. The skin on her face was almost transparent, like paper held against a bright light. A mess of blue veins throbbed in the hands she rested on the arms of the chair. Her white hair was rigid and taut and stuck out at an ungainly angle at the top, where the brush had missed its mark. She didn't turn as he entered the room, or even when her sister called out her name. He went to her.

"Mother? Mother?"

"Oh, Werner, it's you, is it?" She sounded as if she'd last seen him that morning and not five years previously. "Is your wife with you? What's her name again?"

"No, Mother, Ingrid's not here," he said, kneeling beside her. He took her hand. It felt like it could disintegrate just by his touching it.

"What about Hilda, is she here?"

"No, Mother, it's just me."

"What age is she, nine?"

"Yes, that's right. You remembered."

He brushed against a table by her chair, rattling a teacup on its saucer.

"My son," she said, and a smile spread across her lips.

"I can't stay long. I'm leaving today. I don't think I'll ever be able to come back again."

"Oh?"

"I wanted to see you, to tell you you're always in my thoughts."

"Your father's gone."

"Father died in '31. You moved here from Vienna to live with Helga ten years later, remember?"

"Of course, and what of your brother, Klaus? Have you seen him?"

"He's still with the Philharmonic in Vienna, I believe. I haven't seen him in years."

"Oh." She paused to look out at the well-kept garden outside. "So where are you off to? And why aren't your wife and daughter here to see me?"

"I have to leave. The Allies . . ." He let his hand slip, bringing it up to tuck her blanket in under her chin. "Are you comfortable?" She nodded. "Good. I'm so glad I saw you."

"Was it worth it?" she said.

"What?"

"All the slaughter. All the death. What was won?"

Brack stood up, peering out the window at the sun setting over the mountains. It seemed like the most beautiful thing he'd ever seen. He stood beside her for a minute or more; the only sound that of the clock ticking in the hallway. He bent down to kiss her.

"I have to go, Mother. Please look for my letters."

"Pass on my regards to Ingrid and Hilda. They are wonderful girls."

"Goodbye."

A black-robed priest waited for him a few kilometers past the Italian border. The innkeeper who'd guided him across bade him farewell and left him with the smiling cleric, who shook his hand with vigorous enthusiasm.

"Welcome to Italy," he said. He was young, perhaps not even thirty, clean-shaven and tanned.

"Thank you."

"I am Don Mauro Falcone. I am here to guide you to Genoa," he said in perfect German.

"Harald Berk."

"Please, let me," he said, reaching for Brack's suitcase. "You must be exhausted after your journey through the pass. I have a car waiting, but in the meantime, would you do me the honor of joining me for a glass of wine?"

Don Mauro led Brack toward a small café, where they took a seat in the back despite the fact that there were several free tables overlooking the street.

"Is it safe?"

"I know the owner here. He is one who understands our motivations."

The owner came over and spoke with Don Mauro in Italian for a few seconds before brandishing a bottle of red wine for the two men. He poured each of them a glass. Brack held it up, nodding in thanks to the owner, who smiled and walked away.

"Have you helped many—"

"Refugees? Yes, we've seen many like you in need of assistance come through in the last months. There are so many displaced souls after the war."

Brack took a sip of his wine. It tasted like a Tuscan summer's day. He took a few seconds to respond. He was puzzled. *Why are these clergymen helping former SS men? Don't they know Hitler hated Catholics?*

The young priest seemed to read his thoughts. He put down the wineglass. "You've done a lot for the Church over the last few years. Now, let us do something for you."

"Thank you," Brack said, no less confused than before.

Five minutes later Don Mauro led the former SS officer to a car parked three hundred meters down the street. The younger man took his suitcase, depositing it in the trunk before opening the door for him. The tiny car shook as Brack sat down. A minute later they were on the way to the town of Merano. It had been almost three weeks since he'd left Lüneberg Heath. He'd met almost a dozen contacts along the way. Some had been former SS themselves, while some saw helping him as a job, the means to the end of getting paid. But he couldn't understand why a priest, and an Italian one at that, would want to help him escape.

He doubted the young man knew what Brack had done personally, but he must have known what the SS had done. Or perhaps he didn't. The newspapers had reported about some partisans killed at the time, but had mentioned little of their age or gender. It was only after the war that any of the details of their operation emerged. He doubted it was possible for any Italian to understand what they'd been trying to do on that mountain south of Bologna. He turned to look out the window. The car rolled on.

"Where are you from?" the priest said after a few minutes' silence.

Brack sat up, almost startled. "From Vienna—Penzing, in the western suburbs." It was a few seconds before he realized he had told the truth. *Idiot.*

"My mother was from Wilhelmsburg, just a few kilometers away."

"Not too far away. That's a beautiful place. She was Austrian?"

"Yes. My father was from Milan. I grew up there." Don Mauro stopped talking for a few seconds as they slowed to let some sheep spill across the road. The farmer waved to him and they were driving once more. "I met Bishop Hudal in Rome after the war."

"Who?"

"Bishop Alois Hudal—he's an Austrian, based in the Santa Maria dell'Anima in Rome. Are you Catholic?"

"No."

"You will be soon." The priest took one hand off the steering wheel, using the other to reach for a pack of cigarettes. The car veered as he took one out and put it between his lips. He reached down for the matches that were beside the pack.

"Let me," Brack said. He lit the cigarette for Don Mauro.

"Thank you," he said, rolling down the window. "I struck up conversations with Bishop Hudal. We spoke many times. He opened my eyes to the dire threat of the Soviet hordes and their desire to destroy everything godly, everything that we hold dear."

Brack wondered if the young priest was telling him all this to impress him or to justify his actions. Either way, a friend was a friend in these dark times. The fact that the Nazis had no love for the papacy was irrelevant. They both shared a common enemy. He stayed silent as the young man continued.

"The bishop told me that the only hope for Christianity in Europe was to eliminate the Soviet threat, and that was what Hitler knew and was trying to achieve. He reminded me of our sacred duty to help those most in need and to preserve a certain moral character, a certain type of person, willing to fight against the communists. We've got to keep a reserve—a reserve we can draw on in the future."

Brack and Don Mauro stayed in a castle that night, in a monastery the next. He felt himself coming back to life. The hope that he might be reunited with his family, able to live out his days in peace with the ones he loved, the ones he had done all this for, filled him with happiness. He longed to speak to Ingrid, to hold her again. He began to believe that he'd make it to Argentina, and that Ingrid and Hilda would follow. He thought of Ingrid, her beauty. He hadn't been with another woman since they married, ten years before. What would have become of them if Hitler and the Nazis had never swept to power? Maybe they still would have met and lived out their lives together, but what kind of a world would it have been? *A world overrun by Bolsheviks? We had no choice in what we did.*

Ingrid had sacrificed the family life she craved for the war effort—just like he had. His commitment to fighting for the betterment of his people and the world as a whole had come before anything else. She was a good woman. The thought of being with her again brought a deep contentment to him before he yielded to a serene sleep.

The lighthouse at Genoa cast its beams across the old port, just as it had for four hundred years, illuminating Brack's path to freedom. He had been staying with Father Eduardo Dömöter, a Hungarian priest who spoke of the National Socialist dream of a better world over dinner every night. Brack had been here ten days now, in the church of San Antonio. Don Mauro had been right; he was a Catholic now. He had been baptized into a new identity, and together with his letter of reference from Dömöter, that had been enough to obtain Red Cross travel documents. An overworked Red Cross official had stamped the papers and taken his photograph and fingerprints. It had been hard to contain his excitement. He was Harald Berk now, a refugee. Soon he was fully accredited and ready to make passage to the New World. On his last night before sailing, Brack accepted Dömöter's invitation to attend Mass and receive his blessing. It was the first time he'd been inside a church since he'd rousted the partisans from one on the first day of the Monte Sole operation.

The old priest accompanied him to the docks the next day. Brack wore a new suit, bow tie, and black hat. He thanked Dömöter one last time before the old priest shuffled off to help the next man who was coming that very night. Two other SS men Dömöter had helped stood at the bow, staring off into the blue as the ship departed. Franz Rostock, who had been a commander of an SS Panzer division, asked the question they were all thinking.

"What do you expect of Argentina?"

"I don't know. A place with no memory, perhaps? I just want to see my family again."

They stood there in silence for several minutes. All signs of land diminished, and there was only blue swirling sea around them.

PART III

CHAPTER 11

May 1952—Cape May, New Jersey

Even though they were fifteen minutes early, they had to squeeze into the last two seats available at the back of the church. The ceiling fans swirling above their heads wafted down cool air, but James still took off his jacket and hat, piling them onto his lap.

Penny reached to him, putting a hand on his forearm. She had never gotten to know the chief, had only met him a few times when she'd come to visit. She never had the need for someone like him. Not like James had.

James looked up and around. Most of the faces he'd known growing up were here. Everyone who mattered in this small shore town was here, as well as many who did not. The mayor was in the front row along with the local congressman. Clyde Miriano, a local drunk who the chief had brought in dozens of times for public disturbance, drunkenness, and brawling, sat behind them with several of his friends. Few had known the chief better. A large photograph of William Brody as a young man in his police uniform sat on the altar. The casket was adorned with the bright-yellow and pink flowers he'd wanted.

"Those flowers are so beautiful, so bright," Penny said.

"He knew what was coming. He almost knew the day," James said. "It was the calm in how he reacted that struck me. It was effortless."

"He knew he'd lived a good life. Look at all the people here."

"They're lining up outside too."

The standing room at the back of the church was full now, and an anxious crowd milled around in the sunshine beyond the doors.

"He told me in his letters that he wanted this—his funeral—to be a party. He wanted people to celebrate what he'd given them, not mourn what they'd lost."

The priest emerged from the sacristy and went to the family. He then went back inside for a few seconds before coming back carrying a record player. He set it down, took a record from one of the altar boys, and laid it on the turntable. An audible laugh came from the crowd as the sounds of Rosemary Clooney's "Come on-a My House" filled the church. The lively beat had people bumping against one another, and many were smiling by the time the song ended, including the priest, who began by saying, "Only Bill Brody would invite everyone to his house at his own funeral."

The ceremony passed: The new chief of police spoke of the incredible influence Bill had had on him and the town as a whole. The mayor told of afternoon drinks and Bill's beloved Eagles, and the local congressman eulogized about how the city had lost a giant of a man. James kept his feelings hidden. He didn't want to cry in public and certainly not in front of his baby sister.

The ceremony ended, and James and Penny shuffled out of the church. Martha Goodwin, his ex-girlfriend from high school, was there with her husband and their three boys, dressed in suits. The sides of Martha's hair were streaked with gray and she looked ten years older than she was, but the lightness in her voice suggested a contentedness that he'd not found.

"How are you?" she said. She wrapped her arms around him. "You look wonderful." Her husband reached a hand forward and James shook it as Martha let him go. "Is this Penny?" she asked.

"Yes. All grown up now."

"You were a baby when I saw you last," Martha said.

"I'm twenty-five now. Married."

"Where's your husband?"

"At home looking after our baby."

"Oh, that's wonderful. I'm so happy for you. The last time we met I brought you to the arcade and we got taffy."

"I remember it."

"And you, James, you're married too, I hear? To a Mexican lady?"

"There's a lot of them in Mexico."

"She's not here?" Martha asked.

"No, she couldn't make it." James wondered what she was doing at that moment, whether she was playing tennis or at the pool at her father's house.

"What do you do there?"

"I'm a writer, at least I'm trying to be. I work for an English-language newspaper in Mexico City, although I do dabble in Spanish from time to time."

"Mexico City. You've come so far, and here we are still in Cape May."

"She gets homesick if we go to Atlantic City for the day," her husband said.

"Oh, I do not," Martha said. "Never mind old George. He loves to tell a tall tale."

"It's true," George said, holding his hands up. His youngest child, a boy who looked about ten, tugged at the cuff of his suit. "We should go."

They said their goodbyes with a promise to talk at the Brody house later on. Penny and James stood a few minutes outside the church, the crowd dissipating around them.

Penny turned the key in the ignition and the engine of her car faded out. A tiny picture of her husband, Joe, sat on the dashboard. He was an engineer, a veteran of D-Day, a part of the war people still remembered. He looked after her well and was a good man. Their wedding three years before was the last time James had been in the States, and the last time he'd seen Chief Brody. The old man hadn't been able to make it to Mexico City for James's wedding in '50. The sickness had already taken hold of him. James got out of the car. The sun was bright above, and the leaves on the oak tree over the chief's house rustled in the gentle breeze. It was like stepping into his memories. The night Brody had brought him back here and cleared out his daughter's old room for him was as fresh in his mind as if it had been the night before.

"It's like coming home in a way," he said.

"I understand that. I feel the same way about Aunt Katie's. I try not to think about the old house."

"I hadn't even been down that street in years, even before I left."

Several other people walked up toward the Brody house, old neighbors who greeted James with handshakes and embraces. Most of them knew Penny too, and made the same remarks that Martha had. She took them with good grace and smiled. Inside, bottles of cold beer sat in the corner beside a table with a selection of wine. Children scuttled around carrying toys. Most people had plates of food, and the lively music playing threatened dancing at any moment. Angela Brody, the chief's wife, sat in the corner, flanked by her four grown daughters. "Come with me," James said as he made for them. Angela stood up with tears in her eyes as soon as she saw him.

"Oh, James," she said. "You came all the way from Mexico."

He felt her tears wet the inside of his collar.

"Of course. I had to. I had to."

He felt the emotions stir in him, but he fought them back. He balled his fists, digging his nails into his palms as he stood back. Each of her four daughters stood up to hug him in turn. He had lived only with the youngest. The rest were married and gone by the time the old man had taken him in, yet they still cried as they embraced him, as if he were one of them. He pulled up a chair for himself and one for Penny. They all remarked how beautiful she was and how proud they were of him. They didn't ask many questions about Susana, James's wife, just pointed out how lucky she was to be married to him. People came and went, and Angela stood up to talk to most of them, but James and Penny never moved. The daughters wouldn't have let them. The ladies asked a thousand questions about James's work, about what he'd been doing these last years since they'd seen him.

"What he really wants to write about are his experiences during the war," Penny said.

"In Italy?" Marcie, Angela's eldest, asked.

"Yeah, no matter where life takes me, my mind gets drawn back there. I think about my time there most days."

"I remember a night you were visiting here, in '47. You remember too, don't you, James?" Angela, who'd rejoined them, said. James nodded. "You told us about that place—Monte Sole, wasn't it?"

"Yes."

"What was the girl's name?"

"Liliana."

Penny stayed silent. She'd heard the story in graphic detail over the years, but had never asked him to stop, had always listened whenever he'd wanted to speak of it.

"Did you ever find out what became of her?" Angela asked.

"No. It was as if she just disappeared into thin air. I gave up trying a few years ago."

"Well, you're a married man now," Penny said.

"Yes, I am." He raised the beer and took a sip. Angela stood up to speak to the ex-mayor. James waited for her to sit down again before he continued. "I saw some terrible things, things I'd like to forget, but which shouldn't be forgotten. The places I was and the things I saw are never mentioned, anywhere. I mean, I've barely ever seen or read any mention of the mountain I was on with the partisans. The people who died there don't deserve to be forgotten. I owe them more than that." It was late now, long since dark, but several children were still up and playing. The party was still going, just as the chief had requested. James waited until the children were far enough away before continuing. "I read last year that one of the men responsible for Monte Sole was jailed in Italy."

"That must have been satisfying," Angela said.

"He was one of two men punished for what happened there. The other was a general called Max Simon. I followed the Nuremberg trials and all the others since. A lot of good was done, but none of the other dozens of Nazis from Monte Sole have stood trial or even been accused. They're all still out there, walking around, living their lives. So that's what I want to write about, and that's who I want to expose. I'll get there," he said, finishing his beer.

"There's something I want to give you," Angela said. "Come with me." She took him by the hand and led him upstairs. It had been years since he'd been up the staircase—not since he'd lived here—and the memories were so thick he felt like he was going to drown in them. He passed a framed picture of him and the chief from a fishing trip they'd taken in '40. He picked it up.

"That was the day I caught my first brook trout."

"I'd like you to have that," she said. "But there's something else." She disappeared into her bedroom for thirty seconds before coming back out, a letter in her hand.

"Bill wrote this to you last week. Two days before he passed." She handed it to him. "He loved you like the son he never had."

"I loved him too," James said. "I really did."

The dark of night outside had turned the window of the hotel lobby into a mirror, and he reached out to touch it with one finger. The operator's voice came on and, after a delay of a few seconds, so did Susana's.

"Hello," she said in Spanish.

"It's me. What time is it there?"

"Just before dinner."

"Is tonight the reception?"

"Yes, the British ambassador should be here soon. How was the funeral?"

He imagined her there in her father's house in an evening dress. Stunning. "I'm glad I was here. It was hard, but—"

"I never tried to stop you."

"I know that," he said. "I wish you could have been here."

"You know I couldn't go there with you," she said. "Have you been drinking?" He knew this was coming. This was the reason he contemplated not calling at all. He'd wanted to hear her voice, just not this tone.

"I had some wine with dinner. I was with Penny and some old friends. We had some whiskey."

"I thought we were past this." Her anger was obvious now. He closed his eyes. "You promised me . . . ," she said.

"I'm mourning the chief. I . . ."

"Oh, James, I don't know what to say anymore. I've asked you so many times . . . I'm sorry about your friend. I know he was like a father to you, but you promised me."

"I know. I know, I'm sorry. Penny didn't know. She doesn't know."

"About your drinking?"

"I haven't told her."

"You tell her everything else."

Penny sat on the other side of the lobby, reading the newspaper. This was the first time he'd seen her in a year, since his drinking had gotten bad, since the nightmares had come back. She had no idea.

"I wanted to talk to you about something else."

"What is it, James? I really need to go."

"I got a letter from the chief. He wrote it to me a few days before he died." He reached into his pocket and took out the piece of paper. It was in Angela's handwriting. "It's short. Can I read it to you?"

"Of course."

"'Dear James. You make me proud every day of the man you are. I love you as my son, because that's what you'll always be. There's just one last thing I want you to do for me, one last piece of advice I have left to give. Go see your father.'" The words were catching in his throat now, and he could hear something on the other end of the line too. "'Give him the chance to earn your forgiveness. And if he doesn't, give yourself the chance to say goodbye and move on. You've been a prisoner of what he did for too long. Time to fly free. When I think about you and my four girls, I know I'll die a happy man. Do this last thing for me. Love, Bill.'"

The pause on the end of the line lasted so long he had to say her name to make sure she was still there. Her voice came through laden with emotion. "Maybe he's right. Maybe you do need to see him. You need something. We both know that."

"Penny won't come. She told me to go. She doesn't need to."

"I think you should."

"It'll mean staying a little while longer, a few days at least." For a moment he thought she'd tell him not to come back at all.

"I'll be here when you get back. Good luck."

"I love you," he said.

She hesitated before answering. "I should go," she said and hung up the phone.

The rain sheeted down from a slate-gray sky as Penny pulled into the prison parking lot. James wore the same suit he'd worn to the chief's funeral, cleaned and pressed for each occasion. She turned the engine off, and they sat in silence a few seconds, listening to the rain pelting the car. They hadn't spoken much during the ninety-minute drive from her house in Philadelphia to the prison. Who knows what might have been said if they had? Easier to report on what happened after the fact.

He hadn't asked her to come, but accepted when she volunteered to drive him. She never said she didn't agree with what he was doing, just that she didn't want to see their father herself. She reached across and took him by the hand.

"I'll be here for you when you're done."

He nodded and put his hat on. He opened the door and then his umbrella and walked to the front gate.

Friends, family, and men in suits he could only presume were attorneys waited at each of the other tables in the visitors' room. The bars on the windows, and the guards standing upright in each corner of the room, left him under no illusion as to where he was, and where his father lived. A door opened at the end of the room and several men came through. A tall man with a dark beard hugged a small child before kissing a woman dressed in a fine suit and matching pink hat. An old man greeted a man about his own age, and a young man cried as his mother took him in her arms. His father was last through the door, wiry and thin in his prison uniform, his face unshaven, his eyes dark. James didn't know whether to stand or not, whether to look at him or not, to hug him or not. His father nodded as he came to the table and offered James a handshake. His hand was cold, and James let go of it to sit down.

"So what are you doing here?" his father asked. "Not one visit in the last fourteen years, and now you decide to come? What gives?"

"I live in Mexico now."

"What you doing there?"

"I'm a journalist." His father pulled out a pack of cigarettes and lit one up. James had his own on the table but didn't touch them. "I'm married."

"Oh yeah?" he said, puffing out a plume of white smoke. "Mexican señorita?"

"Yeah."

"Good for you, son."

It didn't feel natural to hear this man call him that, but he ignored it. He thought of Chief Brody. Why was he dead and this man alive? He thought to ask him how he was and what life was like in here but realized that he didn't care.

"Were you in the war?" his father asked.

"Infantry. In Italy."

"I was stuck in here."

James resented his tone—as if he would have served his country.

"You asked why I'm here? I came back for Chief Brody's funeral."

"Oh, jeez, that guy? You came from Mexico for that—"

"Don't say it. Just don't. He told me to come and see you."

"So that's what you're here for? To see if I'm sorry?" He leaned forward and stubbed out his cigarette in the ashtray in the middle of the table. "Do I regret what happened? Yes, I do. I'm in here because of it. But did anybody listen to me when I told them that she drove me to do it, that it never would have happened if she hadn't been so crazy?" He threw his hand with the last word and reached down for another smoke. "I was under a lot of pressure then, drinking too much too, I admit that, I do, but I never would have done what I did if she hadn't been on me all the time."

"You never would have beaten her to death in front of me, with a metal rod, if she hadn't nagged you? Is that what you're saying?" It was all James could do to restrain himself from reaching across the table to grab this man. He was glad Penny hadn't come.

"There were a lot of things you couldn't see. It was a hard time for me."

"You beat her and you beat me, and you forced me to watch as you beat her to death in front of me."

"I'm not proud of that."

"You're not proud?"

"I'm doing my time. I don't need you to come in here and lecture me about—"

"There's nothing she could have done to deserve that. Nobody deserves that."

"I was trying to make you into a man, can't you see that?"

James thought back to those nights alone on the mountain in Italy, to what he'd seen the SS do to the people there. Had his father's cruelty prepared him for what he'd experienced in the war, or was the strength inherent in him, dormant, waiting for the right time to show itself?

"I'm here to tell you that I forgive you for what you did."

"I don't need—"

"Shut up, just shut your mouth." A guard came over to the table. He didn't say a word, but the message was clear. "I don't care what you have to say. Not now. Not ever again. You asked me why I came here? To tell you that you've got no power over me—that I'm leaving you behind."

"How wonderful for you," his father said.

"You'll never hear from me or Penny again."

"What difference does that make to me? You never come see me one time in fourteen years? Your own father? And I'm meant to miss you when you say you won't come again?"

James stood up, knowing that this was a moment he'd replay in his mind the rest of his life. "I'm done here," he said to the guard. "Goodbye, Dad."

He strode down the hall toward the exit. The rain was coming to an end, and he saw Penny's face in the car as the guard let him through the gate. *That's that. Now, on to Monte Sole.*

PART IV

CHAPTER 12

September 1956—New York City

James let his fingers dance across the keys, paying attention not so much to the words he was typing but to the feelings. This wasn't poetry, but without any emotional resonance, what was his writing worth? He wasn't in the business of laying out technical manuals. He scanned his desk, his eyes falling on the framed picture of him and the chief on the fishing trip in '40, holding up the trout. He stood, letting his fingers fall away. He glanced at the page, his eyes falling on the words "Nazi" and "conditioning"—and "Monte Sole."

The setting sun cast swathes of gold over the city like some great loom. It reminded him of Mexico City; memories of Susana tumbled into his mind. He wondered what she was doing. It was five thirty there. She was probably shopping with her friends, or having cocktails with her new husband, or tending to their new baby. The sound of Harry Bailey's typewriter jarred him back into the moment, and he returned to his seat.

> *History is not past, but merely an extension of the present, to which all people are tied.*

He took a deep breath and began to type again.

How? That is the question that we all should be asking. How could the most civilized, modern, culturally advanced society in Europe do what Germany did? We all consider ourselves civilized. We eat with knives and forks and walk upright. We might go to the theater or listen to the works of Beethoven, Brahms, Chopin, or Bach. We might read what are known as the "great" novels or perhaps just the newspaper. We teach our children good manners, not to hit, to share their toys. Is this what makes us civilized?

Werner Brack was ostensibly the picture of civility. The son of a composer, he was taught music from an early age—by the age of six he could read music and play the violin and the piano. He was known as a bright, talented, and cultured boy, and he flourished in the Vienna preparatory school his parents enrolled him in. He went to the University of Vienna, studying business, unsullied by the horrors of the Great War due to his age. Werner left university in 1932, graduating top of his class. He took a job in a local bank and was set to join the upper echelons of Vienna society, a business leader and patron of the arts. But then something happened. A change. Werner Brack joined the Nazi party in 1934 and, after Nazi Germany gobbled up Austria, moved to Munich to join the SS. He met and married Ingrid, the daughter of a local grocer who wore shiny Nazi pins on his coat as he served his customers. When the war that Hitler had set his state up to wage inevitably came to pass, Brack was among those who swept aside the Allied forces in Belgium and France. He was sent to the Russian front and took control of a new elite unit. He was decorated many times, adored by his men.

I witnessed this man—this educated, cultured man, this bastion of Viennese society—ordering his soldiers to open fire on a crowd of women and children. I saw him fire his pistol into heaps of corpses to finish off those who had escaped death the first time around. I saw the houses burned to the ground on his orders, their inhabitants still hiding inside. I saw unspeakable things that still haunt my nightmares.

What is the root of his acquiescence? Where does this evil come from? Why did this man, and so many thousands of others, commit such horrific acts? How are human beings able to devalue the pain of others so frivolously? What is this "civilization" that we're striving for? Do we have it in us to be civilized, or are we nothing more than animals, responding to the most potent stimulus?

Harry Bailey, one of the other staff writers, began speaking beside him. "You writing about Nazis again?"

"Who told?"

"Your fingers on the keys were my first clue."

"I'm that predictable?"

"Hey, if it ain't broke. Your last piece, about Monte Sole . . . I haven't seen Stover smile like that in ten years. I barely knew the guy had teeth."

"I've had worse editors."

"Where? In Mexico?"

"Actually, you're right—he's the worst."

Harry held up an envelope. "Well, here's something that might cheer you up."

"You getting married at last?" James said.

"Think you need a woman for that. No, this is addressed to you, ended up on my desk." Harry handed him the envelope, resting his elbow on the side of James's file cabinet.

"You going to watch me open it?"

"Apparently I am."

James took a letter opener from his desk. He pulled out an elegant ivory-colored card. A decorative pattern outlined the exquisitely rendered calligraphy.

"You are cordially invited to the charity ball to be held at the Landay residence on Saturday, sixth of October," James read aloud.

"Where is it?"

"The Upper East Side."

"Someone's going up in the world," Harry said.

"Sure beats a night at home with the roaches," James said. "I have no idea who these people are, however, so there's that."

"Give it here," Harry said, and James handed him the invitation. "Leonard and Ruth Landay. I think I've heard of them. Yeah, I remember now. This Landay guy's not more than thirty, but richer than Croesus."

"Old money?"

"Is there any other kind? His granddaddy invented some drilling mechanism for oil extraction or something. He makes more money brushing his teeth in the morning than we do in a year. The wife's an heiress too. Comes from the Hawley family. You don't know them?"

"I have no idea what they want with me." James shrugged.

"My name on that invite?"

"Nope. Just mine."

"Damn, I could use a rich chick in my life. You're obviously going."

"Of course, I wouldn't miss this."

The taxi dropped James off outside the apartment block, and the door-man rushed to get the door. James reached into his pocket to tip him before proffering the invitation. The doorman gave him a knowing look and led him to the elevator.

"Take the gentleman up to the Landay residence," the doorman instructed the elevator operator, who closed the gate without a word. They ascended in silence. James took the time to inspect his cuff links, rubbing specks off the tuxedo he'd rented.

"How do I look?" he said to the elevator operator.

"Stellar," the young man said with the barest of glances.

"Much obliged."

They reached the top floor. "Here we are, the Landay residence."

It was the only apartment on the floor. An elderly man in a white tuxedo jacket answered James's knock. James nodded to the man as he walked past. Several people in evening dress stood at the end of the hallway, and James excused himself as he pushed past them and into the foyer. A waiter offered him a glass of champagne from a silver tray. James declined. A string quartet played Vivaldi in the corner. He went to the mahogany table, fishing for the caviar he knew would be there. He dipped in a cracker, relishing the salty taste. He stood facing the room a few seconds in a futile attempt to recognize any of the faces drifting past. A beautiful woman stopped beside him. James was about to speak when her considerably less attractive husband came to whisk her away. *Just a regular Saturday night . . .*

He picked up a glass of water before ambling into the next room. *It's times like this I miss drinking.* A dozen couples danced there, drenched in the sparkle of a thousand lights adorning the walls and ceiling. An attractive middle-aged woman stopped beside him. They talked for a few minutes about these parties and how tired she was of them. She would have rather been home with her kids, even if they were teenagers now. She clinked his glass and walked away to find her husband.

He moved to the doorway, where he heard a piano playing, and moved toward the sound without knowing why. He followed it out of the room with the dance floor and into a parlor a few yards down another hallway. "Clair de lune" by Debussy became more lucid with each step he took. A crowd of eight people stood around a grand piano, and as the crescendo came, the people parted so he could see the pianist.

Liliana's face—a face he'd seen only in his daydreams these last twelve years—came into view.

He put his water down. She hadn't seen him, was still playing the piece. A handsome man said something to her, and she looked up to smile at him before focusing back on the keys. James stood frozen, waiting for the music to end. The seconds went like weeks, and he still had no idea what to say. *Is this why I'm here?* She drew her fingers away from the keys at last, and he went to the piano, ignoring the small masculine crowd surrounding her.

"Liliana?"

"James. You're here." She stood up, luminous in her black sequined dress and heels. The other men's eyes followed her. He held out a hand, awkward in his movements. She reached past it to embrace him, and he took in her aroma, the feel of her against him, the softness of her hair against his cheek. They both laughed as she drew away.

"I had no idea why I was here. I didn't think I'd ever see you again."

"Surprise," she said, waving her hands in faux theatrics. "Would you like to go somewhere we can talk?"

"Of course. Please lead on. Is this your place?"

"No, it's my stepdaughter's." He looked down at her hand—no wedding ring. "It's a long story," she continued. "Let's go outside. I don't think it's too cold." She took a glass of champagne from a passing waiter and led him outside.

Her Italian accent had faded. They stepped out onto the balcony, where four other partygoers were admiring the view. She led him past another couple to the railing, and the city lights twinkled all around them. James peeked down at the street, thirty stories below.

"Your stepdaughter owns this place? Ruth Landay?"

"She and her husband."

"You're married?"

"I was. My husband died last year."

"I'm sorry."

"Thank you. It's all right."

The smell of cigarette smoke filled his nostrils as someone else on the balcony lit up.

"I was married too."

"Was?"

"I'm divorced now. No need to be sorry. She's back home in Mexico City, married to someone more suitable."

"You weren't suitable?"

"Not to her family."

"We've still so much in common."

He drank her in with his eyes, not quite able to believe that she was standing in front of him. She was still so beautiful—the girl he'd met in the barn on Monte Sole. She shone among these people, the "elite" of New York society, as she had in the darkness of that night.

"How?" James asked. "How did you end up in New York?"

"I remember that last day I saw you in the hospital in Florence," she said.

I sat at your bedside for twelve hours the day you awoke, he thought, but said nothing.

"I had nothing. Everyone, and everything, I knew was gone." She stared out into the night. "It was Thomas, Dr. Hawley, who set me up with the job in the hospital. You remember him, don't you—the doctor who was tending to me in the hospital?"

"I do."

"For some strange reason, he asked me to marry him. Stranger still, I said yes. I came back here with him after the war. I've been in New York since '46, living as Liliana Hawley. Thomas was handsome and charming and a good man. He was twenty-five years older than me. I'm two years older than his daughter, Ruth. She doesn't care for me much. Her brothers are the same."

"You never had children of your own?"

"Thomas didn't want any more. He just wanted a wife. His children's mother died before the war. What about your tale of woe? Let's get the misery out of the way first."

A car horn sounded on the street below them. A young man threw down his bike and began arguing with the driver. *Different world down there.*

"Seems like a good idea. I met Susana when I was working for a newspaper in Mexico City. It was my first job out of college. I was down there for three years."

"What was it like?"

"I loved it, and we were happy there together for a while. But my father-in-law didn't approve of his only daughter's marriage to a poor gringo from a fishing town in New Jersey. That, and other issues, wore us down. We divorced. I moved here in '55 when I got the job at the magazine."

"And I thought I was a sad case . . ."

"You're not the only one," James said. "Do you like it here?"

"New York? Yes, I suppose I do."

"You never thought to go back?"

"To Italy? To what? There's no one left to go back to." She was either unaware or unconcerned about the other party guests standing only a few feet away. He was just about to speak when she began again. "Thomas left me some of his inherited fortune when he died. I got enough money to last a lifetime—a pittance compared to what the children got, but somehow they still resented me for it." She took a sip from her champagne flute. A feeling of discomfort crawled across him. The other guests were talking in whispers now, barely making an effort to disguise the fact that they were listening in to their conversation. He wanted to get out of here, to take her with him. And then what?

He thought of her father, her sisters, and her mother—Liliana covered in their blood, wading across the river where he had found her.

"How do I look?" she said.

"You look the same."

"I look twenty? Have you ever considered a career in fiction?"

"How do I look?" he said, turning the question back on her.

"Older, but cleaner."

"The Stella Rossa's bathing facilities left much to be desired."

"Apparently," she said.

"Did you read my article?"

"I did. It gave me quite the . . . to see it all written down, what we went through."

"I hope it didn't dredge up too many unpleasant memories."

"You can't dredge up what's on the surface already."

Her hands shook. James hoped he was managing to conceal his nerves. The war hadn't ended for him when he left her hospital bed in Florence. That end came six months later in Bavaria, but the picture of her never left him during all that time. He'd thought of trying to go back to Italy then, but it had been impossible. She had faded from his mind as the years passed. Just her essence remained, an impossible standard for every other woman to live up to. The impossibility of her.

"I tried to find you after the war," he said. "I had hoped you would contact the chief's office."

"I'm sorry . . . I was married. I needed something. Thomas was there."

What if I'd been there? "I get it," James said. "I wondered if you'd see the article somehow."

"And here I am, just a few blocks away, and I have a subscription to the magazine."

"I tried to pay homage to your family. They were the only ordinary people I got to know in my time . . ."

"You did well," Liliana said. "I still think of them every day . . . and who my sisters would have become . . . They were so young."

James could feel the eyes of the other people on the balcony on them.

"I never got a chance to tell you—but I saw your father when he fell . . . holding off the Germans. He saved our lives."

"As you saved mine," she said.

"I could say the same for you."

"Shall we go somewhere and talk?"

"I think we should," he answered.

Two minutes later they were in the elevator, leaving together. He had no idea of what would follow—just that he wasn't ready to say goodbye. They lived in the same city, and had for more than a year. What if they'd met when she'd been married, or when he'd been with Susana? That didn't matter now. Her husband was dead, and Susana may as well have been.

"Good evening, Mrs. Hawley," the operator said.

"Hello, Fred," she replied. "How's your daughter?"

"Much better. She wanted me to pass on her thanks to you."

"I'm so pleased."

It was silent for a few seconds before anyone spoke again.

James wanted to ask what she'd done to help the elevator operator's daughter but didn't. There was so much to ask, so much to say.

"Have you worked all these years? I always wondered what you'd make of your talents," he asked.

"Thomas never wanted me to work. He said that wasn't my role."

"Is that why you learned to play the piano?"

"I had to do something to fill my time. I spend most of my days volunteering for children's charitable foundations around the city—it makes me feel useful. But enough about me. Did you speak Spanish when you moved to Mexico City?"

"Not at first. I told the editor I did, though."

The elevator came to a halt, and they exited the lobby doors without another word. It was a warm evening for the time of year, and Liliana went without a coat.

"Do you ever think about those two boys we took with us on Monte Sole?" Liliana asked.

"Luca and Luciano? I do."

"Me too," she answered. "I try to remember them when the pain comes. I try to remember that not everyone died on that mountain."

"Thanks in large part to you," James said.

Liliana deflected. "Have you seen your father?" she asked.

"I went to see him in '52, more as a favor to an old friend. Never again."

"What about Chief Brody?"

"He was the old friend."

They crossed the street together, then waited in silence for the light to change. James wanted everything he said to be brilliant, or witty, or profound. He knew how big these moments were. He wanted to tell her about the chief but didn't want to dwell on it.

"He wrote me a note before he died, left it for me at his funeral."

"I'm so sorry," she said, stopping on the sidewalk to take his hand. "I know how much he meant to you."

"Thank you. But look, it's not all a sob story with me. My sister's wonderful—married to a man I don't want to beat up. They live in Philadelphia with my nephew and three nieces."

"She was the next person I was going to ask about. That makes me happy. Do you get to see them often?"

"About once a month, whether it's me going to see them or them coming here. I missed them too much when I was in Mexico. I'm trying to make up for it now."

The wind blew up as they stopped outside a bar he'd never been to. It was classy enough that he didn't feel too overdressed. She didn't seem to care. She pushed open the door without a word to him and took a seat at the bar, ordered a glass of wine. He ordered a soda water.

"I quit drinking a couple of years ago."

"Good for you," she answered. She took a long breath in. "Your article brought me back, the sights, the sounds, the smells. Your writing brought it into a clarity I hadn't experienced since I was there."

"Your approval means a lot."

"Nobody in this country has heard of it. The murder of hundreds has been forgotten. All for nothing . . . ," she said as she picked up her wineglass. "I assume you heard about Walter Reder, the other commander of the SS during the . . . massacre."

"Yes."

"You made brief mention of Werner Brack, the man who ordered my family murdered, the SS officer at the graveyard that day."

"I'm writing another article with more of a focus on him. I've done some research into his life."

He reached for a bowl of peanuts the bartender had put out.

"How?" she said. "Who have you been talking to?"

"Ex-SS officers. It's hard to find many willing to talk, but they're out there. I found one on Long Island who knew him. I have some connections from my time in the service too, and I even managed to track down his aunt Helga in Innsbruck, Austria."

"Where is he?"

"That's the one question I can't get an answer to. His aunt recalled him coming through for a few hours in '48, ostensibly as a goodbye, but they never saw him again."

"Are you familiar with Simon Wiesenthal?" she said as she took another sip of wine.

"The Nazi hunter?"

"Yes. Have you had any dealings with him?"

"I spoke to him on the phone in Vienna last month—for the story I'm writing now."

"What did you make of him?"

"He's a braggart. I don't doubt his sincerity in finding Nazis, but I'm not sure I'd trust him entirely."

"I've been in touch with him myself, asking about Brack. I figured because he was in Austria, he might know something . . . but nothing. I mean there are rumors . . ."

"That's the hardest part, separating the rumors from the truth," James said. "Do you mind if I smoke?"

"Only if you don't offer me one."

He opened the cigarette case. "I've been meaning to give it up. I did quit, but then the divorce . . . you know the rest."

"I only smoke on special occasions," she said as she leaned into his lit match.

"I'm honored." He lit his cigarette before shaking the match out and grabbing an ashtray. "There are rumors everywhere. Brack is in Syria, in Egypt, in Chile, in Argentina. Martin Bormann escaped . . ."

"Or that Hitler escaped. That Hitler planted a body double and is in South America. You don't think that's true?"

James took a drag of his cigarette. He'd been writing about escaped Nazis for about six months or so now and had grown used to the conspiracy theories and cranks. The first letter he received detailing that Hitler was alive and well and living on Long Island had caught him by surprise, but it hadn't taken long before they exhausted him. He'd heard dozens of reports about Martin Bormann, several about a doctor named Josef Mengele, and even some about an SS officer named Adolf Eichmann. They were all lies. These men weren't hiding out in Queens, or Tampa, or Kansas City, although he didn't doubt that some other SS men might have been, and the cranks detracted from the search for real criminals who may have come to the US. "No, I don't. I've spoken to my contacts. They're almost positive the Soviets have Hitler's remains."

"What about Brack?"

"No one knows. The man just up and disappeared. It's strange."

She stubbed out the cigarette after only taking a few drags. "What is?"

"How he escaped, how so many ex-SS have. Where are they going? Who's helping them? Why does no one care?"

"I still see his face." She took a drink. "You have another cigarette?" He pushed the case over to her. "I still care. The thought that Brack is out there, living his life, when he took my family's lives, when he took mine . . ." She reached for the matches herself, illuminating her face as she struck one. "I felt bad for Thomas . . . loving someone incapable of loving him. I thought it might fade over time. I certainly thought it would have faded by now."

"You thought what would have faded?"

"The echo of the war inside me—what happened on Monte Sole." She stood up. "I should go."

Would it make any difference if I asked you to stay?

"Can I walk you home? Is it far?"

"I'll get a taxi."

James followed her onto the street. She had already hailed a taxi when he reached her.

"I'd love to share my work with you—before it gets published. I'm meeting with an ex–special agent who used to track down escaping Nazis."

"I'd like that very much. Here's my phone number." She procured a slip of paper and a pen from her bag. "I'm home most nights. Goodbye, James." She climbed into the taxi.

He went back to his stool at the bar.

"Pretty girl," the bartender said. "An old friend of yours?"

"From a past life."

Liliana reached her apartment and pushed the door open, able to keep up her pretense of strength just long enough to get inside. She slumped to the floor, the ghosts of her family and hundreds of others cut down by SS bullets and bombs swirling around her. Reading James's article had accelerated the stream of her nightmares into a swift current. *Seeing him was worse.* She swung her arm back to shut the door and then sat back against the wall, feeling ridiculous in her evening dress. *I knew this was coming,* she told herself as the tears came.

A few seconds passed before she got up and went to her room. Her makeup was ruined now, splotched and running down her face. She took her dress off and laid it on the bed. The apartment she'd bought with Thomas's money was entirely silent save for the sound of the traffic on the street outside. Everything was as she had left it. This was not what she had known growing up. There had always been noise in the house. One of the girls would be singing, laughing, or teasing her, or her mother would be shouting up the stairs. Her cousins would be playing noisily in the courtyard outside, or her father and uncle would be yelling in the fields behind the house. Never this. Never silent like this.

James wasn't the first man she'd spent time alone with since Thomas died. Six months after the funeral was when men she knew seemed to collectively acknowledge that enough time had passed. Sometimes she accepted their invitations. Some were good men. Some were not. None of them interested her enough to be more than a distraction. *Why tease any suitors anymore?* They deserved better. Anyone would.

She hung the dress in her wardrobe along with the others. She slipped on a dressing gown and went to the painting. None of her family had ever sat for a photograph. She didn't have anything to remember them by. After Thomas died, and after the photos of his ex-wife had finally come down, she'd commissioned an artist to paint her family—from her own descriptions. It had taken several efforts to get it close to right, and she'd hung it in her bedroom so they could watch over her as she slept. Her father stood with her mother at the back, with Lena and Martina smiling in front of them. In the dark, it almost looked like them.

"I met James tonight," she said in Italian. "It was awful. Wonderful too. I'm going to see him again. I think he's going to be able to help me. I won't say too much now. I don't want to promise anything I can't deliver." She went to the window, staring down at the traffic below for several minutes before she emerged from her stupor.

Her father's eyes seemed to bore a hole in her from the painting. "I haven't forgotten the promise I made to you on Monte Sole." She could almost hear his words again, urging her to leave hate behind. "I'm trying, Babbo. But it's hard."

She went to the corner desk and flipped the light on. The drawer opened with a smooth swishing sound, and she took out a leather-bound box. Several folders lay inside it, each filled with papers. She took out the top folder and opened it on the desk. A newspaper clipping with a picture of Walter Reder being led into court sat on top of stories about Martin Bormann, Klaus Barbie, Josef Mengele, and of course, Hitler himself. She withdrew a list stamped with the emblem of the Counter Intelligence Corps, running her finger down it until she found the name of Werner Brack.

The CIC had compiled this list of Nazi war criminals but was doing nothing to find them. All of the names said "location unknown" beside them. The dossier she'd begun compiling on Brack lay underneath it, containing just his SS photograph and war records. She'd bribed an official in Germany to get them.

She took the picture of Brack in her hand. "Where are you?" She put the picture back into the folder and placed it back into the box. "They may have forgotten about you, but I haven't."

CHAPTER 13

Rivulets of water slithered down the window beside him. *Can I think of something or someone other than Liliana Nicoletti, or Hawley, or whatever her name is now?* The night before, in his dreams, he had been back with the Stella Rossa, back with Jock and Karoton and Gianni, on the hill overlooking the massacre in the cemetery. He saw the blood-covered figure bolting, felt the wind in his face as he ran toward the slaughter and heard the sound of the others shouting after him.

After that night on Monte Sole, he never saw or heard from Jock or Karoton or any of them again.

Now he peered through the window at the passing gray figures under black umbrellas. A man came in, shook off his own umbrella, and said something to the hostess, who directed him to James. The hostess took his hat and coat, discolored from the rain, and James stood up to shake his hand. The man was also in his midthirties, and he offered a firm handshake.

"Peter Laughlin," he said with a discernible Boston accent.

"James Foley. Thanks so much for meeting with me."

Laughlin took a seat and ordered a scotch.

"I read your article," Laughlin said. "That was quite the experience you had and quite the woman you met."

"She was extraordinary." *And I just met her again.* "I hear you had some unique experiences yourself in the CIC."

Laughlin took out a pack of cigarettes. "Want one?"

"No thanks."

Laughlin took a few seconds to light the cigarette before he began. "I was recruited out of the army at the end of the war—assigned to catch Nazi war criminals. We were based out of Rome."

"I never made it there."

"Beautiful city. Food like you wouldn't believe—not that we had much time to enjoy it. It wasn't until I was there a few weeks that I realized the sheer scale of what we were facing—an overwhelming tide of criminality. The world had never seen anything like it before. We just couldn't deal with it." He took a drag from his cigarette and pulled over the ashtray. "We dug up evidence of dozens of war crimes—it wasn't hard to find."

"There's a 'but' coming . . ."

"But we were massively underfunded, completely understaffed. We were an afterthought to a forgotten promise."

"The promise to track down all Nazi war criminals?"

"Yeah. The establishment of a war crimes commission was too little too late. It should have been founded in 1941, 1942, not during the chaos at the end of the war. It was a total disaster. We had millions of German prisoners on our hands, many thousands of war criminals among them. We knew that, but to keep them alive we had to release hundreds of thousands of them." Laughlin picked up the menu, running his eyes over it for a second before resuming. "How hard would it have been to put on a different uniform, or adopt a different name, even if we did know to look for them? I questioned hundreds of men, but I knew for every Nazi criminal we arrested, we were letting ten go." Laughlin stubbed out his cigarette as the waiter arrived at the table with the scotch and to take their order.

"Why do you think that happened? Why didn't you get the funding and the support you needed?" James asked once the waiter had left.

"The usual reasons—politics and a shifting agenda. The Nazis were crushed. The acute need shifted to combating the Soviets. No one was extraditing from the East to the West and vice versa."

James took a notepad out of his pocket and wrote down a few things in shorthand. Laughlin spoke quickly, and James struggled to keep up.

"No one shared information," Laughlin continued, "and a scramble began to extricate assets from Europe to help in the new war against the Soviets. The new enemy is potent, powerful, and dangerous and has overridden and destroyed the ability to prosecute Nazis." Laughlin took a sip from his whisky. "The Cold War has created a situation where it's nearly impossible to meaningfully pursue these guys."

It was ironic that the Nazis' worst enemies, the communists, had saved many of them from paying for their war crimes.

"What about Nuremberg and the other big trials?" James said. "Do you think that people thought that justice had been done after the leaders were jailed or executed?"

"Seeing the likes of Frick, Kaltenbrunner, and Göring answering for their crimes probably did bring a sense of closure to the general public. People wanted to move on, to wipe the slate clean. For instance, in November 1946 the British cabinet took the decision in principle to discontinue war crimes trials. They knew it wasn't over. It had barely begun."

"So our allies in Britain just gave up?"

"Not so much gave up as wound down. And not just in Britain either. Our budgets were cut. We were told to focus on what we could gain from the Nazis."

"What we could gain?"

"Some of these Nazi officers had spent years fighting the Soviets. Who better to supply us with the intelligence we needed than those who'd seen it firsthand? We established what we called a 'ratline'—a conduit for extricating informants and defectors out of the Soviet-controlled zones to safety in South America, via Italy, with new identities arranged by the CIC."

"Who were these men?" James asked the question but had heard of the ex-Nazi rocket scientists working in Alabama, led by a man who had designed the rockets that had pummeled London near the end of the war, Wernher von Braun. In truth, he didn't quite know how to feel about scientists who'd worked for the Nazis now helping them in their fight against the new enemy.

"Scientists. Spies. Midranking soldiers and SS men."

"Were there war criminals among them?"

"Yes. I suspected it at the time, but I'm positive now. We extricated an SS and Gestapo man named Klaus Barbie. I found out his nickname was the Butcher of Lyon. Seems our friend had a penchant for personally torturing and killing French prisoners. I met the man, and I knew what we were doing was wrong, but we had our orders." Laughlin finished his scotch and motioned to the waiter for another round. "The higher-ups wanted his knowledge of British interrogation methods that he'd experienced firsthand and the identities of SS officers the Brits were using to their own ends." Laughlin stopped for a moment to look out at the rain belting down outside. The waiter came back with the food, laying down the plates. Neither man spoke until he'd gone. "The old war was over. We had to equip ourselves for the new one, even if that meant a deal with the devil. It was difficult work to do."

"I read about Barbie," James said. "The French wanted to hang him, but he disappeared. Why did the CIC defy our allies?"

"He knew too much by that stage. He knew the names of too many of the German spies we'd placed in various European communist organizations. We were suspicious of the communist influence in the French government too, but I can't help thinking that someone ordered it just to avoid the embarrassment of admitting that we recruited him in the first place. Someone was covering their own ass."

"What about the other Nazis who escaped?"

"Aside from helping our government extract assets, we were also tasked with finding Nazi war criminals. We were undermanned and underfunded, but that didn't blunt our determination to do what we thought was right. I tried to offset the dirty jobs by doing some justice—when I was allowed."

James wondered what he would have done in Laughlin's place. What could he have done? Laughlin was powerless without the backing from his bosses.

"What did you find?" James asked.

"I found a lot. We knew thousands of Nazis had vanished. I had two questions." He counted them on his fingers. "How did they escape on their own, and how did they systematically disappear? If you'd told me where I'd find the answer, I never would have believed you. I came upon a nest of escaped war criminals from Croatia. Croatia was a Nazi puppet state during the war. The leader, Ante Pavelic, ordered massive purges that killed half a million people."

"I didn't know much about them."

"Few did. After the surrender, the entire Croatian regime disappeared. We discovered a whole load of 'em hiding in the Vatican."

"The Vatican? With the pope? Did you try to arrest them?" James said. He was on his fourth page of shorthand notes now.

"We tried. We couldn't. Vatican sovereignty meant we couldn't touch them." Laughlin cut into the steak he'd ordered, taking a few seconds to chew before he spoke again. "That was when the whole game came into focus."

"What game?"

"We discovered a network to game the International Committee of the Red Cross for issuing travel documents. Millions were starving and displaced after the war. One of the only ways to get assistance for international travel was to get ICRC papers. But they needed a preliminary document to get one. With the help of friends in the Vatican, various Nazis were rechristened and got that document, and that, along with a letter from a renowned priest or bishop, would get them the travel documents. From there they were free to travel. This was a system. This was done hundreds or thousands of times, mainly with the help of clerics like Kronuslav Draganović and Alois Hudal. And we couldn't touch them."

"They had immunity?"

"That, and we received orders from above to stop the investigation. We were brought home, and no one else continued the work we were doing. To the best of my knowledge that was the first and last investigation into the illegal Nazi ratlines."

"Why would the Catholic Church want to help fleeing Nazis?"

"They had the same enemies. The Nazis were fanatical anticommunists, and the Church was terrified of the Soviets rampaging across Europe and destroying their church. That's how it began."

"But how could these fleeing Nazi criminals have aided the Church against the Soviets after the war? What power did they have, hiding from the Allies?"

"It wasn't a policy of the Church at large, more like a penchant of certain clerics who had sympathies for the Nazi or Ustaša cause. The Church never sanctioned those clerics, but the pope never condemned their actions either. The maverick priests and bishops running the ratlines did so without interference from their colleagues."

Laughlin took a moment to finish his meal. James flipped through his notes, unable to quite believe what they said. Growing up, he had attended Mass every Sunday with his mother and sister, worn his best clothes, greeted the priest on the way out with a handshake. The notion that the church Father Smith represented helped to harbor some of the worst criminals in history didn't sit well with him, and he wondered what the old cleric would have said about the idea himself.

"Why were the orders for you to stand down issued?"

"We were never told. Maybe the top brass wanted to protect their own ratlines and didn't want the embarrassment of the illegal ratlines exposing their own dirty secret. Perhaps it was something else, but you see a pattern here, don't you?"

"Yes. So where did they go?"

"South America mainly. The Perón government in Argentina had always had a chummy relationship with the Nazis, and there were hundreds of thousands of Germans there already. There couldn't have been anywhere easier to melt away from sight."

"And there were never any attempts to pursue them down there?"

"The appetite wasn't there. The people moved on. The Allies turned a blind eye except when it was convenient. The government in Argentina protected them. What could we do? Nazi hunting largely became a pursuit for private citizens—Jews looking for personal justice—or the Israeli secret service."

"You never had any more dealings with escaping war criminals?"

"I did some work on my own. I was in contact with a diplomat in the Argentinean embassy. I managed to turn him. The Perón government fell in November 1955, and the welcome mat for fleeing Nazis was rolled up and put away. I stayed in contact with my guy. He sent me this a few weeks ago."

Laughlin reached into his pocket and took out a photograph, pushing it across the table.

James held the black-and-white photograph in front of his face. Perhaps twenty people stood facing the camera in front of a podium adorned by a portrait of Hitler. A large Nazi flag hung on the wall behind them, a white circle with a swastika in it. A man in a suit seemed to be preparing to address them. James turned over the photo and read the date on the back.

"April twentieth, 1954. They're celebrating Hitler's birthday."

"It seems some things never change," Laughlin said.

"Where was this taken?"

"I don't know. He didn't say and hasn't responded to any of my inquiries since."

"Why did he send it to you?"

"To taunt me, or as a joke, or a clue? I really couldn't tell you."

"Where is this diplomat?"

"Buenos Aires."

"Would he tell where this photo was taken?"

"For a price, maybe," Laughlin said. "Men like Juan Carlos Ospina don't tend to have many loyalties past themselves. You can keep the photo. I've got no use for it anymore. Banging my head off a brick wall got a little tiresome after a while. I'm a private citizen now."

James put the photo on the table. "Where can I find this Ospina? Do you have an address for him?"

"No. I only know a restaurant he frequents. If I were looking for him, I'd go to the ABC in Buenos Aires—who'd have believed—it's a German restaurant."

"Do you have a photograph of him?"

"You're not thinking about going after him?"

"I want to keep my options open."

"I can send one—to the magazine." Laughlin hesitated a moment. He reached for another cigarette but left it unlit on the table beside him. "Be careful, Mr. Foley. These are dangerous people, and not to be trifled with. If they were to catch wind of anyone trying to expose them . . ."

"Thanks for talking to me, Mr. Laughlin. You can rest assured that your anonymity will be respected."

"I wish you well," Laughlin said, wiping his mouth with his napkin. He threw it down on the chair as he turned to James one last time. "Don't forget what I told you. These are the worst kind of people."

"Thanks again, Mr. Laughlin."

He sat there staring at the photo after Laughlin had left. Five minutes passed before he put it away and got back to his food, which was now cold. Without realizing it, he finished the meal and paid, and found himself struggling through the rain, back to the office a few minutes away.

"Evening, Sam," James said to the security guard at the front door. He shook off his umbrella and put it in the holder.

"How are you? Don't you guys ever go home to your families?"

"I might if I had one."

There were few people in the office at this time on a Tuesday evening, and the silence that pervaded was punctuated only by the sound of the cars on the street below.

He pushed back the typewriter on his desk and laid out the notepad, his shorthand scrawled on page after page. The thought of thousands of Nazi war criminals living their lives in peace tore at him, and he slumped back on his chair. The ashtray on his desk was clean. He lit a cigarette, letting the gray smoke billow out of his mouth.

What now? Was he going to pursue this story? Laughlin's warnings were a stark reminder of the savagery these people were capable of. *Nothing more dangerous than a rattlesnake when you turn over the rock he's hiding under.* But it wouldn't be his job to arrest any fugitives—just to expose them. How could he sit on this story, after all that he'd seen? *This is about more than me now.* The photograph was useless without some kind of verification. There was nothing placing it in modern-day Argentina—it could have been taken in some local Nazi party meeting in Berlin or Stuttgart in 1944. It meant nothing without Ospina's word. It was a tease for now, nothing more.

He took the photograph out of his wallet, placing it on his typewriter, searching for something. The man on the podium was dressed in a suit and looked like any middle manager. There was nothing remarkable about him or any of the rest of them. The women were plain but well dressed. Some faced the camera; others seemed focused on something else. James studied the photo for ten minutes, but there was nothing—no sign of where and when or who these people were—except the portrait of Hitler and the swastika decorating the podium and wall. The date on the back seemed to mock him. *What I wouldn't give for five minutes alone with that guy on the podium . . . I'd get answers.*

He wanted to call the generals in the Pentagon and alert them to what they almost certainly already knew but had chosen to ignore because of the Red peril. Simon Wiesenthal's number was in his address book, but what use would calling him be? What could he do? This could be another hoax.

He finished his cigarette and began typing out the notes he'd taken at the meeting with Laughlin. The lights went off around him, and he raised his head. A custodian called out, and James answered. The lights went back on. He began typing again. The phone was on the wall a few feet from his desk. *She said she was home most nights . . .*

He took the paper from the typewriter and read the words out loud.

The Allied Betrayal of the Victims of the Nazi Regime.

The paper fell from his hand. It was time to go home.

Two days later, James sat alone in a café. He'd thought of little but Laughlin's interview since the two had met. What Laughlin had told him weighed on him. *Those bastards.* At least his editor, Stover, had agreed with him—this was a big story. But the photograph was the linchpin, and without verification it meant nothing. Stover wouldn't stop him from going to Argentina, but he wasn't going to sponsor him to do it either.

He paid for his coffee and made for the phone booth in the back. A middle-aged man in a suit held the receiver and motioned to James that he would just be a moment. He explained to his wife that he wouldn't be home tonight. The man handed the receiver to him with a shake of his head, wishing James better luck. The phone rang three times before she picked up.

"Liliana?"

"James, I was wondering when you'd call. Did you meet the CIC agent?"

"I did. I've been trying to figure out how to write the story ever since. There was a lot that he said I wasn't . . . expecting."

"You want to talk to me about it?"

"I was hoping we could meet."

"How about tonight at eight? You know Giannini's on Second Avenue, between Seventy-Seventh and Seventy-Eighth?"

"That's in two hours. Are you sure?"

"Positive. Can you make it?"

"I'll be there."

James was ten minutes early, and she was already there. She stood up as the hostess brought him to the table.

"I'm sorry. I hope I didn't keep you waiting."

"You kept me this long," she said, holding her thumb and forefinger an inch apart on her wineglass.

He didn't know how to comment on her chic green dress, her lustrous hair, her perfect, barely there makeup, so he didn't. He kissed her on the cheek, his nose full of her perfume as he drew away.

"Thanks for seeing me at such short notice," he said as he shifted into his seat.

"I told you I don't have much of a social life, and I only live a few blocks from here."

"You walked?"

"I walk most places if I can."

The restaurant was packed. White tablecloths covered small tables, and the conversation was loud, almost boisterous. The mahogany-paneled walls were decorated with posters in Italian, and the smell of fresh pasta hung in the air.

"Did you have any problems getting a reservation at such late notice?"

"No. They take pity on me once a week or so when I come in here to dine alone."

The waiter came to the table. Liliana addressed him by name in Italian and ordered another glass of red.

"I never did pick up the language. Did you continue your studies after the war?"

"No. A lot of things changed after you left me. I never went back to college."

"Did you ever go back to Monte Sole?"

"Why would I go back?"

James picked up the menu. The waiter returned to take their order. *I can't believe I'm sitting here with you.* James fumbled through ordering and the waiter left.

"How was your meeting with the intelligence man?" she said.

"Shocking. I thought I had some idea what went on with the escaping Nazis after the war. I feel like a kid now."

"What did you find out?"

James recounted the interview for the next ten minutes. Her appetite for detail was unquenchable—she had questions for every point he made and comments for every conclusion. Every revelation hammered her. Her spirit had visibly flagged by the time he stopped.

The waiter returned to lay the food down on the table and then receded without a word.

"I've kept up to speed with any news of Nazi criminals in the newspapers over the years. Thomas used to tell me to forget about the past, but he had no idea who I really was. How could he . . . when I didn't tell him?" She took a sip of wine. "We stopped sleeping beside each other. He couldn't take it—couldn't take my thrashing around and the calling out in my sleep. He could never understand that the war wasn't over for me—not while Brack was still free and there was no justice.

I've been able to do what I wanted since he died. I don't have to repress my pain anymore."

"I'm going to write this story and expose these people," James said.

"To what end?"

"You don't think these animals should be exposed?"

"Your readers might spit up their coffee." Liliana shrugged. "And you'll get some award where you can go on stage and look handsome in your tuxedo, but nothing will change."

"I'm a journalist, not a cop, Liliana."

"The police aren't interested in finding them . . ."

"I'm not a Nazi hunter," James said firmly. "The Mossad or the other people who are out there catching these people can use the information that I make public. At the very least, the public deserves to know that the institutions they're putting their trust in have let them down."

"I've met with Nazi hunters and private detectives," Liliana continued. "The only information they need is where these animals are and how they can get them out. They're protected by the establishment in Europe and in the countries they're in."

"We have to expose the people protecting them," James insisted.

"The people in Germany aren't interested. No one wants to even mention what they were doing eleven years ago. Most of the people in the civil service are the same as were under the Nazis. It's pointless going to most of them for information. Their sympathies haven't changed since the end of the war."

"What are you saying?"

"Your story is good and noble, James, but it's not going to do any good."

"You don't know that," he said. "If it changes public perception—"

"What? The United States government is going to start cooperating with the Soviet Union to find and prosecute war criminals? The governments in South America, and Syria, and Egypt are going to stop harboring them?"

This wasn't what he'd expected—he had thought she'd feel hopeful about the chance to expose such a great wrongdoing. But she seemed close to tears. This wasn't what he was here to do. He wanted to comfort her, not destroy her. She seemed to be barely holding on. He wished he could reach out and take her pain away, to still the echo of the past that reverberated through her.

"I inherited four million dollars when Thomas died," she said. "I didn't ask for it, and it was never the reason I married him. I have an empty apartment and all this money I don't have the first idea what to do with. But, James, I'd give it all to see Brack hang for what he did to my family. I'd give everything I have in this world to see him answer for his crimes."

"There's not a day that goes past that I don't think of it. That's what drove me to write these stories—to do something."

"The desire for justice is all I have left," Liliana went on. "It's driven everyone else in my life away. It's all I have—to see justice done for my family."

James thought of the photograph in his wallet. Sensing that Liliana needed a minute alone to collect herself, he excused himself to go to the bathroom. *Liliana, look what they've done to you.* He splashed cold water onto his face and thought back to who she'd been. He'd seen glimpses of that person tonight, but they were few and far between. The girl he'd met in that barn on Monte Sole in 1944 was almost gone.

A man in a gray suit and silk shirt entered the bathroom. Had he been speaking out loud? The man brushed past James on his way to the stall.

James took out the photograph. *It's like it's mocking me now.* She had the money to do this. Perhaps bringing her along could give her some sense of closure, could allow her to get on with living her life. They could help each other. He still needed her, even after all these years. Needed or wanted? He put the wallet back into his pocket, the photograph on top of it.

Is this going to push her over the edge? Am I being selfish here, playing with her grief for my own ends? The stall opened, and the man glared at him again, washing his hands in seconds before leaving. *She knows they're out there. She's anything but naïve. Give her the opportunity to make up her mind for herself.*

Liliana was eating her rigatoni when he returned to the table.

"I'm sorry you haven't had the life you deserved," he said.

"I don't think being deserving has much to do with what we receive."

"I can't let this go," he said. "I have to expose these people."

"Write your story, then. I don't doubt your sincerity, James. You're a good man." Her fork clattered onto the plate. "It's funny, but you're the only person I know who ever met any of my family. You're the only person in this whole city, in the country, who knew them."

"I feel privileged to have met them."

"I don't know if you're a gift or a millstone around my neck."

James was taken aback. But there would be no better opening. "Maybe this will help you decide," he said, reaching into his pocket. "I got this from the CIC man I met."

Her face changed as she saw the photo. "It can't be . . ." He could barely hear her over the din of the restaurant. "It can't be."

"I'm sorry. I didn't mean to upset you . . ."

"Where did you get this?"

"The CIC agent got it from an Argentinean diplomat. I think it's meant to be a tease or a joke or something. The people in the photograph are celebrating Hitler's birthday."

"It's him. It's definitely him," she said, holding the photo up.

"Who? What are you talking about?"

"It's Werner Brack!" she shouted. "There. There. In the back, beside the bald man."

"What?"

"Right there," she said, pointing again.

James squinted to see the figure at the back, his face covered in shadow. "Are you sure it's him?"

"I've seen that face in my nightmares for twelve years."

James walked around the table, crouching beside her. He'd seen photos of Brack before—when he was younger or in his SS uniform—and while this man bore some resemblance, it was impossible to tell. The man's body was hidden, along with half his face.

"I can't say I recognize this man as Werner Brack," James said. "I've seen photos of Brack, but I couldn't say this was him."

"It's him. I know it is. Are you blind? Look at this," she said, reaching into her bag. She pulled out Brack's SS photo.

"Where did you get this?"

"I bribed someone in Germany who got it from the KGB. It seems Brack is wanted by the Soviets too."

James held up the photo she'd given him, examining it. "I'm sorry, but I don't think this is the same man." The man in the photograph seemed smaller than Brack, with a wider face and shoulders—it wasn't the same man. Perhaps she was seeing what she'd so desperately wanted to all these years.

"It's him. I know it is."

"I never saw him up close, but I don't think this is enough to go on . . ." He handed the SS photo back to her.

"Where was this taken?"

"I don't know. The diplomat never said. The only information I have is what's written on the back."

"He never said where?"

"No."

"Birthday celebrations," she said, biting down on her lip. "Two years ago. Give me a cigarette. Light it for me, would you?"

He lit two from the pack, handing one to her. She seemed to try to inhale the entire cigarette at once.

"So how do we find out where this was taken? Where is this diplomat?"

"He's in Buenos Aires. As far as I know, he's the only one who can verify it."

"How can we get ahold of him?"

"I don't know much about him. I know the name of a restaurant he frequents, and I'm waiting for a photo of him from my CIC contact."

"When is this photo coming?" She stubbed out the cigarette.

"I don't know. My contact said he'd send it soon."

"And where is your contact now?"

"I'm sure he's home with his family," James said. "Pull back the reins a little here."

"Pull back what? What are you talking about? I've been looking for this man since the day he killed my entire family, this is the best lead I've had in twelve years, and you ask me to pull in the reins?"

He stood up and went back to his seat opposite her.

"The diplomat's name is Ospina. Juan Carlos Ospina. He lost his job when the Perón government was overthrown."

"So we get the photo to identify him, then we go to this restaurant, and we speak to him."

"We?"

"Yes, James. We. It won't be the first time we've faced impossible odds together. When can we leave?"

"I spoke to my editor about going down there already. He's not stopping me, but he won't pay for it."

"I'll take care of the travel arrangements. You write the story."

He wanted to reach out to her, to assure her that this man wasn't Brack, that she was chasing ghosts.

"If we go, I go to expose the Nazis in that town. I'll write that story, but I don't believe this man is Brack. This isn't evidence."

"This man, this devil, is Werner Brack. I know it. I've been looking for proof for years. This is it."

There was no convincing her. He could go with her and write the story, or else have her go alone, likely to meet up with some mercenary down there who'd take advantage of her fragile emotional state. She might never come back.

She barked something at the waiter in Italian and stood up. "The meal is taken care of."

"No, please."

"There's no need, James. I own the restaurant. Please call me when the photo of Ospina comes through, and we'll make the necessary plans to leave. I have to be alone now. I'll be in touch."

CHAPTER 14

Liliana waited for James at the plane, dressed in a chic red suit and matching hat. She greeted him with an embrace and, once he'd handed his bag to a waiting attendant, led him up the stairs into the plane. Men peeked over their seats as she made her way to her own, though she seemed to pay them no regard. They were headed to Miami, the first leg on their trek to Buenos Aires.

They hadn't met since that night in the restaurant, almost two weeks before. She had been evasive when they spoke on the phone—just letting him know where and when to meet for their flights and that she'd taken care of everything. James didn't know what to expect now they were to travel together.

"This calls for a celebration," she said as they sat down. She flagged down the stewardess, a young girl with shoulder-length blond hair and a smile that seemed permanent. "Excuse me, miss, but this is the first time my fiancé has ever had the pleasure to fly."

"How exciting!" She seemed genuine in her enthusiasm. "How about some champagne to mark the occasion?"

"Not for me," James said. "But I'm sure the lady would love some."

The stewardess left.

"I've flown before—to and from Mexico City."

"Details." Liliana shrugged. "They love fawning over first-timers."

The stewardess arrived back thirty seconds later, champagne glass in hand. "Enjoy your flight," she said. "If you need anything, just call."

"Cheers," Liliana said. "Here's to finding what we're looking for." James resisted the temptation to ask exactly what that was. He'd wait—until they were in the air at least. They sat back as the stewardess announced they'd be taking off.

"So we're engaged?" James asked.

"Don't get any ideas, though. This is a business trip."

"Of course."

The engines began the cacophony that would last all the way to Miami. James relaxed. He enjoyed the feeling of climbing into the air, of leaving everything behind.

When they were allowed to get out of their seats, they talked to the people around them. The free booze and party atmosphere on the flight lent itself to getting to know people. The other passengers all presumed he and Liliana were together. Why wouldn't they? It was almost an hour before they had a moment alone.

"One thing we never discussed is what to do if we find Brack," James began. "The Argentineans will never extradite him, not even with Perón gone. I'm going down there to write a story. What are you going to do?"

"I'll report his presence to the local police."

"What if they're not interested?"

"Police not interested in the presence of murderers in their community? Ridiculous. Excuse me, I need to use the bathroom."

James settled back in his seat and took a sip of his soda water. *Surely she doesn't believe that,* he thought. *She must know the futility of reporting Brack to the police. So what is she planning to do?*

～

James brought his fingers to his eyes and tried to rub days of grit and tiredness out. The sunset became a golden haze at the end of the runway, blurred by dust and jet fumes. A gust of wind blew up, almost taking Liliana's hat off. He took Liliana's bag as the fatigued throng of passengers trudged toward the terminal building for Buenos Aires.

They'd been through a dozen airports in the past week. Jorge Newbery airport, their final destination, looked much the same as the others. He wiped sweat from his brow, looking back at Liliana. She was talking to a young married couple from Buenos Aires who had been in Rio on their honeymoon. Her talent for languages hadn't diminished— her Spanish was perfect.

Time to speak alone had been in short supply. When they'd stayed in hotels in between their flights, they each had a private room —despite the cover they had assumed. On the few occasions he'd brought Brack up, she had remained as elusive as smoke dissipating in the breeze. He felt uneasy, but reassured himself it wasn't Brack in the photograph anyway. And even if it were—finding him would be next to impossible. *I'll protect her,* he decided. *I'll try to direct her energies toward something productive.*

Liliana and the young couple caught up to him.

"Please call us when you're in the city," the young man said. "We'd love to take you both out to dinner."

"That's going to be difficult. We're only here a few days and have a packed schedule. Perhaps next time we pass through?"

The young lady still wrote down their phone number to give to Liliana and said goodbye.

They were alone. Liliana's façade seemed to melt away immediately. "I feel twenty years older since we left New York."

"You don't look it."

"You're a good liar."

A few minutes later a taxi steered them toward their hotel.

"Do you speak English?" James asked the driver in English.

"*¿Qué?*" the driver said.

"*Está bien,*" James replied. Then, to Liliana, he continued in English. "We can talk. What are you doing here?"

"What do you mean? You know why I'm here."

"Cut the crap. We're here now. Time to level with me."

"I haven't forgotten what you did for me all those years ago," Liliana said.

"You didn't answer the question."

She reached into her bag and took out lipstick and a mirror. Her lips made a light smacking sound as she pressed them together. "I don't see why we have to discuss this now. You said it yourself—the chances of us finding him are so small."

"But what if we do?"

"You didn't even think that was him in the photograph."

"You wouldn't have come down here if you didn't."

"Why not? It's not like I have anything better to do—my charitable foundations can survive without me. And I owe you. I want to help."

The driver stopped at a traffic light. A street seller came to the window. James waved him away.

"You don't owe me."

"Yes, I do. For saving my life during the war," she said.

"You saved me. I needed you then, and I need you now."

"It doesn't seem like much has changed." She put the lipstick back into her bag. "You're trying to do something noble and true, and I know you want to help me move on with my life."

"I am, and I'm worried that—"

"You're a good man. You always were." She took his hand before letting it go.

"Liliana, I need to know you're not going to do anything stupid. That you won't do anything illegal."

"What are you implying?"

"You know."

"I would never do anything to endanger you," she said.

"What about yourself?"

The taxi pulled up in front of a building with a neoclassical French-style façade. "Here we are," the driver said in Spanish.

She got out without another word and climbed the stone steps. James paid the driver in dollars, which he seemed happy to accept. A young bellhop with a thick mustache—rare on someone his age—took the bags before following Liliana.

"We need two rooms, please," Liliana said at the check-in desk. "One for me and one for my darling fiancé." The clerk eyed James. But whatever he was thinking, he kept it to himself.

"Someone recommended a restaurant for us, the ABC?" she asked the clerk. "Do you know it?"

"In San Nicolás," he replied. "It's close by. Would you like me to arrange dinner reservations for tonight?"

"No. I think we'll leave that for tomorrow. Can you have dinner sent to my room?"

"Of course."

The bellhop led them to Liliana's room first, and she made quick work of their parting. "Good night, darling," she said. "Give me some time in the morning. Shall I see you in the lobby around one?"

"Yes."

"All right, then." She shut the hotel room door behind her.

The bellhop gave him a sly look. "Women, eh?" he said in English.

"Tell me about it."

Liliana descended the stairs twenty minutes after one the following day, luminescent in her blue sundress. James looked at his watch, shaking his head. She just smiled back in response and embraced him, the aroma of her perfume lingering after she pulled away.

"I'm sorry, James." He waited for her to offer an explanation, but none was forthcoming. It didn't matter. "Shall we get some lunch? I'm hungry."

"Is there anywhere you'd like to go?"

"I was out this morning for a while and was told La Boca is the place to see. We can't chase Nazis all day," she said.

"We've no other leads than that restaurant."

"And no reason to believe he'll be there during the day, so let's enjoy ourselves until the real business begins."

"You were out this morning without me?"

She looked back over her shoulder. "Is that allowed?" She didn't wait for an answer as she walked out into the bright spring day.

They strolled through the cobbled streets of La Boca. It was a Saturday, and the streets were alive with peddlers selling art, buskers playing music, and stalls offering a variety of trinkets. Shanty houses lined the street, painted orange and lilac, yellow and blue. The music covered the silence between them.

He didn't think of her as a stranger—she could never be that—but there was a wall around her. It was in everything she did, and in every question and conversation she sidestepped.

They stopped outside a restaurant. "Here we are," she said with a bright smile. "El Ternero Gordo."

Just after they ordered lunch, a man in a black suit and matching fedora strode into the center of the restaurant. He threw his hat down as a lady in a tight red dress strutted over, laying her hands on him. The band started up and the couple began the sensuous ballet of the tango. The energy of the dance was infectious, and the crowd was drawn in.

"What was it like living in Mexico City?"

"I loved it. It had the same vitality as the streets here. It's a beautiful place."

"What was your wife's name?"

"Susana Ortega, of the venerable Ortega family." James shook his head. "What was I thinking?"

"You think she was too good for you?"

He accidentally put his soda down on his fork, knocking the utensil onto the ceramic tile floor. Then he almost knocked the soda over as he reached to get it. "Too good for *this*?" he said, laughing. "Not good enough, more like it."

"What, then?"

"It wasn't what I thought so much as her father."

"I've met enough rich people in the last twelve years," she said. "They're no better than anyone else, just luckier."

"What about hard work?" he said.

"What about it? You don't think poor people work hard? You think the person scrubbing the dishes in there doesn't work harder than the manager or the owner? Susana's father is an idiot."

He didn't think anyone had ever had the courage to call Susana's father an idiot—certainly not to his face anyway. "I won't argue with you on that one."

"What did she say? How did she react to her family's disapproval?"

"She said nothing at first, but then a lot. It was a gradual process. Maybe I was just a foil to get under her father's skin."

"Then she was an idiot too."

"She's not an idiot. I wasn't a good husband. I had some problems. It would have been a lot for any relationship to get through. It wasn't easy for me—coming home after the war with all those feelings inside. Too easy to try to find the answer at the bottom of a bottle."

"But you've given up drinking now."

"Too late."

"We are so similar, you and I."

"We've been through hard times together."

Liliana took a sip of wine and watched the dancers for a few seconds before she continued. "Are you happy in New York?"

"I am. I love my job."

"You're good at it. Your article about Monte Sole . . . captured the horror of those days. The people who died deserved that. You told their story with dignity."

"That means a lot coming from you."

The dancers finished to raucous applause. The man picked up his hat and started going table to table. They both reached into their wallets for cash.

"It's a strange feeling, being here," she said. "I'm looking at everyone with suspicious eyes. It's almost like they're all a part of this web of criminal conspiracy."

"They're not. Even the Germans here—most of them are just innocent people getting on with their lives."

"Do you think it was the same in Germany during the war? Do you think most people were innocent?"

"Depends on your definition of innocence."

The waiter arrived with steaks that covered the entire plates, and when he left, Liliana said, "I've been trying to understand for all these years—how could they do that? How could they shoot women and children? They lined them up and mowed them down. They burned down houses with the families still inside. What was going on in their minds?"

It was a question he'd wrestled with too. It wasn't easy to talk about with most people. "I don't know. Combat is a horrific, insane, terrifying experience. It can affect men's minds in ways I could never explain."

"But you saw combat. You never did anything like that."

"I was never ordered to."

"That's not an excuse. You were a soldier in the same war they fought in. What would you have done if you'd received the orders Brack handed down to them?"

"I would have refused them." James cut into his steak.

"Why didn't they?"

"I'm trying to figure that out. It's as if some collective psychosis overtook them. I'm sure some soldiers didn't want to carry out the orders they were given."

"The men who chased me from the graveyard were jeering me, calling out disgusting sexual slurs. What kind of animals were they? What happened to them to make them like that?"

He reached across the table to take her hand. It felt good to touch her.

"Please excuse me," she said. "It's been twelve years, but it still feels like last month or last week."

"My story isn't the only reason I'm here," he said. "I want to find some kind of conclusion for you." James set down his glass. "What if we did find him, and he admitted what he did? Would that give you peace?"

"If he sat in front of me, and asked my forgiveness for what he'd done?"

"Yes."

"I don't know."

"I do know one thing," James said. "Killing him won't make the demons go away."

Liliana demurred. "It's not as if we're going to find him anyway."

"I won't be a party to murder. Get that straight right now."

"We need one another."

"Not for that," James said. "You don't think I'd like to see Brack suffer for what he did? For what they all did? But we can't do that. We have to be better than them."

"I would never risk . . . your life or freedom."

"I'm going to ask you again, Liliana. What are you planning to do?"

"I don't know! All right?" She stood up and walked outside. He didn't go after her.

A few minutes later, the waiter returned to the table.

"The lady took a taxi back to your hotel," he said in English. "She said she wasn't feeling well and didn't want to spoil your meal."

"Thank you," he replied.

He sat back and lit a cigarette. A new pair of dancers took to the floor. The band started up once more and the dancers began their cabaret.

They met that night in the lobby. She looked as radiant as before, having changed to a tight magenta dress with matching hat—smart but not too formal—fitting for the ABC restaurant in San Nicolás. He stood as she came down the stairs. He thought to mention what had happened at lunch but knew he'd get the same answer. *All in good time.*

"Are you ready for this?" he asked.

"Of course." She took his arm.

They had studied the photo Laughlin had given him. They both knew every curve and mark on Juan Carlos Ospina's face. With little other solid information to focus on, the photographs had become a minor obsession.

"Can I have the photograph?" she asked.

"Why?"

"In case I need to ask people if they've seen him."

"I think we need to be subtle here."

"Why? We're going to a restaurant to look for a patron. He's a diplomat, not a jewel thief."

"What if he doesn't want to be found? We don't know his circumstances."

"I'll be careful." She held out her hand. "These men will react more kindly to being asked by me, believe me."

"I'm sure they will but—"

"Hand it over, James." Her tone was light, but the message was clear. He reached into his pocket and gave her the photograph.

Gritty darkness had descended on the city. Streetlights lined the roads, blinking through the murk. It was a short taxi ride, not more than ten minutes.

"I'm famished," James said to break the tension in the car.

She reached into her bag for the photograph of Ospina, looked at it for a few seconds, and put it back. "Where are you, Juan Carlos?"

"Let's not scare anyone away. We only want to have a conversation with him."

"This should help," she said, holding a roll of twenty-dollar bills.

"Put that away."

Liliana paid the driver when they arrived, over James's objection.

"You don't have to pay for everything," he said.

"You keep your cash for those pretty girls back in New York."

She was gone before he could argue. The restaurant was narrow, perhaps only ten meters wide. Its glass windows declared what the architecture already made apparent—that it was a German place. The low red roof that slanted down almost over the door was an eyesore. It was as if a German farmhouse had been dropped in the middle of the street. The wood-paneled interior was decorated with German flags and crests, with dozens of black-and-white photos of Teutonic patrons raising beer glasses or eating stew or schnitzel. The host led them to their table in the middle of the room, surrounded by tables of people speaking German.

Liliana's posture was rigid as James helped her into her seat. The waiter appeared a few minutes later. They ordered the first thing they saw—jaeger schnitzel—and he returned to the kitchen.

"I knew it was a German restaurant, but this . . . ," he said in English.

"I know," Liliana said. "It's no secret that there's a huge German population in this city. I just wasn't expecting them all to be in here."

"I'm not seeing our friend," James said. "I'll go to the bathroom, have a look around." He surveyed the room as he walked, pretending to admire the photographs on the walls. Ospina wasn't to be seen, and

James carried on to the bathroom in the corner. *What is this place? Why would an Argentinean diplomat spend so much time in a place filled with Germans?*

When he returned to the dining room, Liliana was showing their waiter something produced from her bag—the photograph. James quickened his pace and got back as the waiter held the picture close to his face.

"I'm new here," the waiter said, "but I could ask around. Can I take the photograph?"

"That really isn't necessary," James said.

Liliana shot him a look that would curdle milk. "No, please ask. We're looking for our old friend. He moved houses, and we lost his address. He mentioned this restaurant in his last letter, so . . ."

"Let me ask the manager. He knows all the regulars."

The waiter turned around and left with the photograph in his hand.

"So much for feeling things out," James said.

They stayed in character as their meal was served, discussing the great things they'd seen in the city that day. Liliana had even constructed a South American itinerary—fabricated entirely for those who may have been listening in. The waiter returned with the picture as they finished.

"The manager's not here, but I called him and he says your friend could be in later. Sit tight." He handed the photograph back.

"That sounds great," Liliana said. "I'll have another glass of red, and another soda for my fiancé."

Two hours came and went, with still no sign of the diplomat or someone who knew where he was. James asked for the bill, but their waiter assured them that they need wait just a little longer and their friend would come. *Am I being paranoid,* James wondered, *or is something going on here?* Soon they were the only customers left, and it was hard to make conversation in the empty room. A man came through the front door. His long forehead and pale skin set him apart from the man they were looking for, but he approached the table and sat down.

"Hello, my name is Carlos Fuldner," he said as he offered a hand shake to James. He took Liliana's hand and kissed it. "I heard you were looking for my friend Juan Carlos? He's not around tonight as you can see, but I know where he lives. I could take you there now if you'd like?"

"Perhaps we could meet him in the restaurant tomorrow night?" Liliana said. "It's not an emergency. We can wait."

"Of course," Fuldner said as he sat back to light a cigarette. "Are you married?"

"No. We're engaged," Liliana said. "We're to be married next year."

"People say it's the best day of your life, and you know what—they're right! And children? What a blessing! I have three myself. Do you want children?"

"When the time comes," James said.

"Is that what you say?" Fuldner said to Liliana.

She hesitated.

"You see," Fuldner laughed. "That's not what she says. She wants children straightaway, don't you, my dear?"

"How perceptive of you," Liliana said as the lock on the front door clicked shut.

"Why are you locking the door?" James said.

"I'm the manager. We're closed," the man who locked the door said.

"Why did you want to see Señor Ospina?" Fuldner said. "He's a close friend of mine, someone who's helped me with sensitive matters in the past."

"We didn't mean any disrespect," James said.

Fuldner sat back, blowing smoke high into the air. "These are difficult times in the city. We Peronists have had to watch our backs these last few months. The bombing in Plaza de Mayo last year was a shock to us all, and then the overthrow of the government—a military coup, no less."

"We don't work for the government. I'm an American," said James. "We both are."

"I've spent enough time in Europe to recognize an Italian accent," Fuldner said, looking closely at Liliana.

"I was born outside Bologna."

"I've never been. I believe it's beautiful."

"It was once," she said.

"You still haven't answered the question—why are you looking for Señor Ospina?" He stubbed out the cigarette on the ashtray in the middle of the table.

"He's an old friend—"

"Stop lying to me. Stop." His voice was soft but stern. "If he were an old friend, you would have his address or phone number or know where he works, but you don't, so what does that make you?"

"We knew him when he was in New York, in 1952," James said. "It's been a while, I admit."

"We really had no idea that looking him up was going to be so much trouble," Liliana said. "I'd happily forget the entire idea right now and go back to our hotel."

"I'd be delighted to let you go once you let me know who you are and the real reason you're looking for my friend."

A loud knock on the front door caused them all to turn. The manager scuttled over to open it. Four men in their twenties walked in, talking to each other in German.

"I thought you were closed," James said.

"These, also, are friends of Señor Ospina," said the manager. "We owe him a lot and are most eager to see him protected."

The men stood around the table without saying a word. James felt panicky. *How do I hold them off while she escapes?* It didn't seem possible. The four newcomers were muscular and fit. He could try against two, but four? *What excuse will get us out of here?*

"We don't mean Ospina any harm," Liliana said. She reached down for her handbag and put it on the table. "We just want to ask him some questions."

"What kind of questions?" Fuldner asked. "Perhaps I could see my way to answering them."

"We want to find someone."

"Who?"

"My father. He disappeared after the war. Ospina may have helped him," she said.

"Who was your father?"

"He was in the SS."

"What's his name?"

"Enrico Tomassi."

The four young men stepped closer. James could feel their breath. He appreciated what she was trying to do, but Fuldner wasn't going for it.

"I've never heard of such a man. I still think you're lying," he said and slammed down his fist. "We have a tight-knit community here. We don't take kindly to outsiders, particularly when they have a laundry list of questions accompanying them. I think we're going to need to teach you both some manners." He stood up and said something in German to the men around the table. A man with piercing blue eyes twisted James's arm behind him.

"Take him out in the alley and teach him some manners," Fuldner said, then turned to Liliana. "And as for you . . ."

James twisted around, freeing himself. Blue Eyes came at him. James landed a punch on his chin and he fell backward. Another man grabbed James from behind.

Liliana reached into her bag.

"That's enough." She pointed a gun at Fuldner's head. "Let him go."

"Careful, you might hurt someone with that," Fuldner said. "Why don't you give it to me?" He held out his hand.

One of the men lunged for the gun, but she was too fast. She stepped back and fired a round just past his ear. It shattered a mirror with a picture of the Black Forest on it. "The next round goes in your head. Let him go."

Fuldner raised his hand. "Do as she says."

The man let go of James, who rubbed his shoulder and went to her side.

"Open the door, Adolf," she said to Fuldner.

"You have no idea who you're messing with. You're dead."

"You think I won't shoot you, you Nazi scum? Now open the damn door."

James shoved the man who had bent his arm to the floor. The other men stood back. She kept the gun trained on them as she backed toward the door. One of the men opened it, and they stepped through onto the street. The door closed behind them. They ran for several blocks before they stopped to talk.

"You have a gun?"

"You're welcome."

"Where did you get it?"

"I arranged to get it through a contact this afternoon."

"Why? What contact?"

"Where would we be now if I hadn't?"

James shook his head, holding out his arm to flag down a taxi. "I can't be a part of this," he said.

"I can't do this without you."

"I won't help you track down this man just to kill him."

"You're using me to get your story," Liliana said. "What's the difference?"

"The difference is that one of us is looking to murder someone. Revenge isn't the answer."

"You call it revenge. I call it justice. Why not? Why are you protecting him?"

"I'm not protecting him. I'm protecting you. This . . . mission of yours will destroy you."

"You killed. I've seen you kill men. Why is this so different?"

"That was war."

"The war never ended for me."

A car pulled up. "Get in," James said. She hesitated. "I'm not leaving you here alone after what just happened. Get in the car."

"I need to know you're still with me."

"We have to be . . . better than them."

"No," said Liliana. "This is everything. I have to . . . I have to do this."

"Please get in."

She did as he asked. He closed the door and gave the driver the address for their hotel. She banged on the window with her forearm. He stood alone, watching the taxi as it drove away.

CHAPTER 15

Liliana raised the binoculars to her eyes, scanning the street outside the ABC restaurant. It would be opening for dinner soon, though the rush wouldn't begin until after nine o'clock. She let the binoculars drop to her lap, rubbing the tiredness out of her eyes. Her bag was by her feet, the gun still inside. The remnants of the sandwich she'd had delivered to the room were lying on the table beside her, but she hadn't eaten much.

She'd barely left the window in the twenty-four hours she'd been in this hotel. Sleep had only come after a fruitless time watching the restaurant the night before, and the nightmares had returned in earnest. *Where the hell is Ospina? Maybe Fuldner warned him. Bastard. What do I do if he doesn't show?* She had no idea what her next move would be. Who could she pay off? She stood up, her knees audibly cracking, and went to her suitcases on the bed. She ignored the one with her clothes and toiletries and opened the other.

She picked up one of several dozen rolls of American bills. Had she brought enough? Would two hundred thousand dollars be enough to bribe whomever she needed to bribe to find him? Somebody knew where he was. That was for sure. Somebody knew where that photo had been taken. James had left the photo for her at the front desk at the hotel, but nothing else. She hadn't seen him this last day or so, not since he'd sent her home in the taxi the night before last.

She'd gone to his room to talk to him, to tell him what her intentions were, to ask him what he was going to do now, or perhaps just to say goodbye. He wasn't there, and she almost did it—she almost left without saying goodbye. Her bags were packed and in the taxi when she'd relented and scribbled a letter that she left under his door. She wondered if he'd even read it. It was impossible to harbor any bitterness toward him—he was down here to do a job, and she'd lied to him. He deserved better. *Everyone whose life I touch these days deserves better.*

She returned to the window, taking her place in the worn armchair she'd dragged over. The hotel wasn't what she had grown accustomed to these past twelve years. It wasn't the kind of establishment Thomas would have approved of. The faded décor reminded her of home, and she drew comfort from that.

She went over the plan in her head again. If she saw Ospina go inside, she would wait in the lobby downstairs until he emerged and follow him from there, on the bike she'd bought if necessary. If he went to his car alone, she would try to talk to him, to offer him a smile, or one of the rolls of bills from the suitcase before he drove away. *And if all else fails—pull the gun.* He wasn't getting away. The fear of Fuldner and his heavies was nothing. So what if they caught her again? She'd buy them off too.

The doors of the restaurant opened, and she spied the manager with the thin mustache peeking out onto the street. He drew his head back inside like a rodent retreating into its burrow. The lights inside the ABC flicked on, illuminating the street through the large glass windows. She thought about what James had said to her before he put her in the taxi. *Am I better than Brack if he dies at my hand? Does it matter?*

Her parents would have said precisely what James had, but they were dead now. She had no one to steer her. She was adrift—a raft in the ocean with no land in sight, surrounded by raging waters. An elderly couple stopped outside the ABC, looking at the menu posted there. They conversed a few seconds before heading inside. Then she heard a knock on the door. "Who is it?" She grabbed the gun from her bag and stood.

"James. Can we talk?"

She went to the door. "What do you want to talk about? I'm not leaving without seeing Ospina."

"Can you open the door?"

She opened it a few centimeters. He was alone. He looked tired, resigned.

"Can I come in, please?"

The door swung open and she walked back toward the window. She raised the binoculars to her face and sat down again.

"Have you come to show me the error of my ways?" she said as she peered down to the street.

"I read your letter."

"How else would you have found me?"

"I was ready to leave. I packed my bags." She heard the bedsprings creak as he sat down.

"How were you planning on getting home?"

"I have enough for the flights to Caracas. I was going to work my way back from there, somehow."

"Is that what you've come for—a handout for your trip back to New York?" She didn't believe the words coming out of her mouth, and it hurt to say them.

"Do you really think that's why I'm here?"

She put the binoculars down, realizing she still had the gun in her other hand.

"You planning on using that?"

"Of course not. I wasn't expecting anyone at the door."

"How can I convince you not to kill this man if we find him?"

"You don't think we're going to find him. You don't even think that's him in the photograph."

"What if I'm wrong?"

"What do you want me to say, James? This man gave the orders to have my family murdered."

"And you survived, Liliana." He went to her, kneeling beside her. "By some miracle, those bullets didn't hit you."

"My mother saved me. The bullets hit her instead."

"I've experienced something like the horror that you've seen. I've felt that deep pain. My father is the only person who prepared me for what I've witnessed in my life . . . I just wish to God you hadn't experienced the same."

Liliana said nothing.

"I think about Luca and Luciano every day," James went on. "They're alive today because of you. There's still so much you can do in life—so much good. That all ends if you murder Brack. When the SS lined you and your family up in that cemetery, you weren't in a position that you were able to choose. Now you can. You can choose to be like them, or you can choose to be better than them."

She felt something stir within her. It was hard to say what. Something. Was there life after this? The past twelve years had been leading to this moment; was she just going to let him get away?

She shook her head. "I can't just let Brack go."

"Then let's find him," James said. "I'll expose him. We'll tell the police. We'll lobby Congress to address this problem—to go after these animals as aggressively as they went after us."

"What about the gun?"

"Keep the gun. I think we're going to need it."

"I'm glad you didn't leave."

"But I need you to promise we do things my way."

"I promise," she said and hugged James close. She felt his sincerity, the inherent goodness of him, and it was contagious. How long would this feeling last? Could she change the path she'd been on for twelve years because of him?

He let his arms go and drew back.

"So you're here for me?" she asked.

"I'm here for you, Liliana."

"Good," she said, "because I really need to use the bathroom. Can you keep an eye on the restaurant?"

He laughed. "Gladly." He took the binoculars and sat down.

She was in the bathroom when he called out for her. The urgency in his voice told her everything she needed to know. She ran out.

"I saw him. I saw our man."

"Ospina?"

"He walked up the street, from that direction." James pointed with his index finger. "I didn't see any kind of car or bike or anything."

"He must have come from the subway around the corner. Watch that place. Don't take your eyes off that door. He's likely inside for dinner, but if he's not, we need to be ready." She was already stuffing money into her bag. "You wait here. I'll be in the lobby downstairs."

"How much are you planning on bringing?"

"I don't know—a few thousand."

James put the binoculars down. "I'm not comfortable letting you go down there alone, particularly with all that money."

"I can look after myself. You need to be up here in case I miss him. But you get down those stairs if he comes out."

"All right, but don't do anything dangerous."

"As if I would." She threw on her jacket and closed the door behind her. It took about thirty seconds to descend the stairs. James would be able to do it in less if he needed to. She took a seat in the lobby by the window on a threadbare, lumpy couch. She waited. An hour passed before the door to the ABC opened and Ospina walked out. He was alone and turned toward the subway station.

She leaped out of the seat and went to the door. Ospina was halfway down the street. James arrived down the stairs.

"Let's go," he said.

She took a cursory glance at the ABC before jogging after Ospina, fifty meters ahead. They slowed to a walking pace once they were within ten meters. She kept walking, trying to regulate her breathing. Ospina turned the corner toward the subway station. The station entrance was only a few meters away, and she followed him inside. He moved through the turnstile. She bought the tickets and followed him through. He was just ahead of them, seemingly oblivious to their presence. They followed him down the stairs toward the platform.

Ospina lit a cigarette and glanced in their direction. She studied the concrete. James did the same. The sound of the train interrupted her thoughts, and the wind came, hot and filthy, through the tunnel. Ospina and the half dozen other riders stepped forward as the train stopped. They boarded the same carriage at the other end, taking a seat ten meters from him. The doors began to close. The train continued a few stops before Ospina got up and strolled to the door. They followed him off the train, toward the exit at the end of the platform.

"How are we going to do this?" James said.

"I don't know. Call out to him? We can't let him reach his house—he'll just lock us out."

"And call Fuldner and his heavies."

They caught up to him at the stairs, just a few meters behind. He glanced back at them, then turned the corner once they were on the street.

"Señor Ospina?" Liliana called out.

He turned to face them. He was in his midforties, balding, with a black mustache, unremarkable in every way.

"Who are you?"

"Someone who wants to talk."

"You're the couple they warned me about in the restaurant." He didn't move—didn't seem fearful. He sensed an opportunity. "Why would I want to talk to you?"

"Because I'll give you five thousand dollars if you do," she said.

"What? Five thousand . . . you're joking? Who are you?"

"I'm a journalist," James said. "An American. My friend here is a concerned citizen. Neither of us means you any harm."

Ospina waited a few seconds. "Five thousand dollars?"

"I have it here." Liliana showed him the rolls of cash in her bag.

Five minutes later he was leading them into the lobby of a hotel, this one considerably superior to the one opposite the ABC. They took a seat in the corner. Ospina ordered a gin and tonic from the waiter, James a soda water. Liliana declined.

"You were looking for me in the ABC the other night."

"Your friend Fuldner didn't seem like the welcoming type."

"I played a part in bringing a lot of his friends to this country. It pays to have a paranoid streak when you're protecting the kind of people he is."

She regretted not ordering a drink. James lit a cigarette, and soon all three were smoking.

"Show me the money. I want to see it again, properly this time, before I say another word."

She reached into her bag and handed him a roll of bills.

"Fuldner mentioned you might be dangerous." He pointed at the glint of the handgun below the money.

"Only when provoked," Liliana said. "The money's yours if you give us the information we need."

"What do you want to know?" He handed the cash back.

"We have a photograph—"

James cut her off. "What was your role in the Perón government?"

"I was a diplomat. I worked in Europe after the war. I dealt with immigration and procuring certain persons of interest to the Argentinean government."

This man, Liliana thought, *is making me sick. How am I going to get through this?* She motioned to the waiter, ordered a glass of wine.

"Nazis," James said. He had his notebook in his hand now and was scribbling.

"On occasion."

"How did the program of bringing Nazis to South America begin?" James asked.

"It was no secret that Señor Perón was a . . . sympathizer to the German cause. But the contacts were made during the war, before he came to power."

"What contacts?"

"Several colleagues of mine went to Europe for the express purpose of constructing escape routes for persons of interest. They organized means, guides, and safe houses. They financed what needed financing."

"They found sympathetic members of the clergy," James said.

"The help from the clergy was invaluable, particularly in getting travel documents for our fugitives, but they weren't the only ones we could rely on. We had former SS men working with us. Our mutual friend, Señor Fuldner, was paramount in establishing the network."

Liliana had to take a deep breath to keep her composure. This man, and what he represented, had stolen the chance for justice from her and thousands like her. It was all she could do to stop herself from spitting her drink in his face. And, instead, she was going to have to pay him a huge sum of money. He was a pawn, a stepping-stone. She contented herself with that.

"What was Perón looking to achieve by bringing them?" James asked.

"The president wanted to build and modernize the country's economy. What better way to curry favor and get money than to look after the ex–power brokers? Argentina had a German community upward of two hundred and fifty thousand before the war." Ospina stubbed out his cigarette and immediately lit another. "Who knows how many now? There are over a hundred sixty German associations in Buenos Aires: social clubs dedicated to German pursuits, literature, sports, drinking, and—before and during the war—Nazism. The foundations were already here. What better place for these valuable German assets to come?"

"What about the common war criminals? Why did you accept them?"

"Some came to help with our military, training our men in espionage and interrogation techniques. I heard the story of one scientist who came to develop a nuclear facility on an island in western Argentina. He strung the government along for several years before they figured out he didn't have a notion what he was doing, but most were an invaluable help. We didn't discriminate. We accepted those who needed our aid."

Liliana was unable to remain silent any longer. "What about the victims of these monsters you accepted?"

"That wasn't our concern. The war was over. We had much to gain. We formed a close trading partnership with Germany that exists to this day. German cars, trucks, buses, and even entire factories flooded into Argentina in exchange for US dollars to finance their economic miracle. And of course, the powerful took their piece of the pie. One shipment of Mercedes cars went directly to Perón's office. He kept four for himself and gave the rest to friendly judges, prosecutors, politicians, and journalists as 'gifts.'"

"What about the rest of the international community? The Allied powers?"

Ospina took a sip of his gin before he continued. "If they knew what we were doing, they kept silent. Their focus was elsewhere. They prosecuted the big names, but there were so many others that the average person would never have heard of. They didn't care about a bunch of middle-aged ex-soldiers unless they had something to gain from them themselves."

"How close were you to this process?"

"I saw the files. I saw how they were processed in batches, consecutive numbers stamped one after another, as if on an assembly line."

"How many would you say? Hundreds?"

"Thousands."

Liliana dropped her drink. The wine spilled on the table. She righted the glass but didn't mop up the liquid.

"How many?" she asked.

"Seven or eight thousand, give or take. I'm not sure. I never counted, but the party's over now. The welcome mat's been withdrawn since the coup last year."

"Does that mean that the new regime will prosecute the war criminals the Perón government took in?" James said.

"I have no idea what their plans are, but I wouldn't count on that. The new government has better things to focus on than upsetting the German population. Can you imagine the scale of that? Weeding out thousands of people living peacefully, many of whom work for the military? I don't see it."

"So the Nazis who settled here—war criminals who slaughtered hundreds of thousands of innocent people—are going to be allowed to live the rest of their lives in peace?" Liliana said.

Ospina took the gin and tonic in his hand, rolling it around in his glass before taking another sip. "Who knows? I had a part to play at one time, but I'm out now."

"Why is Fuldner so anxious to keep you a secret?" she asked.

"He's afraid of exactly what I'm telling you. Exposure is the only thing that can hurt him and his cohorts now."

She wanted to throttle this man, to pull out her gun, to even the score. This country was awash with Nazis. The worst people the world had ever known were all around her. Who knew if the people filing through the hotel lobby had killed thousands? Who knew who was guilty? It all suddenly seemed like too much, and she was having difficulty catching a breath. James seemed to recognize this and put his hand on hers. He paused a few seconds, giving her the time she needed. Ospina just waited until James began speaking again.

"Why aren't you afraid of him?" James said.

"Fuldner?" Ospina shrugged. "I have more immediate concerns—the current regime. I'm a single man, with few ties. It's time to leave, and the money you're going to give me will buy me a house in Brazil or Paraguay, far from the likes of Carlos Fuldner." He raised his glass. "I'll drink to that." He downed the rest of his gin.

"There was something else," James said. "Show him the picture."

She reached into her bag and gave him the photograph.

"Ah," Ospina said. "You've been speaking to my friend in New York. I should have known."

"Do you know who these people are?" she asked.

He didn't answer. The fury was rising in her blood. It was all she could do to remain seated. She grasped James's hand. The feel of his skin against hers was the only thing keeping her from screaming.

"Why did you send it to Laughlin?" James asked.

"A little joke. I thought he'd appreciate what the Allies are trying to gloss over."

"How did you get this photograph?"

"I took it. I was there for their *Führer's* birthday, by special invitation."

"Do you know who any of the people in the photograph are? I'll give you more money." She took the photo out of his hand. "Who is this man?" She pointed to the figure she'd identified as Brack.

"I could lie to you, but I don't remember. I met a few people. I remember the ladies more than the men. They were immigrants. Some came before the war, some came after."

"Was this photo taken in the city? Here?" she asked.

"Oh, no," he said, letting out a laugh. "It might have been, but it was taken all the way out west, in the Lake District in Patagonia. In Bariloche."

"Where?"

"It's a sizable town near the border with Chile. They invited me out there to celebrate with them a couple of years ago. Beautiful place." He stood up. "I've said much more than is prudent. I won't be discussing matters any further."

"How do we find these people? I'll give you more money. How much do you want? Ten thousand?"

"I can't say any more."

"Who are they?" Liliana pressed.

"They're common German citizens of the town."

"Where was the photo taken? A hotel? A house?" she asked.

"I'll need that money you promised me. I've already put my life in danger talking to you."

"Give him the money," James said. "He gave us what we need."

She handed over the money. Ospina stuffed it into his pockets.

"You disgust me," she said.

"I trust I don't need to impress upon you the importance of my anonymity."

"You don't. You have my word on that," James said.

He nodded. "I wish you luck. Bringing these people into this country was never a job I asked for, or even relished. I did as I was ordered."

"Think I've heard that line before," James said.

"Be careful. These are not the type of people to be trifled with." He stood up and walked away without another word.

"We have what we wanted," James said. "He's probably right about it being dangerous here now."

"We leave for Bariloche in the morning."

CHAPTER 16

They took turns driving out of the sprawling city and into the unending plain beyond. Fertile, almost treeless farms and grasslands sped by on either side. Liliana silently repeated the name of the town as she drove. *Bariloche. Bariloche.* It was a beautiful name without a speck of anything sinister. Now she knew. He was there. Not a shred of doubt existed in her mind of that, even if James remained unconvinced.

They'd checked out of the hotels, bought a car, and were on the road by late afternoon. The car wasn't fancy—just something to get them the fifteen hundred kilometers to Bariloche. Spending the money was nothing to her. James understood now; she was sure. He was firm in his convictions in pursuing the story, and making sure she "didn't do anything rash." She looked over at him sleeping in the passenger seat. He was just as brave as he'd always been, just as forthright and strong, and she felt it again—something stirring within her. Something unfamiliar. Perhaps it was the excitement of the chase.

The specter of Brack lurked in her mind. James was the very antithesis of everything he and his Nazis stood for. *It's difficult to believe they're even the same species.* Who were the others in the photo with Brack? Had they murdered innocents, destroying lives in equal measure as he had? She knew every line, every shadow on each of the people's faces. She would recognize any of them on the street.

A policeman in Buenos Aires had told them Bariloche was a tourist city on a lake, and a ski resort come the snows of winter. Neither Liliana nor James had ever heard of it before Ospina had told them. They'd never forget the place now, and they hadn't even reached it yet.

Night descended, and the headlights cut a swathe through the encroaching darkness. James stirred before sitting up.

"Where are we?"

"About twenty kilometers from Santa Rosa, wherever that is."

"Let's stop there."

"Why? We can take turns and drive through the night. We could be there at lunchtime tomorrow."

James reached into his pocket for a pack of cigarettes. "He's not going anywhere—if he's even there. He has no idea we're coming. No one does."

"Except Ospina."

He put the cigarettes on the dashboard without taking one. "Ospina isn't going to breathe a word about our meeting. They'd string him up if they found out."

"I suppose, but—"

"He's going to take the money and get as far away from Fuldner's goons as possible. Let's stop at that town—what was the name of it?"

"Santa Rosa."

"That sounds like a fine place to spend the night." He lit up a cigarette, offering her one. "And let me pay for the hotel tonight. Just this once."

She took a drag on the cigarette. "Just this once." The lights of Santa Rosa appeared through the black on the horizon.

Two hours later they sat opposite each other in a restaurant window. He was in his now-familiar gray suit, and she wore a pink floral dress. He raised a glass of water to her.

"To our quest—may we both find what we're searching for."

She sipped her wine and inspected the other patrons.

"I can't help but feel that they're watching us. I know how ridiculous that is."

"It's easy to think that there's some grand conspiracy going on—that decisions are made in smoke-filled rooms, and that somewhere our pictures are on a bulletin board—but that's not the case. They don't know who we are or where we're going."

"Do we?"

"Sometimes." He laughed.

Liliana took a bite of her linguine and held up her wineglass so that it sparkled in the light.

"I used to go out, pretending I was someone else—a nurse, or a mother of two."

"When you were married?"

"I didn't do it to invite solicitations from men. I brandished my wedding ring like a shield—the only thing I miss about not wearing it."

"Why did you do it, then? Pretend to be other people?"

"To escape. Don't you ever—"

"I suppose I do."

"It was refreshing to be a secretary or a housewife from Long Island. I would make up the circumstances as I went."

"Ever trip yourself up with the details?"

"Never. I remembered."

The memories of those nights were jumbled and ran together. The people she met, the places she went were trivial details.

"I'm not surprised."

A violinist began playing in the corner. They paused a few seconds to listen before continuing.

"What was your childhood like?" Liliana asked. "Apart from what happened?" She felt ridiculous asking, regretted the question as soon as the words left her mouth.

"It's hard to remember one without the other."

"I'm sorry."

"No, it's a normal question. I had a lot of good times. I had friends. I enjoyed school. I played basketball in high school, went to the beach."

"Your home life must have been difficult."

"Yeah, it was, but I still have my sister. Whatever I went through was nothing compared to you."

"All our experiences are unique."

The violinist brushed past their table.

"I tried to forget what happened," James said, "and the war was the perfect cover for that. I had no time to think about the past, so I didn't . . . but I used to say that Susana's parents were the reason my marriage failed."

"You told me you weren't a good husband. Was that true, about her parents?"

"It's convenient to say, but they didn't hate me because I wasn't rich or blue blooded. They hated me because I drank too much and stayed in the office until eleven o'clock at night. They're good people. They wanted better for their daughter. My father-in-law wasn't afraid to tell me."

"And that's why you don't drink now."

"Yeah," he said, swirling the water around his glass. "Drinking started to get in the way . . . of everything. I loved her. She was beautiful. But my mind was always somewhere else, in my parents' house in Cape May or on Monte Sole, so I started drinking too much, working too late, staying out all night, whatever." A streetlight outside flickered and died. "She didn't want a husband she never saw—a drunk. I gave up drinking, but it was too late. We divorced. I didn't fight it. She's married now with a baby."

"That quickly?"

"It's what she wanted. I'm just glad she's happy." He looked around. "Are we done here?"

"Yes."

He motioned to the waiter, who brought the bill in a few seconds. "I'm getting this." She didn't protest, and a few minutes later they were on the street.

"There's a lake just down the way," she said. "Shall we go?"

"Sure."

They walked in silence a few seconds. "What do you think happened to your father?" Liliana asked.

"What set him off that day? I tried to find out when I went to see him in '52—looking for answers I didn't get. He didn't seem to regret killing my mother for any other reason than it landed him in prison."

"Did he say why?"

"He blamed her more than himself. I don't know what the hell I expected. An act of contrition? I should have gotten her out. I should have forced her hand. I don't know what happened to him in the Great War, but I've seen what war does to men with my own eyes." They arrived at the lake. The reflections of streetlights twinkled on the water's surface. She took his hand in hers.

He looked at the expanse of dark water in front of them. "Why didn't she leave him? Why didn't I get her out of there? I wasn't a child. I could have looked after her. What good did fighting him do?" He reached down and picked up a pebble. He held it for a few seconds before tossing it out into the water. It landed with a plop, sending perfect circles out in the dark water. "People came to me after she died. They said she grew up in a similar house to the one she'd settled in, and that her own father beat her much the same as mine did. Maybe that was why she never left. It was all she ever knew."

She had never heard him like this before. "You did the best you could, James. He was your father."

"I did love him, even after everything . . . and he repaid me by beating her to death in front of me."

The ripples had faded. The lake was calm once more—its surface like black volcanic glass.

"It's not your fault. There was nothing you could have done."

"I could have protected her." He bent his head, and her hand found the rough stubble of his face.

"You were a child. It's not your fault," she repeated, and she would keep repeating herself until he believed her. She could feel his tears on her hands, running down her knuckles. "There was nothing you could have done." She pulled his head down, wrapping her arms around his neck to embrace him. He pulled his head back, but she kept her hands on his face, staring into his eyes now, and she brought her lips to his, feeling the firm touch. With her eyes closed, she felt a flame inside her, something foreign and wonderful. All words, all thoughts fell away. It was as if she'd crossed a threshold, and the world she knew was gone. It might have been a minute or more before she thought to draw away.

"We shouldn't have done that," she said. He didn't answer. "We should be getting back to the hotel. It's just a couple of minutes away."

"Thank you for listening to me. I know it can't have been easy, with what you've been through." His voice was different now—stronger, more composed.

They walked on, leaving the lake behind, the atmosphere between them changed. She felt like she was on a carousel. "I'm sorry I kissed you like that."

He didn't respond, just kept walking. The hotel was a few hundred meters away, and they covered the ground quickly.

James followed her up the stairs to their rooms, one beside the other.

"Get some sleep," she said. "We leave first thing in the morning. We can make it there before bed tomorrow night."

"Of course," he said with his hand on his door handle. "Liliana . . ."

"Good night."

The door closed with a click, and she stood behind it, able to breathe at last. *What am I doing?* She flicked the light on, illuminating the simple room. She went to the bathroom and changed for bed. The springs in the mattress whined as she sat down. A similar creak came through the wall from his room next door. *I can't leave things like this. It's time to clear the air, to make him understand that there isn't room for romantic feelings between us.* The mattress sang again as she got up. She felt as far from sleep as she'd ever been. She threw on a dressing gown and marched to the door. It was after midnight. She made sure not to knock too loudly.

He appeared at the door ten seconds later, dressed only in white boxer shorts. The look on his face was hard to place, somewhere between surprise and anger.

"I need to talk to you," she said.

"You'd best come inside, then."

She walked past him and he closed the door. "I wanted to—"

He cut her off with his kiss, wrapping his arms around her as he brought her body tight into his. She kissed him back, forgetting words, letting them fall away like autumnal leaves.

It was past nine o'clock when she woke beside him, a knot in the pit of her stomach. *This is wrong. This is all wrong.*

"What time is it?" he said, rubbing tiredness from his eyes. The clock on the wall gave him the answer.

She slipped out of the bed, her back to him, reaching for her clothes on the floor. "It's too late," she said. Her hands shook as she pulled up her underwear. "I wanted to leave earlier. We're not going to make Bariloche before nightfall."

"It's OK," he said.

"No, it's not. Last night was a mistake. This isn't what I want from you."

He lay back on the bed, moved his eyes from hers to the ceiling. "You had me fooled," he said. "You're pretty convincing when you want to be."

"I got carried away when you told me your story. I'm sorry." She pulled on her pajamas and stood up to find her dressing gown. It was by the door.

"I'm sorry too."

"I can't do this. Not now. Let's keep our relationship strictly professional."

"Strictly professional," he said. He sounded faded and drawn.

"You're a good man, James, and I do care for you, it's just . . ."

"Probably best you go now. I'll see you downstairs in an hour."

She nodded and closed the door behind her. She fumbled with her key and almost tripped as she pushed the door back. She had to clean her room. They had to leave. This wasn't about jumping into bed with the first attractive man she saw. And what if James left her, or Brack caught him and he died? Best to protect herself from that. She was going to have to accept that being alone might just be the price of justice.

The light of the sun had faded hours ago, and thunder rumbled. Liliana was asleep in the passenger seat. He allowed himself a glance over at her before bringing his eyes to the road. They hadn't talked much about the night before. It was best to leave it—for now, at least. A few drops of rain dotted the windscreen, then turned into a deluge in seconds. The barren landscape added to his feeling of driving into a void. He'd seen few cars in the past hours. The only light was from their headlights. It was after ten o'clock. The last sign passed by an hour before. The road was bumpy and uneven, and Liliana jerked awake when they went over a pothole.

"Are we there yet?" She stretched her arms out, sitting up in the seat.

"I think we're about an hour out. We're in the mountains. We've been in the mountains for a while now."

They summited a hill, and a service station came into view.

"Civilization," he said. "Let's stop off and ask for directions. It wouldn't hurt to get some gas either."

They pulled into the gas station. He was surprised it was still open. There was one other car there, a faint wisp of smoke coming from the engine. A teenage girl with blond pigtails stood waving the smoke away from her face as she raised the hood.

"Need some help?" James asked.

"Do you know anything about these things?" the girl said, pointing to the engine.

"Not a lot. I would hope the attendant does."

"There's no one here to help, not until morning."

James walked over to the car. "Let me take a look." He peered into the filthy gray mess of the engine. "I could pretend I knew what I was talking about, but—"

Liliana appeared beside them. "Can we give you a ride somewhere?"

"Could you? That would be amazing. I was starting to wonder how I was going to get home tonight. My parents would have killed me."

"Where is home?"

"Bariloche."

"That's where we're heading," James said.

"Can I come with you?"

"Of course. We need someone to give us directions," he said.

"Thank you so much. Let me get my bag." The girl took a few seconds to grab her belongings and stowed them in the back of Liliana's car. She made arrangements with the station clerk to have her vehicle fixed, and ten minutes later they were on the road again.

Liliana took her turn driving. "What's your name?"

"Alexandra Klement."

"I'm Liliana, and this is my fiancé, James."

"Congratulations!" she said with a smile. "When is the wedding?"

"Next June."

"How exciting!"

"We're looking forward to it," James said. "What has you out so late? How old are you, eighteen?"

"Seventeen. I was out visiting friends. I had to beg to take out the car too, and then it started coughing and smoking. I'm just so happy you two came along."

"Do you happen to know a good hotel in the city?" James asked.

"My parents own a hotel. It's on the lake, and an easy walk into the center of town."

"Sounds perfect," James said.

"Are you still in school?" Liliana asked.

"Yes. I go to the Colegio Aleman."

"A German school?"

"Yes. It's a German-speaking school."

James felt Liliana's hand grip his leg. "A German-speaking school? In a small city like Bariloche?" she said. He was pleased with the cool tone in her voice.

"There's a strong German society in Bariloche. My father is a member of the German Argentinean Cultural Association."

"Sounds interesting. What do they do? I hope you don't mind the questions . . . ," James said.

"No, not at all. It promotes German interests and festivals. We're famous for our chocolate. Every Easter, we hold a chocolate egg festival in the center of town."

"How lovely," Liliana said.

"It is. The chocolate is delicious too. You'll have to try some."

"I'll make sure we do," James replied. "So your family still has a lot of connections with home? Have you ever been to Germany yourself?"

"Not since I was a baby. I was born in Germany, but my family came here in the early days of the war. We lived in Buenos Aires for a while. My six-year-old brother was born there, but not me."

"Why did your family come here?" Liliana asked.

"We don't want to bombard Alexandra with questions, now, do we?" he said.

"I'm just making conversation."

"Oh, I don't mind," said Alexandra. "We're coming into town now, though—I'll direct you toward the hotel."

Alexandra spoke for a few minutes about the town—a ski resort during the winter, Bariloche was built amid beautiful, freezing-cold lakes.

"So the town was founded by a German?" James asked as they drove through the silent streets of the town center.

"Not quite. He was Chilean, of German descent, but the store he ran was named The German, and the town built up around it."

"You know a lot about the history of your town."

"My father talks about it all the time. You know, owning a hotel and all."

"Seems like you pay attention."

They left the car in the parking lot behind the hotel and ascended steps to the front entrance. Alexandra led them to the front desk, asking them to wait while she looked for her mother. A woman in her forties came out of the back room a few seconds later.

"Hello, I'm Ingrid Klement," she said in English.

The same name as Brack's wife, he thought and turned to Liliana, who was staring at the woman.

"You're the kindly couple who picked up my girl?" Her German accent was strong.

"Yes," James said. "She was most helpful with directions and led us to your hotel."

"You're most welcome here. We have one room available. I trust that won't be a problem?"

"No, that'll be fine," Liliana said.

"Fantastic. It has wonderful views of the lake, which is right there," she said, gesturing to the darkened windows five meters behind them. "Daylight will do it more justice."

"I can't wait. I'd also very much like to meet your husband," Liliana said. "Alexandra told us he's quite the expert on the history of the town."

"He'd love to go through it with you, but unfortunately not until tomorrow evening. He's out of town on business until then."

"Very well."

"How long will you be staying for?"

"We're not sure yet," said James. "Our schedule is open."

"That must be lovely."

"It certainly is," said Liliana.

When they were alone in the room, Liliana flicked on the light, illuminating the tasteful décor. She went to the wide window facing out onto the dark expanse of Nahuel Huapí Lake. James put the bags down.

"Ingrid. Her name is Ingrid," Liliana said.

"I noticed that. Of course I did, but that of itself means next to nothing. How many Ingrids are there in Austria and Germany?"

"It's a common name. What about his daughter? Brack had a daughter around the same age."

"We were never able to verify what age the daughter was. It's not evidence. It's coincidence."

"We'll see when the coincidences start piling up. Maybe we won't see it as nothing then."

"I'll take the floor," he said.

"She's German," Liliana said in a whisper. "So is her mother. Her father is a member of the German Argentinean Cultural Association, whatever that is. It sounds like a bunch of Nazis to me."

"Chocolate eggs and German-speaking schools—a little piece of the old country in the Andes," he said.

"The perfect place for any Nazi to hide."

He went to the chair and took his shoes off. She sat down on the bed opposite him.

"The answers will come," he said. "But we need to be careful. We're in the lion's den here. This isn't a big city like Buenos Aires. This is their town."

The moon came out from behind the clouds and spread a cloth of silver on the surface of the lake.

"For now," said Liliana.

CHAPTER 17

The morning light brought the full majesty of the lake and surrounding mountains into view. The spring sun was high in the sky, and she went to the window as the sun cast down gold on the blue water and the mountains that surrounded it. *He doesn't deserve to live somewhere as beautiful as this. He took everything from me, from all of us. Why shouldn't I do the same to him?* The gun was hidden in her suitcase. She took it out. It felt cold in her hand, heavy.

James was still asleep. The scent of him lingered in the air. Lying to him felt like the worst thing she'd ever done. Perhaps he was right, that she'd feel satisfied if Brack merely confessed. Perhaps there was a life worth living after this.

But a confession would leave Brack free to enjoy his life and family in the splendor of this paradise. Exposing him might cause him some sleepless nights. But without the will of the former Allies to prosecute him, little would be done. He would go on living his life in peace, raising his children.

She slipped the pistol back into her suitcase. James was the best man she'd ever known, but bringing her plan to fruition would likely make being with him impossible. It was a sacrifice she'd have to make; the people of Monte Sole deserved no less.

The hotel lobby was half-full, but the dining room was empty—it was well past breakfast time.

"This place seems haunted," Liliana whispered.

"Maybe so," said James, "but look at this view." Massive windows at the back of the hotel highlighted blue lakes and snow-tipped mountains everywhere.

He led her through a door and onto a veranda, where several other guests relaxed with beverages. Alexandra was in the garden—which led down to the edge of the lake below—and she put down her book to wave up at them. She ran up the steps, arriving with red-faced enthusiasm.

"It looks a lot better during the day, doesn't it?"

"It certainly does. It's outrageously beautiful," James said. "Did you hear about your car?"

"My mother spoke to the mechanic this morning. It's all in hand. And what are you two up to today?"

"We'd like to have a walk around and get some lunch," said James. "Where should we go?"

"We're right in the middle of town. Just go out the front, and you're there. There are plenty of places to eat too."

"Thank you," Liliana said.

"Are you feeling well, Liliana? You seem . . . ," Alexandra said.

"I'm fine. Just a little tired."

"My father will be giving a performance in the dining room tonight," Alexandra offered. "He's been doing it for as long as I can remember."

"He sings?" James said.

"No, he plays piano," she answered.

"Well, we'll make sure to be here for it. We'd love to meet him."

They bade the young girl goodbye and walked into town. They could have been in Switzerland or Germany. The architecture of the city was specific in its influences. They strolled past stone houses with wooden shutters. A stone tower stood in the town square that would have looked at home in any German town. *Whoever built this place wasn't hiding anything.*

Liliana waited until she was sure no one was listening before she spoke.

"Did you hear what she said about her father? Brack was a trained pianist."

"I heard her. Plenty of people play piano. Try to calm down."

"I am calm," she insisted.

"Those nails of yours are pretty," he said. They were holding hands, and he lifted them. "But . . . sharp."

She had left marks on his skin. "Oh! I'm sorry."

"Not everyone here is a Nazi—remember that."

They stopped in a café and had lunch like any young couple, talking about the town and home. They spoke about his work and the charities she supported in New York. They left a generous tip and thanked the waitress. It was time to begin.

"I saw a real estate agent up the street on our way into the café," she said. "He's certainly no German with a name like Albert Gold."

"Seems like a good person to speak to," James answered.

She led him up the street to the small office, where a balding man with a well-trimmed beard sat behind a desk.

"Albert Gold. Pleased to meet you," he said in Spanish.

"I'm James Murphy. This is my fiancée, Liliana Andolini."

Gold shook their hands in turn. "What can I do for you?"

"We wanted to inquire about renting property in the area."

"Excellent. Was there anywhere in particular you had in mind?"

"Somewhere outside the town, up in the mountains. Perhaps somewhere you could hike to from here."

"You've come to the right place. Skiing in winter, hiking in summer. Do you ski?" He picked up some papers on his desk.

"I've always wanted to learn," said James.

"Can I ask you a question, Mr. Gold?" Liliana said.

Gold looked up from the papers. "Of course."

"Are you Jewish?"

"Yes." He looked unsurprised to get the question. "I am."

"Is there a large Jewish population in the city?" Liliana asked.

Gold reached for a cigarette case on his desk. "Not especially. Just a few families."

"It's just that I've heard rumors," she said. James gripped her thigh under the desk, but she swatted his hand away.

Gold offered them a cigarette. They both declined. He lit one.

"Rumors?"

"Of celebrations every year for Hitler's birthday. Some say this town is a haven for Nazi sympathizers, and even some who are on the run from justice."

Gold looked at her for a few seconds before he got up and went to the door. He bolted the door and turned the sign on it to **CLOSED**.

"You're American?" he said in English as he sat down again.

"He is. I'm originally from Italy."

"We didn't mean any offense," James said. "It's just that we could be here awhile. Since we're thinking about buying in the area, we want to know what kind of place this is."

"Those people are here," Gold said. "I can't tell German-born citizens from Nazi sympathizers from war criminals, however. They don't divulge that kind of information to those outside their immediate circles."

"Do you feel marginalized being Jewish here?"

"You mean any more so than elsewhere? Not really. The Germans tend to keep to themselves, and we haven't had any outwardly anti-Semitic incidents here. I suspect that they're willing to put aside their prejudices in favor of a quiet life in a beautiful place."

"How open are they?"

"Open, but closed at the same time. The annual celebration for Hitler's birthday is held in a function room in one of the hotels in the city. I don't know how many attend, but it's probably a hundred or so. You've seen the architecture of the town—it could almost be a village in Bavaria."

"It's hard to miss. How often do you come into contact with these people?"

"As I said, it's hard to discern the Germans who've been here for years, or generations, from the Nazis. The immigrants like to keep their traditions alive through their festivals and the German-language school in town."

Pictures of the local sights adorned the wall behind his desk—Liliana even noted a photo of their hotel. One photo showed a large gathering in the town square.

"That's the annual chocolate festival. It's getting more popular by the year."

"I can detect a little German in your accent," James said.

"We moved over in 1939, just when things in Germany became too much to bear."

He stubbed out his cigarette in the otherwise clean ashtray.

"Was there a spike in immigration from Germany in the years after the war?"

"Not that I noticed," Gold said. "Look, I'm happy to answer your questions, but why are you really here? I suspect you have motives other than purchasing property."

"I'm a journalist," James said.

"Ah, so that's it. Well, good luck. I'd like to see my city rid of any Nazi scum as much as anyone," Gold said. "It's digging them out that's going to be the hard part. You can't just burst into the hotel on Hitler's birthday and ask them to come quietly. They may live in peace here, but they're snakes, and if you disturb them—they'll bite."

"I understand," said Liliana. "Thank you for talking to us."

"I'd be happy to answer any more questions, but the truth is I don't know much more. There are rumors they were aided by the Argentinean government."

"Those are hardly rumors anymore."

Gold shrugged. "But the whispers about them indoctrinating children in the local German school, and the true aims of the local German Argentinean Cultural Association, will be less easy to confirm."

"Indeed," James said.

"Perhaps you'd like to look at some properties now?" Gold took a brochure out from under his desk.

The interview, clearly, was over.

Liliana's feet ached from an afternoon of walking the lake and surrounding hills. She went to the room to change for dinner while James waited downstairs on the veranda overlooking the lake. He was talking to a couple from Mendoza when she joined them, their faces illuminated by candles set on the table. James did most of the talking. *Do these people know about the Nazis here?* she wondered. *What do normal Argentinean people think about the government's policy of protecting some of the worst murderers the world has ever seen?* She didn't ask. It was his job to ask those questions, and he wasn't. She stared at the foreboding darkness of the mountains that seemed to enclose them on all sides.

An hour passed before they made their way into the dining room and took a middle table, surrounded by twenty or so other guests. A grand piano sat on the small stage at the end of the room. She was facing away from the stage, so she didn't see the man who came out, just heard his voice.

"Good evening, ladies and gentlemen. I hope you enjoy the music."

Her chair caught between the tiles on the floor when she whirled around. She stood up to lift the legs, almost falling over the table. The man was at the piano now. He began to play. *That voice! It's him!*

"Are you all right?" James said.

Twelve years of searching . . . Do I get the gun? I could finish this now.

She stood up to get a better look at him. He was behind the piano, four or five meters away. He looked up. *It's him.* The face wasn't exactly like the one she'd seen in her mind since the war, but the voice. The voice. She knocked over her water glass, but James caught it before it spilled. He said something, but his words were garbled, caught between the musical notes and the man's voice still echoing through her mind.

She made for the door, trying not to make her labored stumbling too obvious. A few seconds later she was on the veranda, the night air swirling all around her, the sound of Beethoven's Fifth still in her ears. James came out after her.

"What happened in there?"

"It's him."

"It's who? Brack? Where?"

"Playing the piano."

"The man on the piano? The owner of the hotel? Did you even see him?"

"Yes, but I didn't have to. I'd know that voice anywhere."

"Even speaking Spanish?"

"Spanish, Italian, German—I know that voice. It's the voice I heard in the cemetery when they opened fire on my family. The same voice of the man I spoke to at my house when you were hiding upstairs."

He turned away to look out at the lake. She wondered if he believed her.

"We need to go back into that dining room," James said. "We need to find out who that man is. You could be mistaken."

"I'm not. You weren't there . . ."

The door opened behind them and Alexandra walked out. "Is everything all right? I saw you run out. I thought you might have been choking or something."

"We're fine, thank you. She did have something in her throat, but it's gone now. Isn't that right, darling?"

Be calm. Smile. "Yes, I'm fine. We'll be back in momentarily."

Alexandra closed the glass door with a nod. The moon was out now, casting ghostly figures on the rippling lake.

"Just wait a minute here," James said. "I'll get something from the room. Don't move until I get back, OK?"

"I won't."

James turned and left, and as soon as the door closed behind him, the ghosts of the past seemed to ravage her like a plague of locusts. She wrapped her arms around herself to try to stop the shivering that overtook her body. Should she confront Brack tonight? Would he confess?

She allowed herself to wonder, *What if it isn't him?* There was certainly a resemblance, but Germanic men his age had a look about them. It wasn't rare to look the way he did. What if she confronted him? What if she killed him now? No, get the confession first. This man had two children. She had to be sure. The door opened and James appeared once more. It must have been two minutes, but it had felt like hours.

He produced the photographs from his pocket, shepherding her away from the window in case anyone saw. He took out Brack's SS photo first. "This is Brack. But I don't see more than a passing resemblance to the man in the dining room. Brack's got a thinner face and seems taller."

"That's Brack in there. I know it."

"I think the man in there could be the man in the photograph Laughlin gave me, but I don't think either of them is Brack."

"I know. I know it in my heart. That man in there gave the order to kill my family."

"Can you just admit to me that there's some doubt there, that you can't be totally sure?"

"Of course, I'm not completely and utterly sure. There's always some doubt, and I see what you're saying about his face, but . . ."

"I get it," he said.

"We should go back."

"You understand how vital it is that you compose yourself when we go back in there?" he said.

She tried to control her breathing. *Forget the gun. For now.*

"Remember you told me you used to pretend to be someone else?" he said. "Can you do that again?"

"OK."

This would test her acting skills like never before. This wasn't about escaping her life. It was about deciding if another man lived or died.

"Do you need more time?"

"No. We don't want to arouse any suspicion."

"I'm with you, every step of the way."

"Let's go. I'm ready."

James led her through the glass door and back into the hotel lobby. The sounds of Beethoven's Fifth bled from the dining room. He held the door for her. Her eyes were drawn to the man behind the piano like magnets. She kept upright, ignoring the pain inside her, and proceeded to the table. They took their seats. Their food had arrived. And then the music ended.

"Keep your head down," James said. "He's coming over."

"Hello, folks," the man said in English. "I haven't had the pleasure yet."

She was struggling to breathe but managed to speak somehow. "Good to meet you," she said.

"My name is Richard Klement. I'm the owner of the hotel. I believe I have you two to thank for helping my daughter last night."

"It was our pleasure, Señor Klement. She's a charming girl. I'm James Murphy, and this is my fiancée, Liliana Andolini."

"Wonderful to meet you. I believe you had some trouble, Liliana. My sincere apologies."

"That's quite all right." His eyes were different than she remembered—still the palest blue, but somehow changed. He looked younger than forty-six, and had a beard now. He was also less wiry and fit than he had been. But his voice was enough. Christ. She'd heard it in her nightmares for twelve years. "I'm fine now," she continued.

"We're just sorry we missed you playing," James added.

"I'm not finished for the evening. I just had to see how the señorita was doing. Perhaps later you'd allow me the pleasure of joining you for a drink, on me, of course?"

"That sounds like an excellent suggestion. We'd love to."

"It's settled. Until later." Klement bowed and made his way back to the piano.

They waited until the music started before they spoke.

"Are you sure?"

"I think so. He's changed, but his voice . . ."

James reached into his pocket for his cigarettes, holding the pack up to her. "Take one."

"Not now."

"Take one. You need it."

She did as he asked and leaned across the table to light it. She felt frozen in time. *Jesus, what do I look like? Did he see?* If James weren't here, the man at the piano would be dead already. Dead as winter leaves.

They sat there for the next twenty minutes or so, talking little. She tried not to stare, but it was impossible not to. The man seemed not to notice, more focused on the piano keys. Doubt crept into her mind as she watched him, but every time he opened his mouth to speak, those same doubts disappeared like raindrops in a pond. The music ended, and Klement stood to take the applause of the dozen or so diners who'd stayed. He thanked the people at each table personally and ended at theirs.

"I hope I'm not interrupting," he said as he pulled up a chair.

"Not at all. You play well," James said.

"My father lit the flame in me, many years ago."

"Was he a professional musician?"

"No. A civil servant, but he dabbled."

"I love the hotel," Liliana said. *I'm an heiress, on a business trip with my fiancé.* "We own some hotels ourselves in America. Beautiful site, with the lake views. How long have you been here?"

"We bought the hotel in '52. It took a few months to get it into shape, but we had it ready for ski season that year. I'm glad you like it."

"We were looking to purchase some property in the area. This would be ideal."

"Give the man a chance—he just sat down, and you're already trying to buy him out!" James said.

Klement laughed and motioned for another whisky. "It wouldn't be the first offer, but my answer is always the same—it's not for sale."

She sipped her wine. "I had to ask, Señor Klement."

She tried to dispel the thoughts of her family, of blood and death on Monte Sole from her mind. Those memories would do their cause no good here. It was exhausting to concentrate on every word, on every gesture that he made, and the adrenaline she'd felt earlier upon first hearing his voice was draining from her system. At one moment she was sure that Werner Brack sat in front of her, but the next, a niggling voice in the back of her mind cast the shadow of doubt.

"Forgive my fiancée. She has a mind for business, even when we're on vacation."

"A kindred spirit."

Klement's drink came and he raised it. "Here's to profiting from the good business decisions, and to surviving the bad ones."

"I'll drink to that," she said. They toasted and took a sip.

"So what brought you to Bariloche?" James said. "The German influences are apparent, but was there any other reason?"

"I'd been in Buenos Aires for years. I grew weary of the big city and longed for the countryside."

How many dozens of times have you used that line? "How long were you in Buenos Aires?" she said.

He motioned to James's cigarettes on the table. "Could I have one of those?"

"Of course."

He lit the cigarette and sat back in the chair. "We arrived when Alexandra was a baby."

He seemed relaxed, confident, and to be enjoying the conversation. Was he analyzing what they were asking him like she was? Had others come searching for him? Perhaps this was something the Nazis here dealt with every so often. There might have been a protocol they used for those seeking justice.

"You were able to travel during the war?"

"It was just before, in summer 1939. I didn't like the way things were going."

"I can see why," James said. "Were you always in the hotel business?"

"No, not at all. I was a teacher in Germany, but I decided to get into something more lucrative. One has to make such decisions when the children come."

"We hope to have our own someday."

"They're a blessing. I used the money from my inheritance to buy this place and never looked back. I'd never do anything else now. We're happy. My son, Carlos, was born here."

"It seems like you could transplant this town to Germany or Austria, and no one would notice any difference between it and the other places there," Liliana said.

"We have a proud tradition here."

"Alexandra gave us some of the history," Liliana said. "She's in a German-speaking school?"

"As I said, we are proud of our heritage."

"Do you have any family still in Germany?" James said.

"Two brothers, although I don't write as much as I should. You've reminded me now."

"This site is truly breathtaking. I must admit that I'm disappointed you wouldn't consider selling it."

"This is my family home—I intend to retire here and hand it off to my children someday."

"There's nothing more important than family," Liliana said.

"Do you have family in Italy?"

I never said I was Italian, she thought. It must have been the accent. That was explainable.

"Yes. My two sisters, Lena and Martina, are both in Bologna. Have you been there?"

"No. Never. I hear it's quite lovely."

Why did I mention my sisters' names in front of this monster? Speaking about them like this gave them life in her mind, and just for a second she imagined what she'd said was true, and they were alive and living in Bologna. Reality intervened seconds later.

"You seem tired. Why don't you go to bed, darling?" James said.

"No. We're just getting to know Señor Klement."

"Richard, please."

"I'll stay here with Richard awhile," James said. "I think it's best if you go to bed so you're fresh for our day tomorrow."

He was right. This was more than she could take right now. The chair screeched on the tiled floor as she stood up. "It was a pleasure to meet you, Richard."

"It was a pleasure to meet you, Liliana. I look forward to speaking again tomorrow." He took her hand. It was all she could manage not to snatch it back from him.

"Yes, of course," she said and turned to walk away. She reached the stairs when James appeared beside her.

"I'm sorry. You looked like you'd seen a ghost."

"I think I did."

"Leave this to me. I'll talk to him awhile."

"OK." The urge to kiss him came like a wave. Somehow it felt like the natural thing to do. She resisted it.

"Go to bed. I'll set everything in motion. I'll gain his trust, and we'll find out exactly who Richard Klement is."

He hugged her, and she made her way up the stairs.

CHAPTER 18

James watched her ascend the stairs, amazed at her fortitude, but dubious about her detective work. Some of the things Klement had said were suspicious, but nothing that couldn't be explained. His wife's name was the same, but his daughter's wasn't, and he hadn't come to Argentina after the war, but before. If he was telling the truth. Perhaps he was a Nazi. Maybe they all were. James went back to the dining room. Klement stood to introduce his wife as James got back to the table.

"I believe you've already met my lovely wife, Ingrid."

"Nice to see you again, señora." James shook her hand. The dining room was empty. Ingrid had a glass of red wine on the table in front of her.

"Is your fiancée all right?" she asked.

"Yes, she's just a little tired. I'm sure a good night's rest is all she needs."

"James and his fiancée were inquiring as to whether we were interested in selling the hotel."

"You were?"

"I informed him that we never would."

"Of course."

"And I told your husband how sorry I was to hear that," James said. "Can I ask you a question? You live so far away from where you're from. Do you miss home?"

Ingrid's clothes looked expensive and new. *Business must be good.*

"I do, but we've made a fine life here."

"Do you have family in Germany? Richard told me about his brothers."

"I have two sisters. My brother died on the Eastern Front during the war."

Even if Liliana was wrong about Klement, Ingrid's apparent deceitfulness was still worth investigating. Maybe it was their facial expressions or the way they talked, but these people were hiding something. He just wasn't sure what.

"I'm sorry," he added.

"It was such a waste."

Klement puffed on a cigarette.

"Your husband told me you came here before the war?"

"That's right."

"Was that because of Nazi policy?"

"In part. We could see war clouds forming on the horizon. We got out just in time. Many people didn't. I can only imagine living under the yoke of Soviet rule."

Klement stubbed out his cigarette. "How much of our beautiful town have you seen so far, James?"

"Some. I'd like to take a hike into the mountains tomorrow."

"It's beautiful. Ski season is over now, but it's spectacular."

"I told you we were looking to purchase property," James said. "The only problem is we don't know anyone here. So I have a proposition for you, Richard."

"I'm listening."

"How about you help us out? You know the town better than most, I'm sure. You're a member of the German Argentinean Cultural Association, aren't you?"

"I'm vice president. How did you know?"

"Alexandra is a friendly girl."

"That she is," Ingrid said.

"We're going to need some help in finding a suitable property. You're a man with business connections, and you know the town. We'd be glad to pay you a finder's fee."

"Why here, in a city you've never been to, in a country you're not from?" Richard asked.

"Why did you?"

"I already lived in Argentina."

"You could go back to Germany tomorrow. The country's rebuilding, and the threat from the Soviets has diminished."

"You're being naïve," Ingrid said. "The Soviets are more dangerous than ever now. The Allies helped them get away with murder at the end of the war."

Said like a true Nazi. "Is that the reason you live here? The Soviets?"

"No. Don't listen to my wife; she doesn't concern herself with politics."

"It sounds to me like—"

"Perhaps you could lock up the basement, Ingrid."

"Of course," she said.

"Good night," James said. He stood and kissed her on the cheek.

"She's a good woman," Richard said, "but I have no idea what's going to come out of her mouth from one moment to the next. Don't listen to that nonsense about the Soviets. We moved here because I didn't want my family involved in the war. We stay here because we've made a successful life." He picked up his empty whisky glass. "You never answered my question."

"What question?"

"Why do you want to buy here, in a city you don't know?"

"Ah," James said. "We're weary of the hustle and bustle of New York. We both speak the language. Liliana fell in love with the place from afar. It's what she wants to do. Easier to change the earth's rotation than a woman's mind."

"You don't need to remind me of that. I'd be happy to help you in your quest. I'll even negotiate on your behalf."

"You could do that?"

"I have a lot of sway as vice president of the German Argentinean Cultural Association."

"Wonderful. I look forward to working with you," James said.

"Perhaps I'll have one more drink. Are you sure you won't have one?" Klement said.

"Not for me."

"I admire a man with self-control," Klement said as he left the table. James lit another cigarette, staring at the gray smoke, thinking about what Ingrid had said.

Liliana was still awake, sitting on the bed fully clothed, when he entered the hotel room an hour later. He hung his jacket over the chair and braced for impact.

"What did he say?" she asked.

"He accepted. We're going to start looking for properties tomorrow."

"All right."

He took out his wallet, matches, and cigarettes and placed them on the table by the wall.

"You believe me, don't you?" she said.

"Maybe."

"What do you mean 'maybe'? It's him."

"Klement doesn't look like the man in the military file you showed me, but there were things the wife said."

"Such as?"

"Like living in fear of the hordes of Reds from the East. She talked like a Nazi. His story seemed solid, but hers . . ."

"He's a skilled liar." She looked at him. "And he's changed. That beard hides his face, but it's him, James. I need to know you're with me . . . I can't do this on my own."

He wanted to believe her. He wanted her to be right but wouldn't persecute an innocent man to appease her. He would help her investigate him but wouldn't let himself be swayed by her emotions. Logic and diligence would lead him on their quest. And if Klement was Brack, they would act. If he wasn't, he would be the key to the door of the coven of Nazis that seemed to exist in plain sight here.

"I'm with you. We'll find out exactly who Richard Klement is."

He went into the bathroom to get changed for bed. He heard the sound of the hotel room door closing, and when he came out, she was gone. He had the thought to go after her but realized he had to trust her and settled down on his blankets on the floor to go to sleep.

CHAPTER 19

James was breathing hard by the time he crested the hill. The lake shimmered aquamarine below them, surrounded by lush green. Snow-dusted mountains rose up in the distance, extending to a cobalt sky. He put down his backpack and took out a canteen. He could feel the sweat on his face.

"Spectacular, isn't it?" Klement said from behind him.

"I can see why you decided to settle here."

"It was love at first sight for me—something I'd never believed in before."

The overarching silence seemed to envelop them. James's mind was back on Monte Sole, with Karoton, Jock, Gianni, and Lupo.

"All this, just a thirty-minute hike from the town," Klement continued. "And there are dozens, hundreds of vistas just like this one. It's a true outdoor wonderland, a natural playground."

"I have my fiancée to thank for taking me here."

"Is she OK on her own? I feel I've been keeping you from her these last few afternoons."

"She's not a hiker. Lounging down by the lake is more her style."

"It's beautiful there, but the water is cold—glacier runoff."

"Noted."

He put his bottle back into his backpack. Klement was a hard man to read. Opaque. James had spent the last three afternoons with him, hiking trails to possible sites to build fictitious hotels in the mountains above the city. Richard hadn't revealed anything about his past. He deflected all of James's subtle questions with the deft touch of an experienced politician. He never queried who his guests were, or if they had the kind of money to make the purchases they spent most of their conversations on. His apparent lack of a past was suspicious in and of itself, but perhaps, like many Germans and Austrians, he was eager to move on from the failure of the Nazi regime.

"I'm fascinated by the German-speaking school."

"It's a good school. Alexandra values the traditions I hold dear. I raised her that way, and Carlos will be the same." He stared out at the horizon for a few seconds. "She's a special girl—the light of my life." Something else came over him. Something James hadn't seen before. "I think of her when I come here. This view is the only thing that compares to the beauty I see in her."

"She's a wonderful girl." James let his words settle before he spoke again. "I'd love to have a look around her school."

"There's no property to buy there—just classrooms where the students happen to speak German."

"I know, but I'd like to see it."

"I could speak to the principal on your behalf and arrange a tour if you'd like. Let's go. I have someone I want you to meet."

Klement set off down the path. James shouldered his pack and followed. They walked in silence until they made town.

"Let's stop off before we head back to the hotel." Klement led him to a small chocolate shop. They pushed through the door, and a bell rang out. The sweet smell of chocolate was thick in the air. "This is Franz Rostock," he said. "Franz, this is James Murphy."

A middle-aged man in a white apron greeted James with a bone-crushing handshake.

"You like chocolate?"

"Does anyone ever say no to that?"

"There are some strange people around," Rostock answered with a hearty laugh.

"Wait until you try some," Klement said. "You'll never taste better."

Rostock produced a plate with samples, and James took a large piece.

"You weren't kidding. This is the best chocolate I've ever had."

"What did I tell you?"

The two men looked on with pride. A few minutes later the three men went out back to have a smoke in the evening sun. James resisted the temptation to ask Rostock about his past. Instead, he sat back as the two men spoke in Spanish for his benefit. He tried to imagine Klement doing the things Liliana was so sure he'd done. It was impossible to know. He wanted her to be right. He wanted to extract a confession from Brack, to expose him and the other Nazis here as the fraudulent scum of the earth they were. He wanted to believe her. Desperately. But sometimes the level of her conviction scared him. Had the years obsessing about this man driven her over the edge? Making sure that Richard Klement wouldn't fall victim to the traumas that she had suffered had to be a priority.

The evening sun was warm on Liliana's face as she walked through the town. She felt alone. Every stranger on the street was a potential enemy. *How do I discern the evil from the mundane here? Perhaps they're one and the same now.* Those who had committed unspeakable evil had taken on the guise of the ordinary person now, but that didn't change who they were or what they'd done. She couldn't stand being around Klement. The mere sight of him made her feel physically ill, so they split responsibilities. James would deal with him—making excuses for her—and she handled everything else. Three days had passed since the performance in the dining room. She had been alone for much of that time. James was on another long hike with Klement that afternoon.

Their host seemed to take pride in walking to the houses and hunting lodges in the mountains around the city. James remained skeptical about what she knew—that this man was Werner Brack—but he was determined to find out whatever Klement knew about the Nazis in the city. The Austrian SS man had yet to crack.

She made her way to Gold's office on Ángel Gallardo Avenue and knocked on the glass window. Albert Gold lifted his head. She pushed the door open.

"Miss Andolini," he said. "To what do I owe this pleasure today? Have you been enjoying the sights of our wonderful town?"

"I've spent a lot of time by the lake. The tranquility there is a sharp contrast to New York."

"Bariloche is a terrific place to raise children."

She took a seat opposite the real estate agent's desk. "I'd like to rent a house—somewhere remote. Somewhere we wouldn't be bothered."

"I thought you were looking to buy."

"We want to find the perfect place. It might take some time. We're going to rent in the meantime."

"OK. I have some places you might be interested in."

Liliana paused before speaking. *Can I trust this man?* They were going to need help from a local. No one else came close to being trustworthy. *How could the Nazis hold sway over this man?*

"You may want to close the shop for the conversation we're about to have."

Gold got up and locked the door before returning to his desk.

"What can I help you with?"

"I was in Italy during the war."

"Where?"

"I'm from a place called Monte Sole, just south of Bologna. There's no one there anymore. The people there were . . . eradicated by the Nazis. I'm one of the last."

It felt good to tell him—to reveal at least part of the truth she was hiding.

"I was wondering when you'd come," Gold said.

"When I'd come?"

"Or someone like you."

"I'm here to do what the police and the governments won't—to find the man who ordered the deaths of my family."

"And you think that man is here?"

"I've already met him."

"Who is he?" Gold said, but stood up before she could answer. "You know what? Don't tell me. I can't be involved. I have family here."

She wondered if he'd say the same if he'd seen what she had. No one could understand what she was feeling unless they'd experienced it themselves. Only James knew what she'd been through.

And she was going to betray his trust. A cold blanket of doubt draped across her. The internal monologue started up once more, distracting her from the man in front of her. She dragged herself back into the moment.

"Do you want a cup of coffee?" Gold said.

She replied that she would, and he went into the back, emerging with two mugs a minute later. He put the coffee in front of her and sat back down. She took a sip and started in again.

"How well do you know the German immigrants here?"

"I know some of them. Not well, but a little. They're good people."

"What of the influx after the war?"

"I'm sure many were legitimate refugees," Gold said. "I'm also sure some were not. The thought doesn't sit easily with me. I lost cousins to the Nazis, my aunt and uncle also."

She wouldn't find a better ally than this man. "And you're able to live among them?"

"I don't know who they are. I haven't tried to find out," he said. "But you have. You say the man who ordered your family killed is here."

Liliana nodded. "I need some advice, and I need a cabin."

"I can't be an accomplice to anything illegal."

"I'll pay cash, weeks in advance." She reached into her bag for a money clip filled with bills and placed it on the table. "I'll give a fake name. The police aren't going to come after you."

"It's not the police I'm worried about."

"If you can't help me . . ."

"I didn't say that," Gold corrected. "What are you planning to do?"

"I need him to admit what he did. I need him to look me in the eyes and confess. That will be enough." It was funny how the more she repeated this lie the easier it became to say it.

"That will be enough?"

"There was a time when it wouldn't have been, but now, yes," she lied.

Gold opened a drawer, took out a whisky bottle and two glasses. He poured without asking.

"You intend to use the property you rent from me to extract the confession from this man?"

"Yes."

"And then let him go?"

"Yes."

He pushed the glass over to her. She took a sip. It burned all the way down to her stomach.

"And how long do you expect this process to take?"

"A few hours."

"I'm assuming your man was a hardened soldier?" Gold asked. "Most likely an SS man. You think he's going to hold his hands up and confess easily? He won't believe a confession will be enough. I hardly do."

His words jarred her. *If he hardly believes me, what does James truly think?* "My friend is a journalist. He's going to expose the Nazis hiding here. Then it'll be up to the Allied governments to act. We need a source. Someone who can expose these people."

"You want that source to be me?"

"You'd remain anonymous. My friend needs to interview you, on the record, about nights like this." She pushed the photograph of the Nazis across to Gold.

He looked at the picture for a few seconds. "I know some people. I could speak to the owner of the hotel that hired this room out. But back to your man. What about when his family comes looking for him?"

"My friend is gaining his trust. He thinks we're looking to buy a hotel in the area. We're going to ask him to come away with us for a night. That should give us the time we need."

"What about your escape?"

"That's where you come in, or at least your advice."

Gold reached into a drawer and took out several folders.

"We have some remote cabins. But this man will be missed. These people are a tight-knit group. They look after their own. And do you think once he's given his confession, *if* he does, that he'll just let you leave?"

"What about the Chilean border?"

"It's almost three hours away."

"Three hours? But we're only forty-five kilometers from the border."

"And if you were a bird, you could fly there, but it's all wilderness. There are no direct roads. You're going to need to find another way." Gold picked up a pencil and tapped it on the desk. "How much money do you have?"

"A lot."

"I know a man with a seaplane," he said. "He lands it on the lake, takes the richest tourists for sightseeing tours of the mountains."

"Would he wait for us? Would he remain ready?"

"For the right price."

"How about ten thousand American dollars?"

"I'd imagine that would do it."

Gold took a hard pull on his whisky and then lit a cigarette.

"I have no intention of putting my family in danger," he said. "Let me organize the seaplane, and I have a property that should be ideal for your purposes. I just need to know you're not going to use it for . . ."

"I'm not going to kill him. I don't want to die here or end up in a jail cell."

If James doesn't want to flee with me, I'll go alone. If that's what he chooses, he can fend for himself. The thought of that—of deserting him—stabbed at her insides like a red-hot blade. *Perhaps he'll see sense—that I have to do this.*

Gold stood up and went to a filing cabinet. He took out a sheet of paper with a photograph of a cabin attached to it. "This cabin is far enough out that no one will come by. It's best you don't rent it, and you just go there. I'll give you a key you can dispose of. It should look like you broke in without my help."

"I understand."

"When are you planning on doing this?"

"As soon as our man agrees to come away for the night. The day after tomorrow, most likely."

Gold produced a key and a map from his desk drawer. "Take these. You'll have to find your own way up to the cabin. I'll call my friend with the seaplane. He'll require money up front."

"I'll give him half and then the rest when we're away."

She took several rolls of notes from her bag and laid them on the desk.

"I see you came prepared."

"That's five thousand," she said.

"He'll agree once he sees the money. You can contact him directly after that. I don't want my fingerprints on whatever it is you're planning."

"I won't mention you, no matter what happens."

"I wish you luck on your quest. I hope you find what you're looking for."

"Thank you, Señor Gold—for all your help. I can pay you for your trouble."

"That won't be necessary," he said. "Just promise me you won't do anything stupid."

"You have my word."

Ingrid Klement greeted Liliana as she arrived back at the hotel. *Her face seems to hide a myriad of truths.* Getting to those truths without raising suspicion would be the trick.

"Are the men back yet?" Liliana said.

"Not quite. I'm expecting them anytime now, though."

"It seems like James has been gone for weeks."

"Just between you and me, it won't get any better when you're married," Ingrid said as she shuffled some papers on the desk. "Will you be joining us in the dining room this evening?"

"I think we'll be dining out tonight."

"Very well."

"Perhaps we'll catch the end of Richard's performance later. I noticed the sign that he'll be playing tonight."

"Yes."

The front door opened behind them, and James and Klement walked in. James went to her, kissing her on the cheek.

"How was your day, dear?"

"Marvelous. How was yours?"

"This town, this area, is truly a wonder," James said.

"I'm ready to do some hiking myself, at last," Liliana said and turned to Klement. "Did James fill you in about our plans for tomorrow? We'd love for you to come."

"I believe there's a hotel in San Martín de los Andes you want to see?" Klement said.

"Yes," James said.

"It's too far to go there and back in one day, so we'll be staying the night, returning in the morning," Klement told his wife.

"If that's OK with you, Ingrid?" James said.

"I suppose so," she said.

"Our friends here are making it worth my while," Klement said, "and I look forward to spending the time enjoying their company."

"As you wish, Richard."

CHAPTER 20

Liliana woke early. It was paramount that no one see her smuggle the bags downstairs to the car. They weren't checking out, but they'd never see this hotel again. She had paid in cash, another week in advance. *We'll be long gone by then.* She'd called the pilot Gold had recommended the day before, and they'd met him after dinner. The plane would be ready. He would have it in place this evening.

The light of sunrise was creeping below the curtains. She drew them open to reveal the freezing waters of Nahuel Huapí Lake. The bags were packed. The gun was in her suitcase, tucked under her clothes.

She thought of her family. *Who would they be now if the Nazis hadn't come? Who would I be?* Her father would still be working the land, scraping a living from the gray soil of Monte Sole. Her mother would surely be as strong as she'd ever been, tending to the house and baking the bread Liliana could almost smell. *I'm twelve thousand kilometers away, but I never left.* Her sisters. *What would my sisters be doing now?* Would they have submitted to the male-dominated world of Monte Sole? Would they have spawned a dozen children between them? It was hard to imagine them submitting to middle age before they were twenty-eight, like her mother and grandmother had. No. They would have embraced the modern world. She pictured her and her sisters coming back from the city to the old house, their parents coming out to greet them. She felt her family with her and wallowed in their love until the visions fell away like water through her fingers.

James left the room first, then came back to tell her the way was clear. She walked in front of him down the stairs, the suitcases hidden by her body. He deposited the cases in the trunk, and she went back for the rest. James went to the dining room. She heard him speaking to Klement as she passed. The door to their room was open, and the last case was on the bed. She took it and closed the door behind her. Several other guests descended the stairs in front of her, impeding her progress. Alexandra was at the bottom of the stairs in her school uniform.

"You're not leaving us, are you?"

"No. We're just going away for the night. Your father is coming with us to check out a property we're interested in."

She seems oblivious to who her father is. How could a monster like Brack have raised someone like her? Her brother appeared beside her in the same uniform and said something to her in German.

"Have you met Carlos yet?"

"No. I haven't." She put the suitcase down. "How old are you?"

The boy looked up at her with gray-blue eyes. "I'm six. How old are you?"

"I'm thirty-two."

"We'd best be getting off to school now," Alexandra said.

"Of course."

"Will I see you and Mr. Murphy tomorrow?"

"I expect so." The lies tore at her. This girl would know. She'd always know the woman who killed her father. The fact that he deserved it wouldn't matter to her.

"Until later, then. Perhaps we can go down to the lake with Carlos."

"Yes. That would be great." The two children left without another word. Liliana paced away, shoving the door open, and was outside again. She put the last bag in the car, taking a few seconds to breathe. *Her father is a monster. She and her brother will be better off without him.*

She took as long as she dared by the car before making her way back inside.

James was at the breakfast table with Klement, and both men stood up to greet her.

"Are you ready for our hike today?" Klement said.

"I'm not sure," she replied. "There's a property we want to show you before we head to San Martín de los Andes, but it's a two-hour hike up the mountain. I can drive and meet you there." She took out a map and pointed to it, making sure no one else could see.

"Too much for you?"

"I'll leave the sweating to you two. I'll meet you up there at about eleven?"

"And we can make our way to San Martín de los Andes from there," James said.

"I'm looking forward to seeing this place." Klement stuffed a piece of bread into his mouth. "I haven't spent much time in that area."

"We're excited," she said. The knife in her hand shook as she held it, so she put it down.

"We'll set off after breakfast. We should be there to meet you on time."

"I'll prepare the way."

They sat there talking for another ten minutes. The effort of focusing on the small talk of the sights they'd see and the area was almost too much for her, and it was with some relief that she excused herself.

The men set out a few minutes after breakfast, and she said goodbye to James with a kiss. She stood on the street a few seconds to make sure they weren't returning. She went back to the hotel room. It was impossible to wait there. Impossible to sit or stay still.

The road to the cabin wound out of town and up the mountain. All signs of civilization, apart from the rough-hewn dirt road she was driving on, disappeared. They had come up here yesterday after meeting with the pilot. The cabin would be perfect for whatever was about to happen. *Don't forget what Gold said—he isn't going to confess readily. He has other Nazis to protect.* Turning over the stone would expose the entire nest. Her promise to James drifted into her mind. She saw the innocent faces of Carlos and Alexandra, waiting at the bottom of the stairs in the hotel. *I'm still better than him, even if I do this, better than all of the murderers. I just wish I could honor my word to James, give us the chance of a future.*

She brought the car to a stop on the dirt track outside the one-story cabin. The woods started a meter from the sides and back of the house. She pushed the front door open. They had left it unlocked overnight, and she had left the key in Gold's mailbox. The sparse interior of the cabin was untouched—a table, chairs, a couch, and an empty bookshelf. A thin layer of dust came off the table where she touched it with her finger. Silence. She went to the small veranda at the front of the house and sat on the step. Waiting.

Klement assured James that he knew where they were, knew where they were going, but James wasn't so sure. They had been hiking for more than two hours. The two men had settled into a comfortable silence, or so it seemed. *Is this man Werner Brack?* The photograph of the Nazis at Hitler's birthday settled into the forefront of his conscious mind. The resemblance seemed flimsy, yet Liliana had no doubt. *What am I doing? What if this is an innocent man?* It would be up to him to prevent Liliana from doing something they both might regret. He would be the arbitrator, the defense counsel, even. *Every human being deserves that much. He's a human being. He's at least that.*

James pushed an overgrown branch out of his way to reveal a glint of sunshine and a clearing that he recognized. It wasn't far now. They could both end up in jail for this. Would the confession be enough for Liliana? It would have to be. *Do I have to choose between the woman I love and an innocent man's life?*

They pushed through the trees that lined the trail and saw the car parked outside the cabin.

"Looks like she beat us here," Klement said.

James was running down Monte Sole, the wind blowing in his face, the submachine gun in his hand. *Be here now. Answer the man.*

"Yes. She's probably inside. Let's have a look."

"Why would you want to buy this place?" Klement said, looking around. "I thought you wanted somewhere bigger, more commercial? This place is in the middle of nowhere."

He wasn't moving.

"Buy this place? No, but it's a good site. Let's go inside and take a look. Liliana said she'd bring a packed lunch for us."

"I have my own."

"This is Liliana's idea. Can you humor her a little? You're married. You know how it is."

"Only too well."

James walked him up the two steps to the veranda and inside. The place smelled musty. The windows were closed, the curtains drawn. A single white wooden chair sat in the middle of the floor, the other furniture moved back away from it.

"Not exactly luxury accom—"

Liliana stepped out from behind the door. She was holding the gun in two hands, pointing it at his head.

"What is this? What's going on?"

"Take a seat," Liliana said.

Klement looked at James. "Did you know about this?"

James took his backpack off, placing it in the corner.

"What is this about? Who are you people?"

Liliana took another step forward. "Take a seat."

"What are you going to do?"

She raised the gun. "Make me ask again. See what happens."

He took off his backpack and sat down. "I don't know who you think I am—"

"Shut up. There'll be time for all that. James, get the rope. Make sure you tie it good and tight."

"James, please tell me what's going on. This can't be your doing."

James took the ropes she handed him. He tied Klement's hands first, and then his legs and chest to the chair. Klement didn't speak.

"Do you remember me?"

"What? No. What are you talking about?"

"Do you remember the cemetery at Casaglia?"

"What? Where? Untie me." He struggled against the ropes. The chair rocked back and forth on the wood floor. James put his hands on the back of it to hold it in place.

"Do you remember my family? They were among the old men, women, and children that you herded into that little walled cemetery. My mother, my teenage sisters, my grandparents, my aunt, and my cousins."

"I don't know who you think I am—"

"I'm doing the talking now." She whipped the gun barrel across his cheek. Blood splattered the metal and ran down his face.

"Liliana," James said. She brushed him off, her eyes fixed on the man in the chair.

"You ordered them into the cemetery. You had your men set up machine guns and then ordered that they open fire."

Her hands are shaking so much, James worried. *That gun's going to go off.*

A tear rolled down her reddened cheek. "You murdered them. You murdered them all."

"I don't know what you're talking about. I wasn't in the war. I was in Argentina. I've been here since 1939."

"My sister Martina was sixteen. Lena was fifteen. They were beautiful. They were full of life and wonder, and you killed them."

"What is she talking about? She's insane."

"Tell the truth," James said. "That's all she's looking for. If you can do that, we all get to walk away from here."

"She's out of her mind."

"I wouldn't say that again if I were you," James said. She hit him with the pistol again, and his head rocked back.

"Please, I don't know what you're talking about. I'm sorry your family died in the war, but—"

"So you're sorry?" She held the gun centimeters from his face. "Look at me. I said LOOK AT ME!"

"Calm down," James said. "Let him speak." *This is her moment, but what do I do? Take the gun? Is she going to kill him? No. She promised me.* It was hard to tell the difference in his mind between something he wanted to believe and what he thought was actually true.

"Your name is Werner Brack. You were born in Penzing, just outside Vienna, in 1910, the eldest son of a composer, but you weren't the one who inherited Daddy's gift. Your brother, Klaus, did. He was the one who got to live the musician's lifestyle."

"I don't know who you're talking about."

She punched him, bloodying his lip. His face was already a bloody mess, his shirt stained red at the collar. "Don't interrupt. You left university in 1932, graduated top of your class. A career as a captain of industry beckoned, but something changed. You moved to Germany in 1934 to join the SS, met Ingrid, the pretty daughter of a local businessman, and married. You served with distinction in France, and then Russia, before being sent to Italy with the Sixteenth Waffen-SS Division in the summer of 1944. Your men adored you. They followed your every whim, even when you ordered them to open fire on my family in that cemetery."

"I've never heard of this 'Brack,' I swear to you. I don't know who you're—"

She hit him with the gun again. His blood was on her hand now. He tried to kick out at her but only succeeded in making the chair shift forward a few centimeters. James grabbed him by the shoulders from behind.

"Liar!" she said.

"You're accusing me of being this monster, but how am I meant to defend myself when you won't let me speak?"

"Admit what you did." She pressed the gun barrel into his forehead. "Confess to the murder of my family."

"Stop. Enough." James took her by the arm. "This is useless."

"Listen to him," Klement spat. "I'm not this SS man, or whoever you think I am. I was here during the war. I was in Buenos Aires. I don't know you. I've never seen you or your family before in my life. I can prove it. I can prove I was here."

She shrugged James off and shoved the barrel of the gun into Klement's cheek. "If you lie again, I'll kill you, do you understand? Confess. I need to hear you say the truth."

"How can I confess to something I haven't done?"

James took her arm again. "Stop. We need to talk." She fought against him, but he put a firm arm around her chest, pulling her away. "Stop." He tried to hug her, but she pushed him away. *She's losing it. This needs to end.* "Can we talk? Just for a moment?"

"Please reason with her. She's out of her mind. I have a wife and children."

James took her by her ice-cold hand and led her past the car, only stopping to turn to her once he was sure they were out of earshot.

"It's him," she said. "I've never been surer of anything."

"More sure than you were before?"

"I'm positive now. Did you see the look in his eye? The recognition when he saw me?"

"No, I didn't."

"He's trying to protect the other Nazis in Bariloche. He knows that if he confesses, we'll expose all of them," she said.

A wind blew through the trees and the sun disappeared behind a thick veil of cloud. "You haven't told him that you'll spare him if he confesses. All you've done so far is demand he admits to killing your family. He probably thinks the only chance he has of staying alive is denying it—if he is Werner Brack at all."

"So you think I'm insane too."

"I didn't say that."

"I know that is the man who killed my family and all those others. I'm not crazy."

"I know you're not crazy. I know that. I want you to be right. I want you to resolve this, to leave all this behind and get on with your life in peace. I won't let you become like Brack, whether that's him sitting in that cabin or not."

"Leave if you have to."

"Don't do that. I'm here with you. I've been here all the way, and I'm not leaving now. All I'm saying is that we have to give him a chance to speak. If that man in the chair is Brack, he's changed a lot physically in the last twelve years."

"That's not impossible."

"No, it's not, but if it is him, let's at least find out. Offer him the deal."

"And he dies if he doesn't."

"I can't allow that."

She lifted the gun—stared at it—wiped the blood off the nickel plating. "I don't want to kill anyone . . ."

"Let's hear him out. His story will either hold up or fall apart. If it falls apart—"

"He's guilty."

"Yes."

She went to the car, opened the trunk. A tire iron lay on the dirty fabric.

"Can you get that?"

"Why?"

"We have to show him we're serious."

"Pistol-whipping him didn't cover that?"

"OK, I'll get it myself."

She twisted the tire iron in her hand a couple of times and walked back toward the house. James followed her inside. Klement was where they'd left him—bloodied and tied to the chair.

"What are you going to do with that?"

"Whatever you force me to."

"If you confess to being Werner Brack and to the crimes he committed, we'll let you live. We will leave, and you'll never see us again. I'll place an anonymous phone call to the hotel and have someone come and get you once we're away."

"I've told you already, how can I confess to something I haven't done?" She raised the tire iron. "Wait! Wait!" he shouted. "I can prove it. I can prove I'm not that man you say I am. Stop!"

James took the tire iron from her hand.

"How can you prove that?"

"I was working in the German embassy in Buenos Aires from 1941 to the end of the war. I left when I got a job in a local business."

"What business?" James said.

"I was an accountant for a machine parts factory."

"What was the company called?"

"Hershing."

She tried to grab the tire iron back, but James kept hold of it.

"What was the address?"

"Pinto 4844, in Vicente López. It's not there anymore. They went under after I left."

"Who was the owner?"

"His name was Alvaro Brown. He was Paraguayan, Irish descent. He died in '51. I was at the funeral."

James let the tire iron fall to the floor with a clunk. "That's a good cover story, but where's the proof?"

"Call the embassy, ask for Rudolf Kocher. He was my boss, and the only person still working there that would know me."

"How do you know he's still there?" James said.

"We're friends. He was in the hotel in June for ski season with his family. Call him and end this fiasco. I'm sorry about your family, but I'm not this man you think I am."

"What do you think?" James said.

"I think he's put some work into his cover story," she said.

"I'd like to make the phone call," James said.

"How do we know he hasn't set this up with some friend at the embassy? You said the diplomats were involved in getting war criminals over here."

"I did, and that's true. It could be part of his cover, but it could also be the truth. I can find out by making the call."

"There's no phone here."

"I'll drive back to town," James said.

"You can't leave me here with her. She's crazy."

"I can trust you when I leave, can't I? You're not going to do anything stupid?"

"I won't hurt him. I'll wait for you to get back," she said.

"OK, then. Señor Klement, if that's your real name, I'm going to take a trip back to town. I should be back within the hour. If your story checks out—"

"What? What if my story checks out?"

"We'll see." He went for the door. "Oh, and I wouldn't rile her if I were you."

James walked through the open door into the dull afternoon outside. She was by his side as he reached the car. She put the keys into his palm.

"I love you." The words spilled out of his mouth as if he had no control over them. He opened the car door. "I didn't think I'd say that to anyone again . . . and certainly not like this."

"I love you too," she said, her voice weak. A tear came down her face.

He kissed her. "Don't do anything until I get back. No matter what he says. In fact, you might be better off waiting outside, not talking to him at all."

"You'd best be on your way."

He kissed her on the forehead and got into the car.

She watched the car disappear around the curve, enveloped by the trees overhanging the dirt track. Why did she say that to James? *I'm such an idiot. My feelings don't matter.* Maybe this needed to happen before James came back. It might be best if she was gone when he arrived. The urge to walk back inside and finish this was almost too much to bear. *What if the cover story works out? What if James believes it?* She cursed out loud, balling her fists so hard that her nails almost drew blood. That man was Brack. He was going to confess. He was going to know that she knew before she killed him. She stormed back up toward the veranda, her feet clomping on the wooden slats. She stopped a meter short of where he sat.

"I'm not going to use that ridiculous name anymore. I'm going to call you the name your mother gave you—Werner Brack. So, Brack, are you going to confess?" She reached for the tire iron on the floor. "If you confess, you have my word that I'll let you go." Lying to this maggot was easy.

"Why are you so eager for me to confess to something I didn't do? The war is over."

"Not for me. It's still echoing inside me every day."

"Torturing an innocent man isn't going to bring your family back."

"No, but your confession will go a long way . . . so you have a choice. Confess or die. The choice is yours."

James paused a moment in the car, his hands slick on the steering wheel. Klement's hotel was a few hundred meters away. The pilot and the seaplane were waiting for them on the lake. *What the hell am I doing?* He withdrew the car keys. Klement was convincing. If he was lying, he was one of the best liars James had ever seen. His story seemed airtight, but there was something. It was almost as if he'd practiced it. There was a hundredth of a second's hesitation when he told it. It was as if he were retrieving the information stored in his brain as opposed to imparting it.

Liliana didn't believe him. *What's it going to take to convince her? What if this isn't Werner Brack, and merely Richard Klement, family man? Would she ever recover?* He opened the door and got out. He went into a hotel—they were bound to have a phone. It was in the corner of the lobby. The girl behind the front desk gave him a Buenos Aires phone book. He hadn't felt like this since the war. It was like being in that attic on Monte Sole again, the SS below them, knowing any false move would be his last.

He spoke with an operator, who placed the call. It seemed to take days to connect to the lazy voice on the other end. He asked for Rudolf Kocher. The young man asked him to hold. A man came around the corner, looking to use the phone. James resisted the temptation to shoo him away. *Ignore him.* A voice came on the other end of the line.

"This is Rudolf Kocher."

"I just needed to check a reference. I have a man here who used to work there. Richard Klement?"

"Yes, Klement. He used to be here. Was here for years."

"Can I confirm he was there from 1943 until '47?"

"Yes. That was it. Good man. We still keep in touch."

"You're sure about those dates?"

"Quite."

"Very good. Thank you, Señor Kocher."

James put the phone down. He went to the girl behind the desk and gave her back the phone book. He thanked her and wandered back onto the street. People brushed by him, but he barely felt them. He was numb.

Liliana took a chair and placed it in front of Klement. She turned it around so she was facing him. "Do you know anything about the people that you killed?"

"I've never killed anyone in my life. I'm a family man. You met my wife and children. Please think of them before you do anything."

The thought of Alexandra and six-year-old Carlos on the stairs caused her a second's reflection. Would they be the victims of what she was about to do? But then the voice in the back of her mind reappeared, driving her forward. *Justice is all that matters, and there's only one way to serve it.*

"I should take pause, should I? Take a moment to think? What were you thinking when you killed my family? How many did you kill that day, Brack?"

"This is useless."

"Not if you confess. Cleanse your soul. Not just mine. Yours too. Only you have the power to do that. You can do that now with just a few words. This is your chance."

"I don't know what to say. I've told you already. Your boyfriend will tell you when he comes back."

"Be the decent man that you pretend to be in your hotel, that perhaps you might have been if the Nazis had never come to power."

"We're going around in circles here. Let me go. Just leave. Leave me overnight. Give yourselves all the start you'll be comfortable with. I won't tell a soul."

"Not until you confess," she said, pointing the gun at him again. "Confess. Beg my forgiveness for murdering my family, for sending your men out after me through the gate of the cemetery." *There it is—a flash of recognition in his eyes.* "Yes. I was the one who got away, covered in my family's blood. I ran out. You sent two men after me. They never came back, did they?"

"I don't—"

"Did they?" She pressed the barrel of the gun into his face before striking him again with it.

"Please, stop."

"Confess."

"I have nothing to confess to."

"Have it your way." She stood up and went to a bag in the corner. This wasn't going to work. He was too tough, and they didn't have enough time. She reached in for a cut-throat razor.

"What are you going to do with that?" Klement said. He tried to scramble backward but only succeeded in rocking the chair back and forth.

"I think this will reveal who you are."

The car pulled up outside.

"Your friend is back. He won't let you do this."

"Oh, I think he will."

"James," he screamed. "Stop her. She's gone insane."

The car door closed, and James entered the cabin. "What's going on?" She held up the razor. "You're doing that now?"

"Doing what now? Don't let her."

"I called the embassy."

"And you spoke to Kocher? Did he tell you I was there during the war?"

"He told me you were there from '43 to 1947, not from '41 till the end of the war like you said."

"I told you he was lying," she said.

"He got the dates wrong, but I was there in 1944 during the operation you mentioned. I was in Argentina. He got the dates wrong. It's an easy mistake."

"It could be a mistake, or it could be that he got the dates wrong on the cover story you fed him," James said. "That's quite a discrepancy."

"You don't believe him, do you?" Liliana said.

"I don't know. I really don't know."

"This should help you decide." She wielded the razor.

"Go ahead," James said.

"What? You're going to let her cut me? Don't do this."

"Confess."

Klement hesitated a moment. "I already told you . . . I don't know this Monte Sole place you're talking about."

"Wait," Liliana said. "Wait." She lowered the razor. "I never mentioned Monte Sole. I never said that."

"You did," Klement spluttered. "I heard you."

"No, she didn't. Neither of us did. It's over, Brack. Time to confess," James said.

"I don't know what you want me to say. I'm not this person you're looking for."

"How about I get that daughter of yours up here?" Liliana shouted. "Confess, or I'll go into town and tell her exactly what you did. I know who you are."

He hesitated a few seconds before he spoke. "You can tell her all you want. She's proud of her family and what I did in the war."

"The war?"

"Yes. The war. She's the future of our movement in Bariloche."

"What do you mean?" James said.

"You don't think we're going to skulk in the background of this country forever, do you? We mean to take power. It's young, powerful people like Alexandra that will make that possible." Blood spattered on his shirt with his laughter. "That name. I could never get used to it.

It's a strange thing, renaming your child at age eleven, but she's such a clever girl, and she knew it had to be done. She was so steadfast." Brack coughed a few times, licked at the blood on his lips. "So I've confessed. Leave her alone. Leave me alone. Be on your way. You've made enemies more powerful than you know."

"Why? Why did you kill women and children? The men fled up the mountain. No one thought you'd come for us—the ones left behind," she said.

"I was a soldier following orders, that's all there is to it."

She dropped the razor and jammed the barrel of the gun against his temple. "Soldiers don't kill unarmed women and children. Only monsters do that."

"Let him speak." James pulled her away. "Put the gun away."

She let the gun fall by her side, still holding on to it. "It was more than just 'following orders.' You could have refused. You could have gone after the Stella Rossa. You knew the women and children—my sisters and my mother and my grandparents, my aunt and my cousins—you knew we were innocent."

"The Stella Rossa only existed because of the support of the local population," Brack spat, blood running down his chin.

"That didn't give you the right to massacre innocent women and children."

"It was war. We were protecting our men." His tone was dismissive, patronizing.

"Against women and children. Why? Why did you do it?" She was centimeters from his face now.

"You wouldn't understand. You said you'd let me go if I confessed."

"I was there on Monte Sole," James said. "I was a soldier. I saw what you and your men did. I saw the heaps of corpses you left behind. Hundreds of women and children."

Brack took a few seconds, the silence heavy in the room.

"We were brought in from Russia," he said. "The top brass knew who to call when they wanted a nasty job done. The Russian front was hell on this earth. I must have killed a hundred, or more, with my own hands. In Italy or France, the British or the Americans would attack with tanks and artillery and with men here and there, but in Russia, they came at us like swarms of bees, thousands at a time, some of them even unarmed. We'd shoot and shoot and shoot. Killing was nothing to us. We didn't take prisoners on the battlefield, and neither did they. Civilians were enemies too. We'd shoot them on sight as quickly as any Ivan soldier."

James reached into his pocket for a pack of cigarettes.

"Can I have one of those?" Brack asked.

James lit one and held it to his mouth. Brack took a few drags before continuing.

"We hated the partisans most, though. More than anyone. They caught my junior officer and his radio operator. My best friends. We found them the next day. They cut off their penises and sewed their mouths shut and let them bleed to death. Young men with their whole lives in front of them. More of my men were captured, and the partisans tortured and burned them to death. My men . . . I wanted to murder every partisan for what they did to us, and I tried. That's what we became known for—eliminating partisans, and we were good. The best. I would have killed every man, woman, and child in Russia with my bare hands if I could have."

"I'm Italian, not Russian."

"And they called us to Italy. Every time we pulled the trigger, we thought of our dead brothers, and then we did it some more." Brack spat the cigarette out of his mouth onto the floor. James stamped it out. "We egged each other on. Any SS soldier who showed any doubt was a coward, and you couldn't rely on cowards in battle. We all wanted to get home, and if killing was the price of getting back to our families, we were happy to pay it. We never gave your people a second thought."

"Do you remember the cemetery at Casaglia?" Liliana said.

"I remember two of my men died chasing you. I mourned them. Your people were nothing more than targets on paper. The only difference was there was more to clean up."

"Do you regret what you did?" James said. "Do you regret joining the SS and doing those things in Hitler's name? Hitler failed. He was beaten. Was it all in vain?"

"I know what you want me to say, but the answer is no. If there's one thing clear to me, even all these years later, it's that if it wasn't for Hitler, the Russians would have swept all the way across Europe, and no one would have been spared. That's something the Allies never understood. We weakened the Soviets enough to save the civilized nations in Western Europe. That's why we still celebrate Hitler and what he stood for."

The sun was setting outside now, the wind howling through the trees. No one spoke. Liliana struggled to control her body. She wasn't going to cry in front of this man.

"You have your confession," Brack said. "Let me go."

Liliana raised the pistol again.

"What are you doing?" James said.

"I'm sorry, James. I do love you."

"You said you'd let me go."

"Shut up," Liliana said through gritted teeth. "Nothing you can ever say matters now."

"I can't let you do this," James said. "He's a cockroach. A stain on the scum of the earth. He's not worth it."

"I've been waiting twelve years to do this."

She brought the gun back to bear on Werner Brack. The weapon shook in her hands.

A tiny smile spread across Brack's face. "Do it," he said. "You don't have the guts."

"Don't listen to him," James said. "You pull that trigger and you're lost like he is. Don't do it." He held his hand to her. She glanced at him and curled her finger around the trigger. "I know what hate can do. I've felt what you're feeling right now, and I think I would have killed my father if I could have. I thank God every day I was never given that chance."

The words barely registered in Liliana's consciousness. She felt empty inside. Everything faded around her, even the look in Brack's eyes as he stared her down. She was back in the cemetery, the smell of wet grass, the wind, the red walls. She saw the bodies and heard the SS man singing that aria—"Largo al factotum," from *The Barber of Seville*. This was the reason she'd survived that day—to pull the trigger. To finish this. The only justice here was death, and she was here to deliver justice.

James lunged at her, went to take the gun, but she was too fast. She spun around, pointed the pistol at him.

"No. You don't get to take this away from me."

"You pull that trigger, and everything good inside you dies."

"That doesn't matter now."

"I never thought I'd want to see my father again, but I went, only because the chief asked me to. It was the last great thing he did for me. I had to see him, to try to forgive him to move on with my life."

"You're asking me to forgive him? Are you insane?"

"I'm asking you not to kill him."

"Do it," Brack repeated.

But then, softly at first, and growing ever louder, she heard the echo of something within her. Her father was with her again. He told her when they were hiding in that attic in Rioveggio that he'd get her through, and she heard his words to her again. *"Don't let what you've seen here change who you are, my love. Don't let the evil that the SS scum have inflicted imprison you. You will survive this—I'll make sure of that. And when you do, you must live the most wondrous life, beyond any of our simple imaginations. Don't let their hatred live. Leave it behind, and you will have won."*

She let the gun fall to her side.

"You don't get to have any power over me anymore. Not now. Not ever again," she told Brack.

James took a step toward her and she handed him the gun.

"I'm sorry, James. I know now. I choose you." He took her in his arms. And she was back on Monte Sole, late for dinner. Her sisters laughed. Her father raised a glass, and Mamma laid down the food. Nonno and Nonna were smiling at the end of the table, and her cousins and aunt and uncle all turned to see her.

"It's time to go," James said and led her toward the door.

"Are you just going to leave me here?"

"That was the deal," James said.

"I'll be sitting in my own filth all night. At least let me use the bathroom. Is there a toilet?"

"Take him to the bathroom in the back." She stepped out onto the veranda, the day fading all around her. The breeze had brought a chill, and she felt herself shivering. *These moments will dictate the rest of my life, and who I'll be. I'm ready to go on,* she thought to herself, and realized she believed it. *Finally.*

He emerged from the bathroom in the back of the cabin with James holding the gun behind him. Liliana stood at the door, about five meters away. She took the tire iron in her hand to put it back in the car.

"Are you going to make me get back in the chair?"

"Hurry up. I'm not in the mood for games," James said. The SS man sat down, and James tied the ropes behind the chair once more. She walked outside. *I'm letting you live, Brack, but the world will know your name.* She was at the car when James came to her, taking her hand.

"I'm sorry," she said. "I thought killing him was the only way."

"I understand—"

His words were cut short by a crashing sound from inside the cabin. James let her go, running toward the sound, the gun still in his hand. He reached the veranda when Brack lunged at him, brandishing a piece of the broken chair. Brack swiped the gun out of James's hand. It fell to the floor in front of them. She ran toward them. James was unbalanced, and the SS man punched him in the jaw, knocking him onto the mud at her feet. Brack took his opportunity to scramble for the gun and got his hand on it first.

"Run!" James shouted. "Go!"

He got to his feet just as Brack leveled the pistol to fire. He pulled Liliana along with him as the sound of the weapon exploded. A bullet hit the car, leaving a round hole in the back door. She had the tire iron. *What use against a gun?* James pushed her toward the car, but there was no time to get in. Brack was five meters behind them.

"Split up!" James said. He ran into the trees to the left. She ran right. Brack paused on the top step, cursing as James disappeared into the trees.

The trees were thick around her, and she leaped over a broad trunk in her path. She kept on for a few seconds before coming to a halt. No noise. Not close anyway. Brack had gone after James. She heard the two men running thirty meters away through the woods. She zigzagged through the trees, running toward James, the tire iron in her hand. A gunshot rang out. But there was no scream, and the footsteps through the forest continued. She ran on. The trees opened up to the extent that she could see the two men. Brack was only a few meters behind him. *I have to lure him away from James, catch him out in the open.* Brack would show no mercy. She ran on, aware of the sound of breaking twigs behind her. She was less than ten meters from them. James came into a clearing, a circle in the trees perhaps seven or eight meters in diameter.

"Stop," Brack shouted and fired a shot. "Turn around. Call out for that bitch."

"No. No way. Go ahead and shoot."

"How noble. It seems that—"

She burst through the trees behind Brack. He was turning toward the noise when she hit him full force in the head with the tire iron. The gun spilled to the ground, falling in a pile of leaves. He lunged toward it like a drunk, the crown of his head a bloody mess. She brought the tire iron down again, and he fell onto his back. She picked the pistol up, standing over him. Blood saturated the soil below his head, and his lips curled back.

"Looks like you'll get your revenge after all," Brack said.

"No. You did this."

"Shoot me. Finish me . . ."

"No." She handed the gun to James. "Let's go." They walked back toward the car. Brack tried to say something, but words were beyond him now. He gurgled a few times and then went still.

CHAPTER 21

*December 1956—The mountains around Monte Sole, forty
kilometers south of Bologna, Italy*

Cluttered villages and battered farmhouses climbed the mountains
north of Florence. As James and Liliana progressed farther on the highway, a subtle change came over the landscape. The same big brown-
orange farmhouses still lay wedged into the sides of the mountain, but
the windows were dark, the fields overgrown with weeds. The vines
were dead, the trellises rotting. All color had been drained from the
land—not a piece of washing billowing in the wind, or a cow, or a
ripening orchard. The land was grayish brown. All signs of life seemed
extinguished. The people who had once lived here were extinct, or gone.
Monte Sole was shadowed and silent, cold.

The stone track hissed under the tires of the rental car. They
stopped, and James took the keys from the ignition. Neither spoke.
They climbed the narrow dirt roads to the top of the mountain and
peered down at the uninhabited wasteland below. The mountain villages of San Martino, Cerpiano, and Caprara were deserted now, the
buildings collapsed and ceding to the unkempt weeds that had seized
their opportunity to rule once more.

One old lady still lived at San Mamante. Once there had been
dozens. She was a widow of the massacre. Liliana hadn't known her,

but James convinced her to visit. They knocked on the door of the old farmhouse. The door opened to reveal the wizened figure of a woman likely in her fifties but who looked thirty years older.

"What do you want?" the woman said.

"My name is Liliana Nicoletti. I used to live here."

The woman's gray eyes moved up and down Liliana's smart coat and hat. "A lot of people lived here once. I have no desire to relive history."

She closed the door. He wanted to knock again, but Liliana had already walked away. They went back to the car and left without another word.

They went to the small church first, as the crowd of women and children had done on that rainy morning in September 1944. They were alone as they got out of the car. She led him through the rusty iron gate of the church grounds at Casaglia. The chapel where the cowering crowd was grouped together was just one wall now, and the inscriptions of most of the headstones were worn off.

They took the track toward the cemetery. Monte Sole towered above them as they walked. Neither spoke, but they held each other all the way. They pushed through the cemetery gate.

"This is where they lined us up, the children at the front." The walls of the church were holed and pitted by bullets, and the entire site was overgrown by brambles and bushes. The walls of the cemetery were falling into the ground. "This was where my family died." She pointed up to the hill. "And that's where you came from to save me."

"I'm sorry I couldn't do more."

"You did so much."

They returned to the car and drove to the house, the last place they'd see that day. There was little to see. It had been obliterated in the battle that followed the massacre. The courtyard was overgrown, barely visible, and only a few stones remained of the home her family had lived in for two hundred years.

"It's gone. There's no point to this. I'm ready to leave."

They made their way back to the car. They wound down the dirt roads to the highway. As they drove, the landscape around them seemed to come back to life, the color returning to the world. She stared out the window during the hour it took them to get to Bologna, her head on her forearm.

"There was no one left to rebuild," she said as James parked the car. "Everywhere else was rebuilt, but our people were wiped out, and there was no one left."

"If only the Allies had arrived earlier."

"If only."

CHAPTER 22

October 1958—New York City

Liliana fixed his tie, made sure it was tight and straight, and gave him a kiss. The curtain ruffled as the stagehand curled it back, and James walked out. He looked back at Liliana applauding him, a wide smile across her face, and she blew him another kiss as he reached the podium. She thought again just how hard it was to get used to this.

She thought about what his editor had told them—that this was what they had written the book for, and that they'd better get used to what came along with success. The applause continued after he reached the microphone, and he took a moment to adjust it, raising it to his mouth. He looked back at Liliana again. She stood with her fist balled over her mouth. James turned back to face the crowd.

"Thank you, ladies and gentlemen," he said, and the clapping faded. "I feel so very fortunate to be in front of you tonight, so very fortunate to be able to tell the stories of those who can no longer speak for themselves, for those who I saw murdered. I documented what I saw, and what I found out, by speaking to others and going to South America to see where many of the individuals who perpetrated those crimes fled to."

He spoke for another twenty minutes about Nazis war criminals, the governments that hid them, and the apathy that allowed them to remain free, then he stood back from the podium. "And now I'd like to introduce the bravest, most wonderful person I've ever known, my beautiful wife, Liliana Nicoletti, the last of her family, and the keeper of the Nicoletti name."

Liliana walked out to the podium. The crowd was standing now. James kissed her. She whispered praise to him, but the sound of applause from the crowd was too much and he didn't respond. He went to the side of the stage and watched as she brought the microphone down. The applause lasted thirty seconds or more before she raised her hand to calm the audience.

"My sister Lena would be thirty today. My sister Martina would be twenty-nine. I often wonder what they would have become, who they would have been. I'd like to dedicate my being here today to their memory." She stopped a few seconds to take the applause before beginning again. "They were murdered along with perhaps a hundred others in a cemetery not much larger than this stage I'm standing on. Why? Why them? Why us? Why anyone? We've seen film of Nazis on trial, proclaiming that they had no choice in what they did, that they were merely 'following orders,' as if, somehow, we'll nod and agree and understand their actions. We presume that their punishment would have been so great as to negate any of their moral objections to the unthinkable atrocities they carried out, but what was the alternative? Death to all who refused?

"There's one major problem with this explanation—that in the hundreds of cases my husband and I have read, of the grisliest crimes ever recorded, not one defense attorney in any Nazi trial was ever able to document a single case in which refusal to kill unarmed civilians resulted in the 'inevitable' gruesome punishment. Not once. In hundreds of cases."

Liliana and James had researched for hundreds of hours, had dedicated their lives to it before the book came out. Their wedding had been a wonderful afterthought.

"There were some men who did refuse to murder innocents. Their punishment never approached the hideous acts the men who didn't refuse perpetrated. The men who refused orders were castigated, moved on, given slop duty, or, at worst, and this was on rare occasion, put into punishment units. They were never lined up, in a cemetery, huddled together, terrified, as my sisters, my mother, my aunt, my cousins, and my neighbors were. They were never murdered in cold blood, as my family were."

She looked out into the crowd, imagined her family sitting there, her sisters smiling back at her from the front row. They'd be with her forever, in everything she did.

"Because of what I've experienced, people ask me to come and speak, and ask my advice as if I have some insight into human nature that they never could. There is one question that people ask me more than any other, wherever I've gone in the six months since we published the book. *Could this happen again?*" She paused to make eye contact with several people in the crowd. "The answer is yes. The men who committed these terrible crimes, many of whom still walk among civilized society today, weren't anything special. They weren't picked from prisons or plucked from padded rooms. They weren't hardened criminals or diagnosed psychopaths, just ordinary people. They came from all walks of life. Many of them were educated and intelligent. Many were not. Who knows how many among you sitting here tonight might have done the same thing in their places?"

A gasp came from the audience followed by a swell of murmuring. She waited a few seconds until the noise died down.

"The simple truth is that it takes unimaginable strength to be different. To break away from what your peers are doing is one of the hardest things for anyone, be that person a child in the schoolyard or a twenty-one-year-old SS man trying to gain the trust of his fellow soldiers. These men didn't shoot my family because of some gruesome bloodlust. If so, why didn't they continue their murderous ways after the war ended? Why were they able to rejoin society and live as peaceful citizens in Germany and Austria and Italy and Croatia and Argentina and a host of other places all over the world? It's easy, convenient even, to paint these men as evil. To write them off as monsters and to think we're inherently better than them. It's harder to realize that there's a little bit of that same monster in all of us, and the only real way to stop that monster is to make sure that those with the ideas to destroy that which is good and true don't attain power. Because once they do, and people start to believe their lies, and stop thinking of their fellow human beings as that—as human beings—then they are capable of anything, even the reprehensible evils that I witnessed with my own eyes just fourteen years ago in a country known for some of the greatest art and discoveries that civilization has ever known."

James led the applause from his position at the side of the stage and waited as the crowd calmed once more.

An hour later they went to the reception together, where they were introduced to the dignitaries the university had invited to hear the award-winning cowriters of *The Forgotten Massacre* speak. Most of them seemed more interested to hear Liliana's story. James was glad. She deserved that. It was near the end of the night, as the room was beginning to empty out, when a man in a pristine black suit approached them.

"Avi Rosenbaum," he said.

"A pleasure—"

"You have no need to introduce yourselves. James, I've been following your work for quite some time, and this book . . . well, it's drawn much-needed attention to our cause for justice."

"Who are you?" Liliana asked.

"A survivor. A leader of a group of other survivors seeking the same justice you sought in Argentina. Your writing has awakened the public to the fact that thousands of the worst criminals the human race has ever known are still at large, and there is not the political will to find and prosecute them. Up to this point we have taken things into our own hands—serving justice how and when we can, but you can change this."

"How?" she said.

"By using the profile you've gained with your newspaper and radio interviews to pressure politicians. They need to set up a commission to look into and prosecute Nazis living here, in the United States."

"The crimes weren't committed on American soil," James said. "They can't be prosecuted for them here."

"So we have them deported and have the American government put pressure on the West Germans and the French and the Italians. Even the Soviets."

James felt Liliana squeeze her fingers around his. This was what she was looking for. He thought about his editor's advice once more. The echo of this war hadn't faded yet. Not for him, and especially not for his wife.

"Your story," Rosenbaum continued, "has captivated the public—the beautiful woman saved by the American POW, who went to Argentina to uncover the government plot to help the Nazis. I have some questions: Why did you go to Argentina? Was there a particular person you were following? I read your earlier articles about a Werner Brack. Was it him?"

"No, there wasn't one specific man. Initially, it might have been, but we never heard of Brack again after Monte Sole. He disappeared. We believe he's dead," Liliana said.

"We went there for all the other Bracks, all the criminals who used the ratlines, and are still living free," James added.

James wondered about this man, what he knew. Brack's body had been found the day after they left Bariloche. James contacted Gold a few weeks later. He didn't expect a response, but got one. Gold told them in his letters how the police had come to him about the mysterious

Americans who took the local hotelier out that day. Gold pleaded ignorance, and soon after, when it became apparent the strangers were gone, the matter was dropped. Gold said he thought the Nazis sacrificed one of their own to save their collective skins. Some stones were best left unturned.

"Have you been able to live with that? Without finding the man who ordered your family murdered—even if you think he's dead?" Rosenbaum asked.

"We uncovered the system that protected him and helped him escape. He was one of thousands. If he started us on the path to turn over the rock that exposed the rat's nest underneath—that's enough," Liliana said. "And the journey turned up more than I thought. Maybe I found something else I thought was gone forever."

"I'm happy to hear you found some measure of peace," Rosenbaum said. "Your story has already revealed a lot, but there's so much left to do. Will you help us?"

"Is there a way I can get in touch with you?" James said.

"I'll call the magazine next week—give you some time to think it over."

"If we join with you, we can't be party to any criminality," James said.

"That's who they were. That's what separates us from them," she said.

"That's never what we intend. Sometimes, things get out of hand, however. It's an imperfect world, and justice is an elusive thing," Rosenbaum said. "We want you to politicize this, to make it so that small bands of survivors like us don't have to be the ones to mete out the justice that the governments of the West should. We shouldn't be the ones responsible for this."

"I'll look forward to your call," James said.

They didn't speak about Rosenbaum's offer until they returned home. Liliana was taking off her earrings as she began.

"What did you think of Rosenbaum? You think he's Mossad?"

"Very possibly. Does it matter?"

"Not to me." She kicked off her shoes and went to the window. The lights of Manhattan sparkled like diamonds below them.

The portrait of Liliana's family hung on the wall. She went to it. "I was foundering before, but now I feel strong as an oak tree, my roots deep in the ground. What we did in Argentina set me free."

He took her in his arms. "There's a 'but' coming. I know you."

"But this isn't over."

"I know that."

"There's still so much work for us to do."

"Then let's do it."

CHAPTER 23

May 1984—Ardmore, Pennsylvania

The light was fading. The setting sun cast shadows along the manicured lawn. Liliana finished her coffee and got out of the wicker chair. She brought the cup from the porch to the kitchen sink and set about cleaning up the remnants of dinner. James had left several pots to soak but hadn't come back to actually clean them. *As usual.* Darkness seemed to descend in minutes, and soon the orange glow of the magic hour turned to inky black. She caught sight of herself in the window. Her long hair was graying at the temples—she refused to cut it short like so many of her friends had. James liked it this way too. She dried her hands and reached up to touch the crow's feet extending from her eyes.

She left the kitchen, went to check on him in the study. He was sitting at the brown mahogany desk, tapping on the typewriter. The window beside him was the only space on the wall not covered by bookshelves. Photos adorned his desk—their daughter, Lena, on her wedding day; the day their grandchild, Martina, was born; their son Mark's high school graduation; Penny and her family on the beach; and the old picture of him and Chief Brody fishing. He didn't notice her until she spoke.

"How's the new novel coming?"

"It's a hard lift." He pushed his glasses back.

"That's what you said last time."

"Well, that one was too."

"I'll leave you to it."

He took a sip from the coffee mug beside the typewriter. "I think I've almost had enough for today. I'll be in in a minute."

She went to the living room and flicked on the television. The nightly news was almost over. She picked up a magazine, only paying cursory attention to the broadcast. Then she heard it.

"Walter Rauff, a midranking SS commander in Nazi Germany, was buried yesterday in Santiago, Chile."

She put down the magazine. The report cut to film taken that day in Santiago. Two undertakers, both dressed in brown trench coats with matching ties, carried a simple wooden casket out of a small suburban house. The camera cut to an old man in an alpine hat with a red feather shuffling into the cemetery.

"An aide of Reinhard Heydrich in the secret police, Rauff is estimated to have been responsible for the deaths of almost 250,000 people during World War II through his instrumental role in genocide through the use of mobile gas chambers."

The camera cut to the scene of his burial. Several elderly men ringed the grave, raising their arms in turn to give the Nazi salute.

"A crowd of old Nazis attended his funeral yesterday, giving the infamous 'Heil Hitler' salute, as the world's most-wanted war criminal in the 1970s was laid to rest."

She hurled the magazine at the television, stood up, and switched it off.

James came out of the study into the living room. "What's going on?"

"Did you see the news—the report from Santiago?"

James nodded. "I was wondering when you'd see it."

"We were down there three years ago. They assured us things had changed."

"Things *have* changed," he said. "They're paying attention now."

"Not to Walter Rauff—the most-wanted Nazi in the world—at least until he died. And who are these others at the funeral? I understand the Chilean police are corrupt, but where is the Office of Special Investigations?"

"In that broom cupboard of an office in DC."

"Sometimes I wonder why we even bothered. It took thirty-four years to get that office set up after the end of the war. What use are they? What good have they done?"

"There have been arrests."

"A few men out of thousands." She went to the cabinet and pulled out an unopened bottle of wine. "I need a drink."

"I thought we were saving that for a special occasion?"

"This seems special enough."

She poured herself a glass and carried it out to the sun porch. He followed her out and sat down beside her.

"There was no way they could—"

"Stop, James. I don't want to hear it."

She peered out into the darkness, sipping the fine red wine.

Saturday came, and with it, the kids. Lena arrived first with her husband, Michael, and their baby daughter.

"Mom, are you OK?" Lena said. "You don't look . . . your usual self."

I'm not going to burden them with that news report. "I'm just so happy to see you all. You make me feel like the luckiest woman alive." Lena hugged her. Michael handed her the baby. "Oh, little Martina. You're the most beautiful girl in the world."

They walked into the house together.

"Anyone else with you?" James said in the hallway.

"No. My brother's late—as usual," Lena said.

"I'm sure he got held up at the game."

"What's the matter, Mom? You look like you haven't slept."

"I'm fine."

"You don't look—"

"Lena, leave it," James said.

They continued down the hallway in silence. The smell of pasta swirled around them as they followed Liliana to the sun porch. They put the baby down on a blanket and watched her roll over, cheering every time.

The doorbell rang thirty minutes later.

"That'll be your brother." Liliana got up to go to the door. "Why are you following me?" she said to her husband.

"No reason."

He got in front of her and opened the door—not to Mark, but to Penny and Joe.

"What a lovely surprise," Liliana said. "It's been too long. I had no idea you and Joe were coming." They parted to reveal their grown-up children standing behind them. Liliana almost screamed. "And the kids! What are you all doing here?"

"We heard you had a bad week and needed cheering up," Penny said. She put her arm around her brother.

"Oh God, I'm going to cry now. Come here."

She embraced each one in turn before leading them inside.

"Where are the little ones?" she said.

"With reliable babysitters. We'll bring them again soon," one of Penny's daughters said.

They brought chairs from the kitchen and sat on the porch. James raised a glass. "To Martina, the first of many grandchildren!"

"Give me a few years on that one." Mark walked in, still wearing his Penn State football jersey.

"Did they win?" James asked.

"No, the opposite of that." He took a seat beside Penny, who greeted him with a warm embrace.

The doorbell rang again.

"I'll get it," James said, as Liliana looked at him suspiciously.

He returned a minute later with a man in his late forties, a woman, and two teenage boys. The man wore a gray suit. The woman was in a yellow dress with a bow tied around her slender waist. The two boys were also dressed in suits, the knots in their ties pressed all the way up. One of them pulled at his apparently overstarched collar.

"I had no idea we were expecting company," Liliana said.

"I'd like to introduce our special guest this evening," James said. "This is Luca Vialli; his wife, Greta; and his sons, Mario and Paul."

The man in the gray suit stepped forward, hat in hand. He held up a bottle of wine in his other hand. "It's such an honor to be here. We—"

She cut him off. "Luca . . . is that Luca?" He handed the bottle to her, but she pushed it aside to embrace him. "You've . . . grown so much." They both laughed. "Look at you. Your eyes are the same. I can still see that little boy in you, and in your handsome sons." Tears welled and broke down her face and she embraced him again.

"I wanted to thank you both for what you did for me and my brother," he said with tears on his cheeks. He drew away and placed the wine down on a side table. His wife took his hat. "I'm sorry Luciano couldn't be here. He's still living in Italy. He so wanted to see you. He promised to bring his family soon."

"I look forward to that." Liliana stared at him.

He reached into a satchel his son was carrying and pulled out one of James's books. "I've been living in Brooklyn for thirty years. I read one of your husband's novels and contacted his publisher a few weeks ago."

"I met up with Luca last week. We wanted to surprise you," James said.

"So that's what you were doing in New York?"

"Caught red-handed."

"I'm so happy you brought your family," Liliana said.

"I especially wanted my boys to meet you both. They wouldn't be here without you."

Luca brought his wife and teenage children forward and introduced them again. He reached into the satchel again and gave her a letter his brother had written them, along with a stack of drawings from Luciano's young children.

"I'll treasure these."

"Now we have a perfect reason to visit Italy again," James said.

"We'll all go," she said. "You should all see where I'm from and know what happened there."

James brought in extra chairs from the garage, and somehow, they all squeezed in. The kids went out to the yard to play soccer, and the rest sat and talked.

"Did you know what your parents did for me? What your brother did?" Luca asked. None answered. "You never told them?"

"We didn't speak of that time much."

"What did they do?" Mark asked. "We know they met during the war. We read the articles and the book they wrote in the fifties, but they never mentioned you."

"They did everything a person could have." He sat by the window and told the story, glancing out at his boys in the yard every so often. When he finished, he stood up to hug them once more. "My children have known your names all their lives."

"It's my turn now," Liliana said after dinner. They returned to the porch, and she told them all about the war in detail they'd never known, told them of her family and what had happened to them. When the story ended, she took her sleeping granddaughter in her lap, and James served the best wine they had. They talked long into the night. The cypress trees at the end of the yard swayed in the gentle breeze, and the echo inside her faded into nothing.

ACKNOWLEDGMENTS

Huge thanks to the magnificent Elena Monicelli, the local historian and staff coordinator at the Monte Sole Peace School. Thanks for your incredible help, and all you do to promote peace around the world through keeping the memory of the horrors of those few days in 1944 alive. I'll never forget seeing the cemetery at Casaglia with my own eyes, and taking the same walk that the huddled masses of women and children took to the cemetery down the dusty track. It was a truly humbling experience, and I just hope I've done something in writing this novel to preserve the memory of those lost.

I want to thank my beta readers for their patience with the messy early drafts of the novels I write. I want to thank Jill Dempsey, Betsy Frimmer, Nicola Hogan, Isaac Lepro, Ed and Carol McDuell, Chris Menier, and Morgan Leafe. Thanks, as always, to my agent, Byrd Leavell, who's been with me since we were much younger men with all our hair. Thanks to my personal editor, the fantastic Will Bennett, who goes to show that even if there's no bad language in the book, bad language in the edit notes is always welcome! Thanks to my fabulous editor-coaches, the unstoppable Jenna Free, and the marvelous Chris Werner at Lake Union. Thanks for all the hard work. I hope you enjoy it all as much as I do.

Thanks to my two brothers, Conor and Brian, and my sister, Orla, and all my other friends who support me in lots of different ways.

Thanks to my terrific mum, who's one of the best sounding boards out there and is always willing to listen to new ideas no matter how garbled they may be. Thanks to my ever-wonderful, ever-beautiful wife, Jill, for listening to every single thing I ever spew about my books and what I want to be as a writer. And, of course, thanks to the three crazy boys that have become the center of our lives these last few years. Thanks to Robbie, Sam, and baby Jack for making all this worthwhile. I'm so glad my dream job gives me the chance to spend so much time with you (most of the time).

Oh, and thanks to all my readers for making my dreams of being a writer come true.

You can find out more about the history of Monte Sole and support the peace school there at www.montesole.org/en.

ABOUT THE AUTHOR

Photo © 2017 Jill McDuell

Eoin Dempsey is the bestselling author of *Toward the Midnight Sun*; *White Rose, Black Forest*; *Finding Rebecca*; and *The Bogside Boys*. His novels have been translated into a dozen different languages and have been optioned for film and radio production. Born and raised in Dublin, Ireland, Eoin moved to the United States in 2008 and currently lives in Philadelphia with his wonderful wife, Jill, and their three beautiful and crazy sons, Robbie, Sam, and Jack. Learn more at www.eoindempseybooks.com.